THE PORT

Rachel McLean writes thrillers that make your pulse race and your brain tick. A proud indie author who manages her own publishing company, she has sold millions of copies digitally and hundreds of thousands in print, regularly topping the bestseller lists. She is the author of the Dorset Crime novels and five spin-off crime series, with beloved characters appearing in multiple series. In 2021, she won the Kindle Storyteller Award with *The Corfe Castle Murders*. She divides her time between Birmingham and Dorset and lives with her wife, three children and two cats Cagney and Lacey.

Joel Hames is a Lancashire-based writer of crime fiction, and the editor of million-selling books across multiple genres. Joel's own works include the Dead North series featuring lawyer Sam Williams, and the psychological thriller *The Lies I Tell*. Most recently, he has been working with titan of crime fiction Rachel McLean on the hugely successful Cumbria Crime series.

ALSO BY RACHEL MCLEAN AND JOEL HAMES

Cumbria Crime series

The Harbour
The Mine
The Cairn
The Barn
The Lake
The Wood
The Port
The Marsh

RACHEL McLEAN & JOEL HAMES

CUMBRIA CRIME BOOK 7

THE PORT

Copyright © 2025 by Rachel McLean and Joel Hames

All rights reserved.

No part of this book may be reproduced in any form or by any electronic or mechanical means, including information storage and retrieval systems, without written permission from the author, except for the use of brief quotations in a book review.

This is a work of fiction. Names, characters, businesses, places, events and incidents are either the products of the author's imagination or used in a fictitious manner. Any resemblance to actual persons, living or dead, or actual events is purely coincidental.

Ackroyd Publishing

ackroydpublishing.com

Printed and bound in the UK by CPI Group (Uk) Ltd, Croydon CR0 4YY

CUMBRIA CRIME BOOK 7: THE PORT: THE STORY SO FAR

Warning: this contains major spoilers for the first six books in the Cumbria Crime series. If you haven't read those, we suggest stopping right now, reading those first, and then coming back to this book.

Happy reading,
Rachel McLean and Joel Hames

The Warehouse Raid

With help from Elena, an escaped victim of Myron Carter's people-smuggling operation, the team has raided a warehouse and rescued four women. Two of the women have disappeared, and one, the red-headed Belarusian, may be a perpetrator rather than a victim. But the remaining two have identified DI Ralph Streeting as involved in the operation.

The Downfall of Ralph Streeting

Meanwhile, Streeting has taken control of the investigation into Bobby Silver's murder. Tom has been seconded to his team in Durranhill, Carlisle, ostensibly to assist Streeting and his DS, Mulligan, but in reality to ensure Streeting doesn't conceal evidence.

Streeting has finally been arrested on people-trafficking charges. His fingerprints have been found on a door handle Bobby smeared with Vaseline before she died.

Streeting is insisting that corrupt officers are manufacturing evidence to stop him exposing them. But the team has tracked down the Jeep that Streeting used to flee the scene of Bobby's murder.

Stella goes to collect the Jeep with Denise Gaskill from PSD, and they recover a handgun from the boot – just before the vehicle explodes, leaving Stella with minor injuries and Denise on the brink of death.

With Streeting's release imminent, Stella's colleague Caroline finds his prints on the gun, and he is finally charged with the murder of Bobby Silver.

The Ryan Tobin Connection

Zoe has maintained contact with Tobin, an environmental activist and former employee of Jenson & Marley, one of Myron Carter's businesses.

The body of Tobin's friend and fellow activist Kevin Downes has been found in Elterwater, where Aaron took over the case and has also been investigating Myron Carter's business associate Sinead Conway, whose local theme park development was the focus of Kevin's protest.

After Aaron arrests Downes's killer, a grateful Tobin sends Zoe a set of emails that might implicate Myron Carter in the people-trafficking operation.

Other Threads

Olivia Bagsby, who went on the run after witnessing women being trafficked into the port, has been contacting Zoe, refusing to expose herself but terrified Carter will track her down. Zoe's old boss, corrupt former Detective Superintendent David Randle, has been pestering Zoe for information on Myron Carter's operations and on Olivia's whereabouts. Zoe hasn't told her partner DI Carl Whaley about her contact with Randle; he wouldn't be as forgiving of Randle breaching the conditions of the Protected Persons Programme.

In the closing pages of *The Wood*, Carter's people finally caught up with Olivia – but Randle beat them to it. The pair managed to escape, but Randle was shot in the process.

Now Harriett's role as an undercover PSD officer has finally been exposed, her relationship with Tom has been rekindled.

Nina, who resented Harriett for lying to them all, has to come to terms with the deception as the two teams find themselves working together and with Harriett's colleague Denise in mortal danger. Nina's house has been targeted in a failed attack by arsonists attempting to silence Elena (who was staying there).

Aaron has continued to see police psychiatrist Dr Filey, with his mental health improving. And he and Denise Gaskill have developed an unlikely friendship.

And finally, the Independent Office for Police Conduct

have carried out an investigation into the Hub, and are preparing to deliver their initial report...

CHAPTER ONE

Miles Stringer wiped his bald head and turned away from his crew to look skyward.

Not yet nine and sweat poured off him like he was in the Mediterranean. The clouds gathering over the sea brought welcome relief. Not the menacing storm clouds that halted work, just the gentle sort that offered shade.

"Come on!" He cupped his hands around his mouth. "Pick up the pace! Break in fifteen minutes."

The still morning air carried his voice across the site. Though he couldn't hear their responses, he knew they'd be grumbling about fatigue or boredom or whatever today's complaint was.

Let them moan. They could whinge to his face during the break.

He'd paired them strategically: Liam with Shiv, Ellen with Barney. Only Stacey worked alone – she could spot trouble from her cab that others would miss until they tripped over it. Yesterday's teams had been different, and tomorrow he'd split them by gender. Keep rotating, keep them alert. One driving and scooping, one on ground duty – clearing space, tidying, rolling logs onto forks, checking for debris.

The debris was increasing. Not the stuff from Bobby's old operation, that vanished long before Miles's crew arrived. This was unwanted rubbish: boat fragments, cables, items tangled in incoming cargo. Dead seabirds, rope swings, remnants from when the logs had been standing trees. He'd found designer clothes once – an Armani suit and a single Kurt Geiger boot. Countless pairs of glasses over the years. Adult magazines, before everything went digital.

He'd been sky-watching too long. Turning back, he spotted Stacey lifting a load, that bloody parrot perched in her cab, likely telling her to wipe her feet.

He'd inherited Bobby's dog, Taylor. Stacey had got the parrot. The dog was a nuisance, but Miles reckoned he'd got the better deal.

Beyond Stacey's position, Barney stood back directing while Ellen manoeuvred the forks. They exchanged thumbs-up signals.

But on the far side, everything had stopped. From this distance, Liam appeared frozen in place.

Shiv wasn't moving either. Or at least, her forklift wasn't.

Bloody hell.

Miles tried to be patient with Liam. The lad's girlfriend had been charged with murder in May. Police had even suspected Liam for a while. He'd seemed to recover well enough – too well, perhaps. After abandoning his plans to settle with Bella, he now spent his nights drinking and chasing different girls every weekend.

"What is it?" Miles called, walking towards them.

CHAPTER ONE

Liam remained statue-still. Shiv's head moved side to side, barely perceptible.

"Liam?"

Nothing. If the lad was having some sort of episode, Shiv should be helping. That's what crews did – they looked after each other.

"Come on, lad." Miles closed the distance. "Liam! You turned to stone or something?"

With glacial slowness, Liam raised his arm and pointed to the log pile in front of Shiv's forklift.

Miles approached. A murmur reached his ears, and he saw Liam's lips moving.

"Not again," the lad whispered. "Not fucking again."

Miles hesitated, a chill replacing his sweat. He forced himself forward and looked down.

Not debris this time. Not glasses or cables or dead birds. Half a suit, like before. The top half, wrapped around an arm.

A bloody arm protruding from beneath the log pile.

Not again. Not fucking again.

"Everyone, *stop* what you're doing right now!" His voice boomed across the site. "Don't move!"

"What?" Stacey called back.

Miles raised his palm in a *stop* gesture. She'd understand.

He pulled out his phone with trembling fingers.

CHAPTER TWO

"Another degree?" said DI Zoe Finch.

"Another degree." Her son Nicholas nodded enthusiastically at her on the laptop screen.

She frowned. "You've not mentioned that before."

"I know. But I hadn't mentioned any actual jobs, either. And there are some really interesting courses about. I—"

Shouting erupted in the background, followed by a bang. Nicholas looked away, still grinning.

"Sorry," he said. "Got to run. Speak this weekend?"

"Speak this weekend," she agreed, but he'd already disconnected.

A postgraduate course would suit him. He'd always been able to multitask; if anyone could earn at the same time as studying, Nicholas could. He'd looked well and seemed genuinely excited by the idea.

Zoe stood and walked to the window. After a clear morning, the clouds were beginning to roll in. Autumn came early in Cumbria. An electric blue Audi drove into the car park, taking the corner too fast and bumping the curb.

CHAPTER TWO

Her phone rang.

"Carl," she said. "Everything OK?"

"Everything's fine. Just been talking to Denise. She's desperate to be back."

Zoe smiled. "No surprise there."

It took more than a bomb to put Denise Gaskill down.

"How did she seem, otherwise?" she asked.

"Just impatient. Fine. I mean, you can't tell, can you? She's never been one for sharing. But if she's fit, then we could do with her. At some point we'll have to deal with Streeting."

"You hope," said Zoe, turning to look out of the window again. The Audi had parked, and Alan Markin was slowly emerging from it, one leg at a time.

"I hope. He's a local copper, and he's been charged with murder. You'd think they'd want us to deal with this."

"Us?" Zoe asked.

"Us. Our team, your assistance. Or the other way round. I don't mind. But they won't let us speak to him."

Zoe sighed. This was a rerun of a conversation they'd had a hundred times since January, when DI Ralph Streeting had finally been arrested and charged with Bobby Silver's murder. Streeting was being held on remand in an undisclosed location, no trial date set, and neither Zoe's team nor Carl's had been allowed near him since. From what little Zoe had heard, Streeting wouldn't have spoken to them even if they had been able to get into a room with him.

She wasn't going to have the same discussion. Not again. Anything would be better than that.

"Heard from Randle?" Carl asked.

OK. Maybe not *anything*.

"Not for a while," she replied. "I'd tell you if I had."

She watched Alan Markin limp slowly towards the building. She'd known the IOPC investigation had taken its toll on her fellow DI, but the man looked even worse than she'd expected. Like he'd shrunk, in height at least. There was an awkwardness to his movement, a sort of shuffle and stumble. Any other place or time of day, she'd have thought he was drunk.

She tore her gaze from the window back to her phone.

Carl hadn't replied.

"Carl?" she said.

"I'm here."

"I would tell you. I haven't heard from Randle for weeks."

"OK," he replied, unconvinced.

She understood his scepticism. She was telling the truth now, but she hadn't been for the year or so up to January, when she'd been in contact with her old boss David Randle without breathing a word to Carl.

"It's true," she insisted. "Look, all we know is he's around somewhere, probably in Cumbria, he's got Olivia with him, and he won't stop complaining about his hand."

Randle had been shot in that hand when he'd rescued Olivia Bagsby, a key witness, from Myron Carter's people back in January. It would have saved trouble if the shot had been a few inches to the side, but then Olivia might not have made it out.

"Does he still want to come in?" Carl asked.

"He did last time I spoke to him," Zoe said. "And I promise you, love, that was weeks ago."

"Will you let him?"

She closed her eyes and ran through it again, the pros and cons.

CHAPTER TWO

David Randle, here, in the Hub. The very idea made her flesh crawl.

David Randle, the only person she knew who really understood how someone like Carter operated. And more importantly, the only person Olivia Bagsby trusted. If there was ever a chance of meeting Olivia, of convincing her to give evidence, then Zoe had to keep Randle onside.

"I don't know," she said. "Look, Carl, I've got to go. Aaron's banging on the door."

"Go," he said. "I'll see you later."

As far as Zoe knew, Aaron was sitting in the team room with Nina and Tom. But the Randle conversation was one she and Carl had been through even more times than the Streeting conversation. And never anything new.

Aaron banging on the door was just a white lie. A lot whiter than some of the lies she'd told Carl since they'd moved to Cumbria.

CHAPTER THREE

"You got the book yet?" DS Nina Kapoor asked.

"What?"

She fixed DS Keyes – Aaron, now she'd been promoted – with what she hoped was a challenging look. She'd practised it in the mirror after her promotion, needing a new glare to match her new position. Something that reinforced her seniority.

She worried it just made her look drunk.

"You know what," she replied.

"Something wrong with your eyes?" he asked.

"Christ's sake." Nina's exasperation made DS Keyes grin.

"Sorry. Yes, of course I know what. And yes, I've looked into getting the book."

She blinked. *Looked into getting the book?*

"It's not complicated, Aaron." The name felt odd on her lips, but he'd insisted. "It's a book. You just buy it. Buy it, read it, learn it, pass the exam, become a DI."

"All in good time," he told her.

She glanced across the desk at DC Tom Willis, who sat quietly watching the argument with a smile.

"What the hell are you grinning at?" she said.

"Nothing, DS Kapoor."

She hated him calling her that. He bit his lower lip to stifle a laugh.

"And what's 'all in good time' supposed to mean?" She turned back to Aaron. "You're blocking my path."

"Am I? Last time I checked, you were a DS. Same as me."

"That's true." Tom leaned forward. "She's got the certificates and everything to prove it."

They were ganging up on her. They were right – she'd aced the sergeants' exam with near-perfect marks and a commendation that her mum had plastered all over Facebook.

But being a DS and acting like one weren't the same thing. Not in a team with one DI, another DS, and a single DC. Not when that DC was Tom, someone she'd been with since training, someone she saw as an equal rather than a subordinate.

The solution seemed obvious to Nina. Aaron becomes DI, having already played the part successfully in Elterwater. He gets promoted and takes over the team. They recruit a new DC she can properly supervise, someone who can benefit from her wisdom and experience...

Wisdom and experience? Who was she kidding?

"Seriously," Aaron said, "I will get round to it. I promise. I want to be a DI. But, you know, we already have one of them. So until DI Finch decides—"

"Until DI Finch decides what?" The boss stood by the

door. Nina hadn't noticed her arrival, and from Aaron's face, neither had he.

"Nothing, boss," Aaron said.

Now Nina bit her lip to hold in the laugh.

"Come on. Out with it." DI Finch took a step forward.

She had to know, didn't she? She must be thinking about promotion herself, looking at DCI roles, maybe asking the super to create one.

"I just—" Aaron began, but DI Finch's phone rang. She answered and listened.

"You sure?" She paused. "Really? There?"

The humour drained from her face. Nina's heart raced. Things could turn in an instant.

"We've got a body, folks," DI Finch said.

"Murder victim?"

"That's what they're telling me. Unidentified at the moment, but let's see if we can do better. Aaron, do you mind coordinating from here?"

"No problem," DS Keyes said.

"Good. Tom, Nina, you can go with me." DI Finch headed out of the team room.

"Go where?" Nina asked.

DI Finch paused in the doorway. "Oh, didn't I say? The crime scene. Which just happens to be at the Port of Workington."

CHAPTER FOUR

"Jesus Christ," Nina said.

Zoe couldn't disagree. From this angle, they couldn't see much, but what was visible made it clear the victim had suffered a painful end. Both legs twisted at unnatural angles. The arms were splayed so far apart that the body appeared stretched.

The rest remained hidden beneath logs.

"What's that?" Zoe pointed to where a log had just been lifted, revealing part of a white shirt. They could now tell the victim was male, but something marked the fabric.

"Blood?" Tom suggested.

Zoe shook her head. "No. It's too neat."

Stella Berry, the local crime scene manager, supervised the scene with Chris Robertson hovering by her side – the only pathologist who still insisted on attending every crime scene, and generally made it there before the investigating team. Keisha Middleton from Stella's team stood back, scrolling on her phone. Dr Robertson's latest intern – a muscular young man introduced as 'Bud' – handled the lifting. He'd whispered a correction to his name as soon as the pathologist had walked away.

"Brad," Zoe called. He paused, one log cradled in his arm. "Can you clear that one next?"

Brad placed his log beside the others that might need testing, then lifted the one Zoe had indicated.

The body hadn't been stretched after all. The log's removal showed the arms had been pulled to their limits by the weight above. Zoe hoped the same explained the legs' position. Perhaps he hadn't been tortured. Perhaps this had happened after death.

"It's a bloody drawing," Nina said.

Brad glanced down at the shirt and dropped the log on his foot. "Shit!" he shouted.

"Language, Bud," Dr Robertson said.

"I've broken my bloody foot." Brad winced. "And it's Brad, not Bud."

"I'm sure you'll be fine." Dr Robertson stepped closer alongside Zoe.

Nina was right. A drawing marked the shirt – dark enough to be blood, but with the consistency of marker pen. Neat lines formed a pair of lips with a finger across them.

"Shut up," Brad said, his pain forgotten.

"I beg your pardon?" The pathologist turned.

"No, I mean that." Brad pointed at the body. "It means shut up, doesn't it?"

He looked around at the assembled team, his hopeful smile lingering on Keisha.

"Dur," Keisha said.

Brad's smile vanished.

"I was just—"

"Keep going," Keisha said.

CHAPTER FOUR

Brad bent to lift the next log, revealing part of the victim's face.

"Oh my God." Tom, who'd edged closer for a better view, went pale.

"What?" Zoe asked. Tom had seen plenty of corpses recently – whatever had been done must be horrific.

"It's..." Tom pointed and stepped back.

Dr Robertson moved forward to examine the body. "It's not pretty, but I've seen worse. So has young DC Willis."

"What is it, Tom?" Zoe watched as the DC sank to the ground.

"It's..." Tom met her eyes.

She saw no horror there, no shock. Only sadness.

"It's Mulligan," he said. "It's Kieran Mulligan, from Durranhill nick."

CHAPTER FIVE

"It's OK, Nina," Tom said, aware that his heart was racing.

Nina didn't look convinced.

"It's not like we were actual mates or anything." Tom shifted his weight between his feet. "I worked with him for a couple of days. He was a decent bloke. I liked him, and he didn't like his boss."

His boss had been Ralph Streeting, so that was a positive.

"But I was undercover," Tom continued. "Or sort of undercover, at least. Kieran didn't know why I was there. We weren't really even working together."

As the words left his mouth, he heard how hollow they sounded.

He'd liked Kieran Mulligan. Seeing him dead like this was sad and a shock. But he'd seen worse. They'd all seen worse.

The boss had suggested they look around the site together, hunt down witnesses and cameras. She'd given Nina a meaningful look while making that suggestion – one Tom hadn't missed.

CHAPTER FIVE

Look after Tom.

Nina studied his face, frowning. "I can't tell if you're lying to me. Are you lying, Tom?"

"I'll get over it." He shook his head. "And you don't need to—"

"That's the thing, Tom," she cut in. "I *do* need to. I'm a DS now. I have to be 'supportive'."

The air quotes were almost visible around that last word.

"Doesn't come naturally, does it?" Tom said.

They both laughed.

Their first stop was the entry kiosk. A tired-looking man with an angry sunburn directed them to a security hut – a windowless shipping container barely larger than the kiosk.

Tom banged on what appeared to be the door.

Silence.

He raised his fist to knock again when the door swung inward, nearly sending him sprawling. A woman stood there, smirking. Behind her, screens showed various areas of the Port of Workington.

Including, he noticed, the outside of the security hut. She'd timed that door opening on purpose.

"DC Willis," he said, displaying his ID. "DS Kapoor. You'll know about the dead man. We need your footage from the previous twenty-four hours."

The woman's face twisted.

"Better make it a week," Nina added.

"You'll struggle," the woman replied. "Cameras are bust."

Tom peered at the screens. He could see Dr Robertson and Brad moving the body towards a mortuary ambulance. Another screen showed Keisha and Stella in white suits, climbing through the logs like oversized caterpillars.

"Looks like they're working fine now," he said.

"Yeah. Just got them back online. No footage for the last couple of days."

"Convenient." Nina pulled out her notebook. "Can we take your name, please?"

The woman provided her details and her colleagues' information, plus a USB stick with footage from the five days before the outage. She seemed unbothered by both the corpse and Nina's scepticism.

Outside, Tom blinked in the sudden brightness. "That can't be a coincidence."

Tom nodded. "And I bet that footage is gone for good," Nina said. "A dead cop at the Port of Workington, and the cameras were disabled? This has Myron Carter written all over it."

"And we know what that picture meant, don't we?"

Nina frowned briefly before her expression cleared. "It meant 'keep your mouth shut'."

"And it was aimed at Mulligan's old boss. Streeting."

Nina's phone rang. She answered, listened, then hung up.

"That's the boss. Wants me with Stella, checking things over, keeping an eye on Keisha. You OK to talk to the people who found the body?"

The body. Kieran Mulligan. A decent bloke.

"Yeah," Tom said. "Chatting with Carter's employees. Can't wait."

"We can't all get the fun jobs." Nina winked and walked away.

CHAPTER SIX

The boss was watching.

"I'll stick in the background, Nina," she'd said. "Just ignore me."

Nina balanced precariously on the boards Stella had placed among the logs, kitted out in her white forensic suit, mask and gloves. She could feel the boss's eyes boring into her back. It was almost enough to distract her from what was happening to her left.

Almost, but not quite.

Keisha stood with her hands on her hips, unleashing a torrent of colourful language at three Port employees who were edging backwards, their eyes fixed on her.

"And stay the fuck away from my crime scene," Keisha bellowed.

A woman about Nina's age with platinum blonde hair and protective plasters around her facial piercings spoke up. "We didn't know. We're just here for the shift. No one told—"

"There's half a dozen police cars, a hundred miles of tape

and a dead body, and you didn't know?" Keisha's voice echoed across the Port.

She had a point. The body was out of sight now, but everything else was obvious enough.

The boss had told Nina to keep an eye on Keisha, but wasn't that Stella's job? Nina turned to find the crime scene manager looking back at her, smiling beneath her mask.

"You want her?" Stella asked.

"What?"

"Keisha. You're one of the bosses now. This is what you'll have to deal with."

Nina shook her head. "Only person I'm in charge of is Tom. And Tom's not like that."

"You tried giving your old mate DC Willis a direct order yet?"

"No. No, but..."

"People," Stella said. "They're all arseholes. Just different types."

"You two quite finished discussing the world of management?" Dr Robertson appeared behind them. "Or would you like to hear about the dead man?"

Nina spun around, startled by his sudden presence. The noise – mostly Keisha – had masked his approach.

"You got anything for me?"

"Looks like he was beaten to death," the pathologist said matter-of-factly. "No sign of any specific individual wound that finished him off, but I'd expect to see that when I get him on the table. For now, my best guess is we're looking at a blunt instrument, multiple injuries."

"Any idea what sort of weapon we're looking for?"

Dr Robertson glanced at the thousands of pieces of wood stacked around them. "Again, I'll know more when I've done the PM. Might be able to extrapolate from the nature of the wounds or even extract foreign material if we're lucky. But yes, it might have been a log."

"Can you tell me if it happened here?" Nina asked Stella. "Or was he moved post-mortem?"

"No, I can't tell you. Not yet, anyway. Although, as Dr Robertson here will no doubt confirm, the way the fluids are pooled in the arms..."

"Agreed," said the pathologist. "If I had to guess, the hypostasis suggests he was moved."

"Hopefully Keisha will come up with something more definitive," Stella continued. "If you give her enough time, she runs out of swear words and starts actually doing her job."

Keisha had indeed stopped shouting and was now crouching down, examining a pile of logs.

"She'll be checking the material closest to where the body was found, first," Stella explained. "Looking for anything that might hold prints, blood spatter, or other material that would indicate either the wounds being inflicted here, or the body being transported. I can't guarantee anything, mind."

"OK," Nina said. "Oh, and keep an eye out for—"

"For his phone, yes. This isn't my first rodeo, Nina."

"Good. Sorry."

The phone hadn't been on the body. Almost nothing had been – just those trousers, and that shirt with its chilling message.

Dr Robertson straightened his suit. "Anyway, I'd best get back. Got more dead people to cut up. They're queuing four deep back at the mortuary. I'll get to the new boy when I've got through the more pressing ones, but we're looking at a day or two."

"Fine," Nina replied. It wasn't like she could offer to lend a hand, and if there was anything to be found, the pathologist would find it. In the meantime, there was enough to be getting on with.

CHAPTER SEVEN

Kieran Mulligan was dead, then.

Aaron had met the man once, briefly. He hadn't warmed to him, but that was because of Mulligan's employer rather than the man himself. The death of a fellow officer always came as a shock.

Now he was dealing with the phone company's usual obstruction, making his job harder than necessary.

"It'll take maybe a week," said the man on the line, his Essex accent thick.

"No, it won't. You can do it in twenty-four hours." Aaron kept his voice level.

"Look, mate, I don't know who you've been talkin' to, but—"

Aaron sighed. "Your colleagues."

"You what?"

"I've been talking to your colleagues. A dozen times in the last couple of years. This happens every time."

There had been a team that did it all for them. The

Police Telecom Unit. But for more than two years now, Aaron and the team had been stuck doing it for themselves.

Cuts, and politics.

"What 'appens?" asked the man from the company.

"You lot say it'll take ages, we complain, you say there's nothing you can do, we remind you there's a killer on the loose, you say it's not possible, we tell you it is, and then suddenly we get everything we need in twenty-four hours."

"You what?" the man repeated.

Aaron shook his head. "Look, we can do all that, or we can skip to the end where you give us what we need in twenty-four hours. Your choice."

"Fine. I'll do what I can."

After a quick search for public information about Mulligan, Aaron picked up his phone to call Tom.

"You OK?" he asked when the DC picked up.

"Yeah, fine." Tom's voice suggested otherwise, but that was to be expected.

"You'll tell me if you need to be removed from the investigation? Or if you need to talk to someone? I can check if Doctor Filey's available—"

"Really, Sarge. I just want to find out who did this."

"Good. Then tell me what you know about Kieran Mulligan."

The details were sparse. Tom had seen Mulligan occasionally since Streeting's arrest. His fiancée had moved back to Canada months ago – an amicable split. His only family was in Ireland – two cousins and a stepbrother he didn't speak to.

"Sounds lonely," Aaron said.

"I think he had friends locally, and at the station. Seemed happy enough to me."

"Good. Get some names down. We'll go through them later. I've got a police station to call. DS Mulligan hadn't been reported missing, as far as I can see."

The admin team at Durranhill took three attempts to reach and proved almost as difficult as the phone company.

"Yeah, he didn't report in this morning," said the woman who answered.

"Not that surprising," Aaron replied. "Given the circumstances."

"Didn't answer his phone, either. Says here... Yeah, he tapped out at six last night. Same as usual. No contact since then. Dead then, is he?"

"Can you put me through to his senior officer, please?"

"Hang on."

Ten minutes of muzak later, she returned. "DS Mulligan's senior officer is DI Streeting, and I'm afraid DI Streeting is unavailable at present."

Aaron laughed. *Unavailable* was an understatement for someone on remand for murder.

"Please could I speak to DI Streeting's senior officer?"

After another brief hold, she returned. "That's DCI Carnegie. She's also unavailable."

"Kiki Carnegie?"

"DCI Carnegie, yes."

"Could you get a message to her, please? Ask her to call me as soon as she's available."

"I'll do what I can." The line went dead.

Aaron sat back. Kiki Carnegie – Streeting's boss. He hadn't known. The first Black woman to make DI in Cumbria, and the first to make DCI. He'd always admired her.

And now one of her team was on remand for murder, and another had just been killed.

He was looking forward to talking to Kiki Carnegie.

CHAPTER EIGHT

MILES STRINGER SLUMPED in his chair. "Just bloody bad luck."

"You think it was a random attack?" Tom's eyebrows rose. He'd expected more insight from the shift manager.

"Not him. God knows if the poor bastard deserved it. I mean Liam. Us lot. Picked that area to load up today, could've been anywhere else and not come back for days. Some other sod would've found it. Liam wouldn't be in the state he's in."

Liam sat silent, listening.

The crew occupied separate tables in the Port canteen, now a temporary operations centre after a heated exchange with the manager. The conversation had followed the usual pattern at the Port of Workington: polite request, firm request, threat. The threat had worked. The manager had stormed out, taking a crucial part of the coffee machine in protest.

Miles's crew had gathered here after discovering the body. Claiming Liam needed help with shock, they'd fortified his coffee with brandy. The ratio had shifted until Liam was drinking brandy with a hint of coffee, staring glassy-eyed through the window at grey clouds rolling through blue skies.

"Did you recognise the dead man?" Tom asked.

"What, from his arm?"

Tom nodded. *Fair point.* He pulled out his phone and showed Miles a photo of Mulligan from the police website.

"Not a clue, mate. Sorry. Listen, is this gonna take long?"

Tom opened his mouth to explain about complex investigations when a voice cut through.

"Wipe your feet," squawked the bird.

"Shut that bloody bird up." The process of elimination told Tom that was Shiv. He could see Ellen, and it wasn't Stacey.

"He's not doing any harm," Stacey said. She'd taken in Bobby Silver's bird after Bobby's death. Tom hadn't known she brought it to work.

Shiv's words slurred. "Just shut the bastard up."

Tom's stomach tightened. Liam wasn't the only one who'd been drinking. Shiv had been with him when they'd found Mulligan. The whole crew had been there, but Liam and Shiv had been closest to the body. Now both could barely speak properly.

These interviews had just got more complicated.

At least PC Roddy Chen, the largest officer in Cumbria, sat quietly by the door, ready if needed.

Tom moved between the group, asking his questions, getting unhelpful answers. Not from deliberate obstruction – they simply didn't know anything useful.

None recognised Mulligan's photo, and Tom believed them. The logs had been there for days. Anyone could have accessed the site at night to dump something – or someone.

CHAPTER EIGHT

Miles steered Tom away with a friendly but firm arm around his shoulders. "Look, you done here, pal?"

Tom tried to stop but found himself moving until he stood by Roddy at the door. Message received.

"I think so," he said. "I've got your initial statements, at least."

"Initial?" Miles's eyebrow lifted.

"Well, we'll need to go over those statements in due course."

"At your Hub, is that?"

Tom nodded.

"You know, up to a few months ago, we'd all have come along without thinking twice."

"You're not so keen now?"

"First Victor dies – accident, they say, but who knows? Then Bobby gets shot, we're all questioned, told nothing. That fella gets killed by Liam's girlfriend in May, he gets the third degree. Now some sod's dead in the logs. We'll be more careful with you lot now."

Tom's confusion must have shown.

Miles smiled. "If you want us in, fine, but we're bringing lawyers next time. OK?"

"Fair enough," Tom said. He'd do the same. Truth was, he doubted Miles or his crew would need detailed questioning.

It could have been anyone who found Mulligan's body. Miles was right about Liam.

Just bad luck.

CHAPTER NINE

So far, so good.

Zoe observed Nina for fifteen minutes at the start of her first murder investigation as a DS. She'd asked the right questions of the pathologist and crime scene manager and hadn't antagonised Stella.

A year ago, the two women couldn't last five minutes without sniping. Nina had matured – it had to be that, since Stella certainly hadn't softened. Whatever the reason, they stood talking by the crime scene while Keisha muttered to herself in the background. Zoe smiled, then noticed all three women turn to look past her.

By the time she'd turned around, the men were practically on top of her.

"DI Finch," said the one at the front, a bald and otherwise unremarkable-looking man. "Long time no see."

Zoe's mind flashed back to their first meeting two years ago at the Whitehaven Golf Club auction. He'd been chatting with Sinead Conway and exchanging nods with Ralph Streeting.

CHAPTER NINE

"Mr Carter," she said.

"Myron, please." A smile played on his lips.

He'd been on her mind for those two years – her counterpart across the chessboard. She'd captured his queen when Streeting was arrested, but Carter himself remained elusive. Five tall, muscled men surrounded him now. Pawns, nothing but cannon fodder.

Carter raised his eyebrows at her silence. "Horrible, this." He gestured towards the crime scene. "I can't tell you how shocked we are. I understand the victim was one of your colleagues, DI Finch."

Zoe nodded, wondering if this was a threat like their last conversation, when he'd warned her to stick to safer parts of town.

"I hope you'll be able to cooperate with the investigation," she said.

Nina appeared at her side.

"Of course, of course," Carter replied. "Ah. DC Kapoor."

Nina opened her mouth, but Carter cut her off. "DS Kapoor, I'm sorry. Congratulations on your promotion."

He leaned in close to Nina's face. "I'll be following your career with interest."

Nina tensed, her jaw set and eyes narrowed as she rose slightly onto her toes.

After a stretched moment of silence, Nina smiled. "Thank you, Mr Carter. I'm sure we'll be seeing plenty of each other." She turned and walked back to Stella and the crime scene.

Carter seemed unmoved. He nodded to Zoe. "Get in touch if you need any assistance." He walked away, his entourage falling in behind him.

Zoe joined Nina and Stella. "That was amazing."

Nina was pale and breathing hard. "Yes, boss. That was just... It took all my willpower."

"You did well, Nina. *Really* well."

A grin spread across Nina's face. "It was pretty cool, wasn't it?"

Tom had arrived during their exchange. After a brief update on the crime scene and body discovery, Zoe gave out instructions.

"Tom, can you head over to Mulligan's house? See if there's anything useful there."

Tom nodded.

"Stella, can you—"

"I'll send Caroline. She can meet Tom there."

Zoe could sense Tom's relief. Caroline Deane was much easier to work with than Keisha.

"Nina," she said, "we're heading back to the Hub. See what secrets Aaron's dug up for us."

CHAPTER TEN

"Kiki Carnegie?" Nina bit her bottom lip. "*The* Kiki Carnegie?"

"One and the same." The sarge smirked.

DI Finch looked from one to the other, her brow creased.

"Think we'll get to meet her?" Nina bounced on her toes like a star-struck teenager. "If she was Mulligan's boss?"

"Mulligan's boss's boss," the sarge – Aaron – corrected. "And I don't know. We'll see how things play out."

"OK." DI Finch folded her arms. "Anyone fancy telling me what you're talking about?"

"DCI Carnegie," explained Aaron. "Streeting reported directly to her, apparently."

The boss snorted. "Streeting reported directly to Myron Carter. Who's this Kiki Carnegie? Do we need to get PSD involved with her, too?"

"God, no!" Nina gasped. "Kiki Carnegie – she's a bit of a legend."

"Really?"

"She is, boss," the sarge confirmed. "First Black DI in Cumbria, then first Black DCI, outstanding record—"

"And a name like a tongue-twister." DI Finch shrugged. "Let me know how you go with her. Let's see what Tom's found at Mulligan's house, shall we?"

The updates to the big screen that Jeff from IT had installed allowed them to make video calls directly from it to each other's phones. They hadn't used it yet, but if Tom had anything to tell them, he could show them directly. DI Finch tapped on her phone, then on her keyboard, then sighed.

"Shall I?" Nina offered.

"Yes, DS Kapoor, if you don't mind."

The sarge stifled a laugh. Nina synched her phone with the network, and a moment later, Tom's face appeared on the wall, taking up most of the screen. A little of his face, anyway. More mask and hairnet than face.

"Boss. Everyone. Everything OK there?"

There was a delay between the movement of his lips and the words. Jeff had told them that might happen. Little niggles, he'd said. He'd sort them out.

He was a strange one, Jeff. The sort of man Nina's mum would have called an odd fish. But he knew his stuff.

"All good here," said the DI. "What have you found?"

"Not a lot, to be honest," Tom replied. "All pretty neat and tidy. Look."

He switched his phone to the rear camera and took them on a brief tour of Mulligan's home, a first-floor, two-bed apartment in a modern block in Cockermouth.

"Not bad," said Nina. It was tidier than her place. And there was a balcony, too.

"View of the car park," Tom pointed out. "Nothing to get excited about. Look."

CHAPTER TEN

He pulled open a door to reveal a wardrobe, half empty.

"Claire, that's his ex-fiancée, she left a little while ago. Seems he hadn't got round to filling the space."

He took them into the kitchen, which was clean and well-stocked.

"No pizza boxes or empty cans in the recycling, either," Tom said. "He looked after himself."

"Needn't have bothered," Nina muttered.

The boss shot her a look.

"Hi," said a quiet voice.

The white-suited figure of Caroline Deane appeared onscreen, turning from where she was bent over a side table in the bedroom to wave.

"Anything interesting, Caroline?" asked Nina, trying to make up for her previous comment.

The crime scene investigator shook her head. "Sorry, no. I'll keep on looking, but nothing jumps out. I'd be surprised if anything happened here."

"So what are we thinking?" asked Tom. "Carter, right?"

Nina looked from the screen to her colleagues. The sarge was frowning. DI Finch's lips were pursed.

"Yes," said Nina. "That's my guess."

"I agree," said DI Finch. "Sending a message to Streeting. Don't talk. Not that he's talking anyway."

"Not to us, at least," added the sarge. "And Mulligan himself, Tom – you're convinced he was clean?"

Tom shrugged. "I liked him. He didn't show any indication that he knew what Streeting was up to. Just tried to get on with the job. I know you can't take anything for granted, but I reckon he was clean."

Nina sighed. That just made the whole thing all the more depressing.

CHAPTER ELEVEN

DC Harriett Barnes left her temporary office and took the stairs to DI Whaley's office.

She passed three people on her way: a woman leaning against a wall, and two men talking in hushed tones as they climbed the stairs. The men startled when they saw her, then gave quick nods.

The woman's eyes were red and puffy from crying.

Harriett had only been back at Durranhill for a few days, but this wasn't how she remembered it. Before her stint at the Hub, people had been either friendly or cold – usually cold once they learned she was a Professional Standards Officer. But this was different.

On the fourth floor, she spotted Phil walking towards her. He'd set up her computer on the secure network in her temporary office earlier.

"Phil."

He flashed her a grin. "All OK downstairs?"

She shrugged. It wasn't. Being two floors away from her

CHAPTER ELEVEN

boss was far from ideal. Someone had decided it wasn't 'appropriate' for her to take over DS Denise Gaskill's office while she recovered. Whoever had made that call hadn't considered how inappropriate it was to place her on the same floor as officers she might end up investigating.

"I've just seen a woman crying," she said. "Everyone's walking around like something terrible's happened."

Phil's expression turned grave. "You haven't heard?"

She shook her head.

"Kieran's dead."

The name tugged at her memory.

"Kieran. DS Mulligan."

Her jaw dropped. "I'm sorry, Phil. I didn't realise. I need to call someone."

Tom answered immediately.

"Have you heard?" she asked. "About Mulligan?"

"Yeah."

"Are you OK?" She knew they hadn't worked together long, but sometimes that didn't matter.

"Fine." His tone suggested otherwise.

"Where are you?"

"On my way back from Mulligan's flat. It was..."

She waited.

"It was just what you'd expect. Orderly. Quite stylish. He was... Bloody hell, Harriett. We've got to put Carter away. He can't get away with this."

"You'll get him."

A door opened ahead, and DI Whaley emerged. He spotted her, nodded, and went back inside.

"I've got to go," Harriett said. "Love you, Tom."

"Love you too."

The words sent a shiver through her. She pictured his face as he said them.

He meant it. Really meant it.

DI Whaley cut straight to business when she entered his office.

"You've been through the files?"

"Yes. I've focused on the long-term investigation." She'd taken over one of Denise's investigations, something she and the DI had been quietly pursuing for months. "It seems to point in one direction."

"When you're working with dodgy cops..." DI Whaley leaned back in his chair. "Well, let's just say they're not all as dumb as Tel Cummings. Sometimes you've got your eye on someone because someone else is trying to distract you. Sometimes it's not them you should be looking at."

Harriett knew this. It was basic PSD training.

DI Whaley eyed her. "What have they said?" he asked.

She frowned. "What? Who?"

"The people you think you're looking into. The obvious suspects. What is it they're alleged to have said and done? And is it really them?"

"Well, we don't know. That's what we're trying to find out."

He raised an eyebrow. "Because even if things have been said and done, and even if they seemed to come from your target, can you be sure? Is it really them? Or is it their boss, pulling strings? Is it someone below them, acting independently but using their authority as cover?"

Harriett nodded through his next few minutes of cautions and truisms. She'd spent over a year undercover when she'd started in PSD. She'd handled more investigations than officers with twice her experience.

She wasn't the uncertain rookie anymore.
She was confident now. PSD had a target.
And she was going to help bring that target in.

CHAPTER TWELVE

"Sit down," said Fiona, bending down to the papers scattered across her desk.

Zoe inhaled the aroma before taking her seat. Good coffee. Proper coffee. The kind prepared by the super's assistant, not the awful canteen stuff she'd endured while he'd been away.

"Luke's back from his holidays," Zoe said.

Fiona looked up. "Just this morning. Give it half an hour and he'll have this lot sorted into something that makes sense." She gestured at the papers. "What I'll do when he goes for good..."

"He got the job, then?"

"He'll be moving to work for Becca Grey in a few weeks. He's working his notice – doesn't have to, strictly, but he's a decent chap. Won't leave me until I've found someone to replace him."

Zoe thought replacing Luke would be close to impossible, but kept that to herself. "You haven't called me up here to talk about Luke though, have you?"

CHAPTER TWELVE

"No. Here." Fiona picked up a sheaf of papers.

Zoe reached for it, but Fiona shook her head. "I'll send you the details later. I want to have a proper read first."

"Is that what I think it is?"

Fiona nodded.

About time. The Independent Office for Police Conduct had interviewed almost everyone at the Hub back in January, then vanished, leaving nothing but tension and rumour.

"How bad is it?" Zoe asked.

"You come out of it well," Fiona replied.

Zoe managed a small smile, but she hadn't really been the one under investigation.

"And?" she prompted.

"Me, less so. Apparently, I 'preside over a culture in which officers are led to believe they can act with impunity, and it is only thanks to the actions and ethics of certain other senior staff that things are not significantly worse than they already are'."

Ouch. "That's rubbish," said Zoe.

"Thank you, but I'm not entirely sure it is. Look at Cummings... It should have been obvious something was wrong."

"You can't be held responsible for that. It was a complex criminal gang that had been going for years. You—"

"I'm not talking about the actual corruption. I mean the sort of person he was. Beating people up. Threatening them. When he killed Victoria Speares, it wasn't because he was working for Bobby Silver. It was because he was a stupid, arrogant, violent prick. And we knew it. Everyone here knew it, and they let him get away with it."

"Cummings reported to Morris Keane, not you," Zoe pointed out, feeling disloyal. Morris Keane was a good cop.

"It's my station, Zoe. The shit flows up, and it stops at this desk. Morris tried to get Cummings disciplined repeatedly. Cummings knew how to work the system. If I'd backed Morris up, instead of just letting things take their course, maybe none of this..." She gazed past Zoe towards the window.

"Anyway." Fiona turned back with a forced smile. "I'll send it over shortly. They're giving us a chance to respond before publishing their recommendations."

"We'll back you to the hilt, Fiona."

"I'm sure you will. And meanwhile, one of our own has been killed, and you'll be getting to the bottom of that before you think about politics and the IOPC, right?"

"Right," Zoe agreed.

Fiona looked down at another sheaf of papers – a clear dismissal.

Zoe's phone rang as she left. Front desk.

"DI Finch?" said a female voice.

"Speaking."

"You've had a walk-in, Ma'am. Says he wants to speak to you. Won't speak to anyone else."

"What's it in connection with?"

"He wouldn't say. We've put him in Interview Room Four. Showed him Room Two, and he turned around and started to walk out."

Interview Room Four was the comfortable one. Room Two was very different.

"On my way," said Zoe.

She headed downstairs through custody to the interview rooms. She peered through the glass panel, but the visitor sat out of view.

CHAPTER TWELVE

She pushed open the door. "Hello, I'm DI Finch. I understand..."

He stood in the corner, facing away, but turned as she spoke. His hair was greyer and thinner, more lines on his face, but the shirt was still crisp white, the suit immaculate.

"Long time no see, Zoe," he said, walking towards her.

"David Randle," she breathed. "What the hell are you doing here?"

CHAPTER THIRTEEN

Aaron parked his Volvo outside Denise's house, trying to ignore the concerning noises it had been making lately. The car had been his sanctuary when he'd needed one. Nothing could be seriously wrong with it – just needed a bit of attention.

The house looked ordinary. You wouldn't expect someone like Denise to live here rather than some stark warehouse with metal doors. But here she was in a large detached house on the outskirts of Aspatria, between Durranhill and the Hub.

Her car sat in the driveway, her motorbike stored in the garage. She'd been back driving just three days after leaving the hospital, although the bike was still off-limits for now. A mere car bomb and induced coma wouldn't dictate Denise's choices for long.

She opened the door almost immediately, as if she'd been watching for him, and led him inside where tea was waiting. Though not usually a tea drinker, she'd noticed his preference and always had it ready for his visits.

CHAPTER THIRTEEN

"Heard anything?" she asked as he sipped.

He glanced up, surprised. Could she already know about Mulligan? She was based at Durranhill, but PSD rarely mixed with regular officers.

"About what?"

"Me, of course." Denise traced a finger along one of her fading scars stretching from ear to eye. "When they're letting me back. I've spoken to DI Whaley."

"Why would I hear anything about you?"

"Maybe DI Finch mentioned it."

"Hate to break it to you, but there are other topics of conversation at the Hub these days."

"Likely story." She grimaced at her tea. "Think I'll make myself a coffee."

Aaron started to rise, but caught her warning look and sat back down. He watched her move smoothly around the kitchen, reaching high and low with apparent ease.

"Listen," he said once she returned with her tiny espresso. "There's been a development."

"You look serious. Nothing good, then?"

"We lost a police officer."

Her smile faltered. "Lost? Not one of the team?"

"No – Kieran Mulligan. DS Mulligan from your old station."

"Not my old station, Aaron. I still work at Durranhill. Just temporarily off sick. I remember him – worked for Streeting. But clean, as far as we knew. Well, that's shit. What happened?"

Aaron explained their theory about Carter targeting Mulligan to frighten Streeting into silence. The colour slowly returned to her face, though her scars remained stark against her skin.

"How's your gorgeous husband?" she asked, changing topics.

They chatted about Aaron's home life for a while. Serge had accompanied Aaron before, and Denise had dropped in on them once she could drive again. The friendship between Serge and Denise had been unexpected – as had Aaron's own friendship with her.

"Right." Aaron stood. "Can't waste all my time with invalids."

"Sod off," she smiled.

In the hallway, he paused to admire an elaborate bouquet of roses in what looked like an expensive crystal vase.

"Impressive. Someone's spoiling you. Anyone I know?"

"Sod off," she repeated with a slight laugh.

They bumped fists as usual. She watched from the doorway as he reversed out and drove away.

Something felt off about that laugh. Maybe it was Mulligan's death affecting her, or perhaps those flowers reminded him of similar expensive arrangements in her hospital room months ago.

But what struck him most was how smoothly she'd moved. Too smoothly. And she'd avoided his gaze the entire time.

CHAPTER FOURTEEN

"Not the welcome I was hoping for," Randle said.

Zoe stared at him, open-mouthed, a thousand thoughts racing through her head.

Was Randle a threat? Should she call someone in and have him arrested? Would he be armed?

But most of all, why was he here?

"Sit down," she said, surprising herself.

Randle narrowed his eyes but complied. She reached for her phone.

He shook his head. "No recording, please."

Fine. If he wanted to play it that way. She tucked her phone away, her eyes drawn to his left hand, swaddled in bandages.

"Still causing you trouble?" She nodded towards it.

"I was shot, Zoe. A bullet passed through my hand. These things don't just get better by themselves."

Zoe smiled. This was the David Randle she knew. "Infected, is it?"

"Yes. If you'll recall, I wasn't able to get treatment initially, because I was helping Olivia escape from Carter's thugs."

Zoe tilted her head. "She drove, didn't she?"

"Yes," he responded drily. "I reference, again, the gunshot wound. Difficult to drive, in the circumstances."

"So you might say," Zoe said slowly, "that it was Olivia helping *you* escape, not the other way round."

She was enjoying herself. Of all the things she'd expected when she'd seen Randle in the room, the idea that she'd enjoy sparring with him hadn't crossed her mind. But then, she'd never been able to do this before. He'd been her boss.

"You might say that, Zoe." Randle frowned, clearly annoyed. "But the important thing is that Olivia trusts me. You understand that, don't you?"

Zoe nodded.

"So if you want her help, you need to treat me with a little more respect."

She managed to stifle the laugh, but it still emerged as a small smile. She said nothing.

"Find this funny, do you?"

Did she? She'd enjoyed it, for a minute, but now...

This was David Randle. Here. In the room with her. David Randle, who'd breached the terms of the Protected Persons Programme to contact her, to leave his approved premises, to head north.

But also, David Randle, who'd found Olivia when she couldn't. Who had, despite what Zoe had just said, rescued the woman just as Carter's people caught up with her. David Randle, who knew more about the workings of organised crime than anyone she knew.

"OK," she said. "Fine. I don't know about respect, David. But yes, I'll listen to what you have to say."

Randle rummaged in his pocket and pulled out a blister pack. He popped out several pills. "Water," he said.

Gritting her teeth, she walked to the door and called down the corridor. A minute later, Randle was gulping water from a plastic cup as he swallowed down... How many pills was that? Six? Seven?

He caught her expression. "Don't ask. Right. To business. We've agreed I have some leverage here, yes?"

"Yes," she replied. *Bloody Olivia Bagsby*.

"Good. Well, here's what's going to happen."

"I can't cut you any deals, David. That's all—"

He waved a hand. "I don't care about all that. I'm not interested in the past. I'm here to help you bring down Carter."

"That's what you keep saying."

"And that's what I intend to do. I'll come here as and when required, but I don't expect any trouble."

"You won't get any."

He laughed, a short, bitter bark. "I know I won't get any from you, Zoe. You're no fool. I'm thinking about your other half. DI Whaley. I don't want him trying to find me."

"I can't speak for—"

"It's quite simple. If I get the merest hint of Whaley sniffing around, I'll tell Olivia to get out. And if I tell her to, she will."

"I don't doubt it," Zoe replied, her voice bitter. "Nearby then, are you?"

He grinned. "Near enough. If you need me, I can be here in thirty minutes. Forty-five on a bad day."

She leaned back, watching him, trying to think things

through. What did Randle think he was bringing to the table?

"I don't get it," she said finally. "It's not your help we need, David. It's Olivia's."

His grin broadened. Zoe found herself pushing back against the chair, trying to distance herself from him.

"I gather Ralph Streeting still isn't talking," he said.

"How do you know that?"

He waved dismissively, a gesture that would have annoyed her even if he hadn't been corrupt.

"Doesn't matter. What matters is how I can fix that. If anyone can persuade Streeting to talk, it's me."

Zoe wasn't so sure of that. Ten minutes in a locked room with Denise Gaskill and no cameras on, and Streeting would be reciting his entire life story. But that wasn't going to happen.

"And," Randle continued, "if I know people like Ralph, things are about to get a lot worse for you and your friends here. And no, I don't just mean police officers turning up dead in a timber shipment."

He smirked, waiting for her to ask, again, how he knew. There was no way she'd give him the satisfaction.

"You really expect me to put you in a room with Ralph Streeting?" she said, the true hideous meaning of the words falling into place as she said them. There had been worse meetings in history, she supposed. Despots and murderers, tyrants and maniacs.

"Fine," he replied. "Call me when you change your mind."

He stood and walked out of the room. She didn't even get up, just sat there, thinking. She didn't like it.

CHAPTER FOURTEEN

She didn't like it at all. Randle and Streeting, in a room together. She couldn't think of anything worse.

But at the same time, she couldn't think of a better way to bring everything to an end.

CHAPTER FIFTEEN

"Your round," said Tom.

Harriett looked at her glass. He'd managed to finish his pint while she'd only taken a sip from her gin and tonic. His third pint since she'd arrived, beating the autumn rain by seconds as she slipped through the door of yet another new Tangier Street bar.

She didn't know how many he'd had before that.

"You sure you want another?" She watched his face carefully.

Tom nodded, silent. This was no good.

No good at all.

"I just think—"

"Look, I know you reckon we should just sit down and talk about it," he said. "I get that. But what's there to talk about? He's dead, Harriett. He was a nice bloke and someone, probably Carter, had him killed, and I'm sad about that, and angry, and I want to get drunk."

When he put it that way, it sounded reasonable. The music was too loud for a proper conversation anyway. She

CHAPTER FIFTEEN

made her way to the bar, glancing back at Tom occasionally while she waited.

He was doing as well as could be expected. Sad and angry, like he'd said. And it wasn't worth getting into a row about. Not when they were so close to moving in together.

She smiled to herself as the barman took her order. Two weeks today. Their own place. The two of them. No more lies.

A new start.

She returned to the table. A couple of teenage girls with perfectly made-up faces hovered nearby, eyes fixed on both the table and its occupant. As Harriett sat down, they shot her identical looks of disgust and walked away.

"Looks like I might need to keep a closer eye on you."

"What?" Tom hadn't even noticed them. Which, considering their effort, seemed a little unfair. But this was one of the things she loved about him.

He really didn't notice.

"Given who he was, we might end up working together on this one."

His wandering eyes snapped back to hers. "Eh?"

"PSD, I mean. On the Mulligan investigation."

"Are you kidding me?" His face flushed red.

Harriett mentally kicked herself for mentioning it. "Look, I don't know, right? Maybe I'm wrong."

"Maybe you are. It's not your job to investigate murder." Tom bent to his pint and took a long drink.

"True." She took a sip of her own drink, the alcohol burning her throat – she'd ordered a double, and the barman had been generous. "It's just that DCI Branthwaite has this idea—"

"What's he sticking his nose in for?"

"He's not," she snapped, suddenly irritated. Yes, Mulligan's death was sad. But bloody hell. Tom had hardly known the man. Fine, get drunk.

But don't take it out on me.

"He's not," she said again. "He just has an idea for future investigations like these ones, where it has an obvious PSD angle, but we don't have the expertise to run it without your help."

"Well that's obvious enough, isn't it? We do what we did last time, with Bobby Silver. You come and work with us. You and me get to spend time together, the team benefits from our combined brilliance, everyone wins." He smiled at her.

She smiled back. Even drunk, even in a bad mood, Tom was a million times better than any other man she'd been with.

"Yeah. This is more the other way round. We'd have oversight. And then the experts, like you guys, you'd get seconded to our team."

He stared at her. "Are you kidding me?" he said, again.

"No. We'd still..."

Tom shook his head. "No. I don't like this at all. If it's a murder, you get the murder people running it. We don't try to take over your investigations, do we?"

They did. They had done. Harriett had lost count of the arguments between DI Finch and DI Whaley about it. But best not mention that.

"Look, it probably won't even happen," she said soothingly.

Tom nodded. "Yeah." His attention drifted away as he looked between their drinks and took another large gulp.

"Drink up," he said. "I'm almost ready for another."

CHAPTER SIXTEEN

Carl arrived home before Zoe, which made sense given her new murder investigation. He filled Yoda's bowl with food, but the cat stared at him with such disdain he checked the tin twice to ensure it was the salmon she usually enjoyed.

Her favourite was scraps from the chip shop two doors down, but she was banned from there for good reason.

He cleaned the hot tub, which they'd been using more lately. Then he phoned Denise, who claimed she was completely recovered – likely a lie. She was eager to return to work, and he could use the help.

He listened carefully to assess her condition, but even over multiple house visits, he knew her background in undercover work enabled her to mask her feelings well. These days she was the more expressive Denise he knew, whose emotions ran close to the surface, but those old skills never faded.

"We'll look at getting you back, but don't rush it," he said, ending the call before she could protest.

He spent the next half hour chopping vegetables for pasta sauce, nursing a beer while Yoda watched with apparent revulsion at the meatless meal. He considered a third beer but held off.

Zoe arrived home close to nine, exhausted and hungry. They made small talk over dinner, until he couldn't wait any longer to ask about her visitor.

"I hear—" he began.

"I had a walk-in today," she said simultaneously.

They both stopped, and he gestured for her to continue.

"You'll never guess who it was."

He shrugged, already suspecting.

"David Randle," she said.

Carl arranged his face to show surprise and anger. "He's got some nerve."

"Still thinks he can order me about. Wants to interview Streeting. Says he can make him talk."

"That's ridiculous," Carl said, squinting against the room's brightness. The beer was hitting him harder than expected.

"I thought so, too, at first. But now I'm not so sure." She hesitated. "What harm could it do? No one understands these people like Randle does. He can connect with Streeting in ways we can't – they're basically the same person, just separated by time and distance."

"What harm? David Randle and Ralph Streeting?" He paused to sip his beer, trying to think clearly.

Randle was the reason he'd initially gone undercover. The reason he'd met Zoe, ironically enough.

"Maybe we could have Streeting outside the interview," he suggested, "relaying questions through us?"

CHAPTER SIXTEEN

Zoe smiled. "If we can get Streeting talking at all, that might work. But there's something else."

Carl tensed again. "What?"

"I had to agree we wouldn't track him down. He's got complete control over Olivia. The bandaged thumb doesn't help matters."

"A what? Wait... you agreed not to look for him? Why?"

"Because if we anger him, he'll send Olivia far away. And she'll go – she trusts Randle more than us. The bastard took a bullet for her."

"Not really for her," Carl pointed out.

"No, but she doesn't know that. So you won't try to find him, right?"

Carl nodded, already planning how to locate Randle without anyone finding out. Including Zoe.

CHAPTER SEVENTEEN

SOME MORNINGS THINGS fell into place just the way Zoe wanted them to.

This wasn't one of those mornings.

She'd woken expecting the IOPC report in her inbox, but Fiona hadn't sent it yet. That was fine, Zoe had enough to be getting on with, but it would have been something to read over her first coffee of the morning.

Then there'd been a traffic incident on the way to the Hub. Nothing serious, just a truck with a flat tyre, but a truck with a flat tyre on a narrow, winding country lane could do some damage. Zoe had to perform a twelve-point turn to get herself facing back the way she'd come and hit the main roads into work instead. It reminded her why she never took the main roads if she could avoid it.

Funny how she'd got used to things. Two years back, after decades of Birmingham traffic, the roads here had seemed empty at the worst of times. Now...

Now she was in, at least. In, and picking up the phone to call Nicholas, half an hour later than planned, but better

CHAPTER SEVENTEEN

than nothing. The phone rang in her hand. She cursed and checked the display to see if she could ignore it. She couldn't.

"Hi," she said.

"Have you seen this rubbish?" Stella Berry's voice crackled through the line.

"What?"

"This..." There was a noise down the phone like someone choking. For a moment Zoe was alarmed before she recognised the telltale sounds of Stella's anger. "It's an absolute disgrace, Zoe. Check your priority messages."

"Hang on." Zoe put the phone on speaker and pulled up her internal mailbox on the laptop. She ran a finger down the screen.

There.

'The Office of the Assistant Chief Constable' in the 'From' column.

'Ralph Streeting' in the 'Subject'.

"You still there?" asked Stella.

"Yeah. Just opening it."

David Randle's words from the day before bounced around her head as she tapped the message open.

If I know people like Ralph, things are about to get a lot worse.

There was no text, just an attachment. A document, sent after midnight, a collaboration between the Policy team and the Legal team within Assistant Chief Constable Joe Carghillie's empire. Zoe still didn't understand why Little Joe had so many people working for him, but she'd given up trying to figure that out.

The Legal team made sense. What the Policy team were doing getting themselves involved in a live investigation was something else. Becca Grey's team.

Becca Grey had been sticking her nose into Zoe's investigations for a while now.

She scanned the document, Stella's breath coming short and ragged down the phone.

'...unfortunate position... convincing counter-argument... culture of incompetence and corruption...'.

It was a summary of the investigation, or at least, the understanding of it reached by Becca Grey and Little Joe's legal team. It seemed they didn't know what to do with Streeting.

Ralph Streeting had trafficked people. He'd threatened people. He'd killed people. The evidence against him was overwhelming. The prints on the gun, the ballistics that matched that gun to the bullets that had killed Bobby Silver.

That, and everything else.

And they really didn't know what to do with him.

Streeting's 'convincing counter-argument' was simply that the evidence against him had been assembled by a team of corrupt police and CSIs. There were references to Carrie Wright. To Tel Cummings.

There was a reference to Hussein Mahmoud, and Zoe could tell that Stella had her phone on speaker, too, and that Caroline Deane was reading the report at the same time she was.

"Huz?" Caroline's voice came through, sharp with anger. "They can't bring Huz into this. The bastards can't do this."

Zoe had never heard her swear before.

She read on, skipping from line to line, grabbing the gist of it, part of her astonished that anyone in authority could take this seriously, part of her completely unsurprised.

If I know people like Ralph, things are about to get a lot worse.

CHAPTER SEVENTEEN

Towards the end there was another paragraph, this one dealing with the incompetence rather than the corruption.

Why not? Throw enough dirt, it'll stick.

Inexperience. Arrogance. A lack of accountability. All there. She hit the word 'instability' and stopped, and reread the sentence, out loud.

"Allegations relating to the instability of team members need to be investigated in further detail. More specifically..."

Bloody hell.

Zoe read on, silently, stopped, read it again.

"Sorry, Stella," she said. "I'm going to have to call you back."

CHAPTER EIGHTEEN

"What fresh hell is this?" Nina stared at her phone.

"Eh?" Tom asked.

"Is she... Do you think this is a joke?"

Tom wheeled his chair over and sat beside her. Across from them, the sarge was speaking to someone at the phone company, his tone more patient than his expression suggested.

"What?" Tom peered at her screen.

Nina shook her head and passed him her phone. He studied it for a moment before handing it back.

"I thought she thought you were gay," he said. "You know, you and Elena."

There had been confusion earlier in the year. Nina's mum had believed Nina and Elena were more than housemates. Nina had encouraged that impression to stop her mum's matchmaking attempts with every eligible man in Cumbria. It had worked perfectly until her mum posted about it on Facebook. The next day, someone had tried to burn down Nina's house.

CHAPTER EIGHTEEN

Elena was a refugee from Carter's people-trafficking network. They hadn't liked knowing she was alive and free.

"I told her the truth," Nina said. "After the fire."

"Oh. So she's back to her old tricks, then."

Nina studied the photo in the WhatsApp message from her mum. A respectable-looking man smiled at the camera, wearing jeans and a white t-shirt with yellow flecks. No glasses but a slight squint. Good teeth.

The message read: *Check out this eligible young man.*

He wasn't young. Sixty at least. Well-preserved, but still sixty. An easel was visible at the edge of the photo. Those yellow flecks had to be paint – her mum must have met him at art class.

Another message appeared: *Abed's single.*

"For crying out loud." Nina tapped out a quick reply.

Her phone rang; Stella Berry's name on the display.

Nina typed, *He's older than you!* and sent it to her mum before answering.

"About bloody time," the crime scene manager snapped.

Nina pursed her lips. "And good morning to you, too."

"Is it? First I've heard of it." Stella sounded defeated, not just her usual angry self.

"Something wrong?"

"Everything's wrong. Ask your DI. And as for your crime scene..."

Nina sat forward, wondering if they'd found something at the Port.

"There's too much," Stella said.

Nina sat back. This was what she'd expected.

"A hundred people must have been around that area in the last twenty-four hours. The ones who found him, the previous shift, security walking the edges. Half the samples we've taken for elimination are on the database already."

"Because half of Myron Carter's employees are career criminals," Nina said.

"Precisely. We'll keep looking. Might find something surprising. But as it stands, I don't think forensics are going to crack this one for you."

"OK."

"Bye." Stella hung up.

Ask your DI, she'd said. Nina turned to see the boss herself pushing open the door, her expression grim.

"Aaron," DI Finch called.

The sarge put down his phone. "Yes?"

"Come with me." The sarge followed her out of the team room.

"Looks like he's got more to worry about than an annoying mum," Tom said.

"Just shut up."

Nina knew she was punching down, but you had to punch somewhere. And Tom could take it.

CHAPTER NINETEEN

Aaron's heart pounded as he followed his boss along the corridor. The short walk from the team room to her office stretched endlessly.

His mind raced. The look on DI Finch's face when she'd entered the team room — and now, as she turned to face him in her office — set his nerves on edge. She gestured to a chair in front of her desk, then sat beside him rather than behind her desk. Her face was pale, her mouth drawn tight.

His thoughts spiralled through possibilities. *Had something happened to Serge? To Annabel?*

"I need you to read this." She reached across the desk for a sheet of paper and handed it to him.

Aaron scanned the document. 'Office of the Assistant Chief Constable'. 'Subject A' – *clearly Ralph Streeting*. '... legal implications... policy decisions...'.

Relief flooded through him. This was politics, not personal tragedy.

He read further, his frown deepening at phrases that

jumped out: 'inexperience', 'arrogance', 'lack of accountability', 'instability'.

'More specifically, one individual, heavily involved in a series of operations leading to the arrest of Subject A, although not in the arrest itself, has been showing signs of mental instability for a period encompassing the majority of said operations.'

"Bloody hell," he muttered.

"Look, Aaron—" the boss began.

He raised his hand to silence her, then caught himself. "Sorry, boss—"

"It's OK, Aaron. Take your time."

He reread the key phrase: 'Although not in the arrest itself...'.

The realisation hit him. While the team had been arresting Streeting, he'd been in Elterwater solving a different murder. The report might as well have painted a target on his back.

The document continued: 'Officer X is thought to have suffered severe feelings of worthlessness, both personally and professionally. On at least one occasion, Officer X is said to have expressed these feelings in terms of wishing to "crawl under a rock and stay there".'

"This is..." Aaron trailed off.

"I know, Aaron. It's appalling. They can't use this against you." The boss shook her head, looking as outraged as he felt.

"Did I say that?" He gestured to the paper. "About the rock?"

She considered carefully. "I don't know. It sounds like something you might have said."

He shrugged. The words felt familiar, but he couldn't place when he might have said them.

"There's more, Aaron."

His stomach dropped. "More?"

What followed was a dizzying conversation about David Randle – Birmingham's version of Streeting – who had apparently helped Olivia escape and was now refusing to produce her unless they met his demands. Not kidnapping, the boss assured him, but protection. Randle had taken a bullet, getting her away from Carter's people.

"What does he want?" Aaron asked.

"He wants to help us bring down Carter."

Aaron blinked. "What?"

"He wants to help us bring down Carter," she repeated.

The conversation spiralled further – plans to involve Randle in questioning Streeting, and then, incredibly, a suggestion that Aaron consider taking the Inspectors' Exam.

The boss's phone rang, cutting short their discussion. After a brief exchange, she turned back to him. "Super wants to see me. I'll see you later, OK?"

"OK, boss."

"And Aaron," she added, "don't let any of this get to you."

He walked back to the team room, wondering which 'this' she meant – the report questioning his stability, Randle's involvement with Streeting, or the suggestion of promotion. All of it felt unreal, like he'd stepped into someone else's life.

CHAPTER TWENTY

Zoe took a seat opposite the super.

"I was expecting—"

"The IOPC report?" Fiona said. "I wanted to go through it with you in person, but neither of us has time for that. You'll have seen that nonsense from the ACC's people?"

Zoe nodded.

"It changes things. Makes my position a little less secure. Talk about kicking a woman when... You going to take that?"

A faint buzzing had been going for the last few seconds. Only now did Zoe realise it was her phone.

"No, it can wait." She tapped to reject it without checking the display.

Fiona grunted. "That's not what I wanted to talk to you about, anyway," she said. "I gather you had an interesting walk-in yesterday."

"News travels."

"I am supposed to be in charge of this station, Zoe." Despite the half-smile, Zoe could tell the super was genuinely annoyed. "It's not brilliant when I hear these things from Doug Branthwaite."

"Branthwaite?"

"Apparently, you've been discussing ideas with DI Whaley. Getting this David Randle in on questioning Streeting. Branthwaite's nervous."

Zoe frowned. "Branthwaite wasn't supposed to know about it."

"Just you and Carl, then?" Fiona arched an eyebrow.

Zoe felt her anger building. Not at Fiona. At Carl, who'd gone running to his boss the moment Zoe's back was turned. She ran through their conversation the night before and realised she hadn't asked him to keep it to himself.

No. If anyone had messed up, it had been her. Keeping the super in the dark.

"I'm sorry," she said.

"I gather this Randle has been advising you informally for months, in breach of his Protected Person conditions. Were you going to mention any of this to me, Zoe? Or am I already yesterday's news?"

"It's not that," Zoe protested. "I just didn't..."

Just didn't what? Just didn't want anyone to know. That was the truth of it. Not Fiona. Not Aaron. Not Carl. Certainly not Doug Branthwaite.

She'd known what she was doing was wrong, even if she thought it was worth it. She hadn't trusted anyone else to see the value of the endgame. To see that the risk was worth taking.

"I cocked up," she said. "I think it was right to keep talking to Randle. But I shouldn't have been so quiet about it. And now he's got Olivia Bagsby hiding out with him somewhere not a million miles away, we have no idea where, and if we want Olivia to work with us, we have to keep Randle sweet."

"And he wants to put questions to Streeting."

"Yes. But his questions could be vital."

"Doug Branthwaite isn't so sure." Fiona's tone was curt.

Zoe took a deep breath, resisting the urge to snort. *Typical PSD.* Dot every 'i', cross every 't', everything done by the book.

"I understand PSD are nervous about this," she said, "but really, Randle isn't anything to do with them any more. If they want to report him for breaching his conditions, they can. If they don't, they can step away. The fact is, Randle understands more about—"

"Save it." Fiona held up a hand. "I've been through the man's file. I agree."

Zoe felt her mouth fall open. "You agree?"

"Yes. PSD shouldn't have the final say on this, and I won't let them. I... Zoe?"

Her phone was buzzing again. This time she checked the display before rejecting it, but there was no number shown.

"Sorry," she said.

"Clearly neither of us has time to waste, so I'll get straight to it. I've been through Randle's file, and I've overruled Branthwaite."

Zoe stared at her.

Fiona smiled. "I know. It's a rare day when I can do that, isn't it? But if you think Randle can help, then he's in. I've had to agree that his questions will be put remotely, through you, but he'll be able to see and hear. Is that good enough for you?"

"We can question Streeting?" Zoe asked, scarcely able to believe it.

CHAPTER TWENTY

The super smiled again. "I know. You've been waiting a while, and now you can not only question him, you can bring your pet dodgy cop in with you to help. I feel like Santa this morning. I... Zoe, I think you'd better answer that."

This time, Zoe picked up.

"DI Finch," said a voice she didn't recognise. "This is Emily from front desk. There's a man here asking for you."

"I'll be right down." She ended the call and looked up at the super. "Looks like Randle's turned up just in time to hear the good news."

CHAPTER TWENTY-ONE

"Babe?"

Aaron detected a note of concern in Serge's voice that he hadn't heard in months.

"What is it?" he asked.

"You OK?"

"Of course I'm OK. Why wouldn't I be OK? I just—"

"You don't sound OK, Aaron." Serge's words made Aaron notice the tightness in his own voice. "There's something wrong. Is it… Is it the same problems? From last year?"

They knew each other too well for Aaron to hide anything.

"No, it's not, but there's trouble. Someone's been stirring. Look, I promise you, I'm OK, but I can't talk about it now. Can we discuss it later?"

"If you're sure," Serge said. "I can tell you're—"

The door opened. DI Finch stood in the doorway, her brow creased as she stared at Aaron.

"Got to go." Aaron ended the call and stood, following the boss into the corridor. Neither spoke until they reached her office. They didn't need to – Serge wasn't the only person Aaron knew well.

"He's here," she said.

"Randle?"

She nodded. "I think so. Another so-called walk-in. I want you to meet him."

Meet David Randle?

Aaron followed her down the stairs and through the custody suite to Interview Room Four. DI Finch pushed open the door and stopped.

The man inside wasn't what Aaron had expected. Early forties, shorter than he'd imagined. Squat and well-built, with a completely bald head. Aaron had pictured someone older, taller, more menacing.

The man leaned against the wall, his face chalk-pale. Aaron's gaze dropped to the man's trembling hands.

He turned to the boss, who stared at the stranger.

"Who are you?" she asked.

Aaron felt a flash of relief – at least he wasn't alone in his confusion.

"My name is Christian Ives," the man said in a flat voice.

"What can we do for—" the boss began.

"My name is Christian Ives," he repeated. "And I killed Kieran Mulligan."

CHAPTER TWENTY-TWO

DI Finch pulled the sarge from the room just as the data from Mulligan's phone company arrived. Tom glanced up at Nina.

She caught his eye and winked before looking away, clearly aware of the timing and offering no assistance.

Tom sighed. The phone data wouldn't analyse itself. It was tedious but necessary work he'd done countless times.

Two minutes into the task, his phone rang. He grabbed it eagerly, switching to speaker when he saw who was calling.

"Tom," DI Finch said. "I need you to dig into someone. Christian Ives. He's local."

"Christian Ives." Tom frowned. "Name doesn't ring any bells. Connected to the investigation?"

"Says he is. Claims he killed Mulligan. We're interviewing him now."

The line went dead. Tom turned to Nina, whose expression mirrored his own shock.

"Bloody hell," he said.

Nina shook her head. "Easiest case we've ever had."

CHAPTER TWENTY-TWO

Tom turned back to his keyboard and started searching.

Christian Ives wasn't your typical murderer. He was a respected Whitehaven businessman specialising in property and construction, but not the cheap rental kind. His projects were substantial – industrial sites, housing developments with above-minimum affordable units, schools, even hospital extensions.

No criminal record showed up anywhere.

The image search revealed a decade's worth of news coverage. Ives was unremarkable – medium build, bald, neither handsome nor ugly. Just another face in the crowd. Yet he was deeply embedded in the community.

He'd established a youth foundation in West Cumbria, providing both premises and mentoring staff.

Nina peered over his shoulder. "One of those, is he?"

"What do you mean?"

"You know the type. Public saint, private sinner. Wants to get away with crime? Builds the right image first. Charity work's the oldest trick going. I bet he's up to his neck in—"

"Think you might be right," Tom interrupted, focusing on an image at the bottom of the screen. He enlarged it.

"Bloody hell," Nina muttered.

The photo was from a business deal two years ago – Ives selling his company to a local consortium and donating proceeds to his charity. The image showed the key players mid-celebration.

Ives stood central. Behind him, a tall man in a white suit with carefully maintained stubble had his arm around Ives' shoulders. Alistair Freeburn lurked in the background, apparently the legal representative. Next to Ives stood one of the consortium buyers, Sinead Conway, her dark hair gleaming.

But it wasn't Conway, Freeburn, or the man in white that caught their attention. Front and centre, shaking hands with Ives, stood another figure. His face was turned away in a half-smile, as if sharing a private joke. This was Conway's consortium partner.

Myron Carter.

CHAPTER TWENTY-THREE

"Aren't you going to arrest me?" The man leaned forward in his chair.

"Let's see how we get on, shall we?" Zoe kept her voice level. "But please remember that we've cautioned you, Mr Ives. Are you absolutely sure you don't want a lawyer?"

"How many times do I have to tell you? I killed Kieran Mulligan. I did it. And no, I don't want a lawyer."

Zoe exchanged glances with Aaron. They'd taken the man's prints and DNA. He'd given them his phone, even unlocked it for them.

They'd never had a more helpful suspect. Or one who seemed less likely to be the actual killer.

Aaron leaned back in his chair. "Tell me again about the incident, Mr Ives."

"Again?"

"Please."

Ives let out a heavy sigh. "Fine. I did it at the Port. Where they keep all the logs. I smashed him over the head. I didn't—"

"With what, Mr Ives?"

"What?"

"With what did you smash him over the head?"

"Oh, yeah." Ives' cheek twitched. "A log. One of the logs."

Zoe folded her arms. "You know we can check all this on the CCTV cameras."

"Go ahead," Ives replied.

Either he'd done it, or he knew the cameras hadn't been working.

"Why did you do it?" Aaron asked.

Ives blinked several times before answering. "I didn't like him."

"You didn't like him?"

"That's what I said, yes. We... We had a row. There. In the Port."

"What were you doing there?" Zoe asked.

"I came to see him. To have it out with him."

"How did you know he'd be there?"

"He told me. No. I told him. I don't remember which. It was about three in the morning."

Ives wasn't the worst liar Zoe had questioned in Interview Room Four. But he was far from the best.

If he wasn't responsible for Mulligan's death, he knew a lot more than he should have about it. Time to put that knowledge to the test.

"Tell me, what he was wearing?" Zoe said.

"What?"

"Mulligan. What was he wearing?"

"Oh, right." Ives shut his eyes, his lips moving slightly as if rehearsing something, going over a list of facts.

"A suit," he said finally. "White shirt, suit."

"Anything notable about those clothes?"

"No." Ives' eyes widened, and he shook his head. "Yes, I mean. The shirt. I was thinking you meant before. But it was done afterwards. I did it afterwards."

"Did what afterwards?"

"I drew on his shirt. After he was dead. A finger over a pair of lips. Black marker pen."

"Do you usually carry marker pens around with you, Mr Ives?" Aaron asked.

"Erm, I don't know. Sometimes, I suppose."

Again, he had the facts. Again, he was about as convincing as an infant playing a camel at a nativity play.

"Why did you draw that on his shirt?" Zoe asked.

"He was mouthy. Mulligan was. He talked too much. It was my way of telling him to shut up."

"It was your way of telling him to shut up *after* he was dead?"

Ives stared at her, motionless. He'd stopped twitching, but was so pale she'd already decided to get the custody nurse to take a look at him, or the forensic medical examiner, if there was one in. Just in case.

A buzz sounded, and Aaron checked his phone. He passed it to her, and she read Tom's message.

So there was a connection. She'd expected that. She hadn't expected Tom to find it so soon.

"Tell me," she said. "What do you know of Myron Carter?"

Ives opened and closed his mouth several times. His breathing was shallow, barely there, and he seemed even paler than before, if that was possible.

He definitely needed to see the doctor.

"Nothing," he managed. "None of this has anything to do with Myron Carter."

Despite his obvious lies, it was clear Ives knew something, and Zoe reckoned she might be able to get it out of him eventually. But she wasn't sure she could do it before he had a heart attack or a stroke or something she didn't want to be responsible for.

"Interview paused," she said. It was time to get the man's clothes and hair swabbed. Get the doctor to give him the once-over.

Maybe the break would encourage him to tell the truth.

CHAPTER TWENTY-FOUR

"Hello, who is speaking?"

The woman who answered the phone at Christian Ives' house had an unusual accent. Nina had spent months listening to central European voices, but this wasn't like that. South American, she thought.

"This is DS Nina Kapoor, from Cumbria Police."

"Oh. Why are you calling here?"

"Who am I speaking to?"

"Marissa." The name hung in the air as if Nina was supposed to know who she was and why she was answering Christian Ives' phone.

"Do you live in the house?"

A short laugh crackled through the line. "On thirteen pounds an hour, I would have to work a hundred years to live in this house. I clean the house. Two times a week. But today, nobody in."

Nina sat up straight. "Is that unusual?"

"It is not normal. Mrs Ives is always here, but today, no Mrs Ives. And the front door, it was open when I arrived."

Nina jotted *Mrs Ives* on her notepad and held it up for Tom to read.

Tom nodded and turned back to his computer.

"Do you have a phone number for Mrs Ives?" Nina wrote down the number Marissa provided. "Good, thank you. Listen, Marissa, can you do me a favour?"

"Yes, for the police, of course."

"Good. Please, stay where you are."

Movement caught Nina's eye. Tom was miming pushing something across the floor, then stopping abruptly. Nina frowned at him. He bent, pretending to sweep something into an invisible dustpan, then stopped again.

"And stop cleaning," Nina said.

Tom smiled.

"The police will be with you shortly."

Nina spent a minute reassuring Marissa she'd be safe waiting there, then tried calling Mrs Ives. The phone failed to connect. The door opened, and the boss walked in, followed by DS Keyes.

"Anything?" DI Finch asked.

Nina and Tom outlined their findings, and DI Finch summarised her interview with Christian Ives.

"He didn't do it." She shook her head. "I'd bet my career on it. He didn't do it, and chances are he's got nothing to do with it. But he's scared of something."

"Carter," Aaron said.

"Carter," the boss agreed. "Almost certainly Carter. Where does he live, then?"

Tom displayed two images on the big screen: a photo of a large, modern house, and a map of its location.

"Newbuild, near Cleator Moor," he said.

"Fine. Nina, Tom, you go there. Me and Aaron will—"

CHAPTER TWENTY-FOUR

The boss's phone rang. She listened for a few seconds. "OK." She turned to Aaron, frustration evident on her face.

"That was the super. I've been summoned. No idea what she wants now, but what she wants, she gets. Aaron, keep things ticking over. As for you two, this missing woman and the open front door can't be a coincidence. See if you can find anything at the house. Ideally, the elusive Mrs Ives."

CHAPTER TWENTY-FIVE

Zoe smiled at Luke as she walked past him.

He smiled back.

She stopped, turned around, and checked again. Luke – Fiona's usually stern assistant – was actually smiling. Perhaps it was because he was leaving for a better position. Or maybe after all these months, he'd finally warmed to her.

Then again, maybe he knew she needed a friendly face before whatever awaited her in the super's office.

"Don't sit," Fiona said as Zoe entered.

"Everything OK?"

"Yes. But you don't have time. I've got clearance."

"Streeting?"

Fiona nodded. "You can see him today." She glanced at the wall clock. "In just over ninety minutes. It's turn up on time or don't bother. And he still might not talk."

"Where?" Even a silent Streeting was better than nothing.

Fiona handed over a printed map showing a tiny country lane branching off a slightly larger one east of Pica. Zoe had driven through that area before, but couldn't place either road.

"Where?" Zoe asked again.

Fiona pointed to what looked like a smudge on the paper. "It's a high-security facility you shouldn't know about. I only just found out myself. Twenty minutes to get there."

"Can I—"

"Yes, you can take your bloody David Randle. He won't be in the room, but he'll have a live feed and secure comms. I've got clearance for three."

"Three?"

"You, Randle, Carl."

"Why Carl?"

Fiona's frown matched Zoe's own. "I overruled PSD, remember? Had to throw them a bone. Plus, they've got expertise with bent cops."

Zoe could have argued that point. PSD had more experience than her or Fiona, true. But probably not more than David Randle.

It didn't matter. Carl was coming, no debate needed. And there wasn't time anyway.

She thanked Fiona and headed downstairs, stopping briefly to call Randle.

"Zoe. To what do I owe this—"

"No time, David. Have you got a pen?"

"Give me a moment."

While waiting, she pulled up her maps app. When he returned, she read out the coordinates.

"A scavenger hunt?" Randle asked.

Zoe almost laughed. Streeting was a scavenger of sorts, living off Carter's scraps. Look where that had got him.

"Be there in thirty minutes, David."

"Why?"

"Because we're going to see Ralph Streeting."

She savoured his sharp intake of breath. It wasn't often she got to surprise David Randle.

CHAPTER TWENTY-SIX

"Are you Nina?"

The woman was distressed, her English halting. She'd spoken to Nina on the phone, so Tom wondered why she was addressing him.

Nina still hadn't made it out of the car. She was in there, switching things on and off and muttering under her breath. The promotion to DS had brought an upgrade from the ancient Fiesta to an electric Nissan. Its blue exterior was already turning a greyish brown, and the inside was decorated with the usual assortment of fast-food wrappers. Nina was still getting to grips with the car. Tom hadn't heard the phrase 'range anxiety' until a few weeks ago, but now it came up daily.

"Marissa?" Tom asked.

She nodded.

"I'm Tom. DC Willis. I work with Nina." He gestured towards the car. "Here she is."

The woman was in her forties, with platinum blonde hair and eyebrows plucked to within an inch of their lives. They stood in the driveway of Christian Ives' house: red brick, dark slate and glass. Three floors of understated, upper-middle-class money. A battered Volkswagen Polo sat in the driveway, driver's door open.

"Is that your car?" Tom asked.

Marissa nodded again.

Nina finally joined them, still grumbling.

"I did not go in the house," Marissa said. "After you called. I had only just started then. So I only did downstairs toilet and edge of kitchen."

"Good," Nina said. "And thank you. Do you mind waiting here while we take a look inside?"

Marissa glanced towards her car but gave a reluctant nod.

"We won't be long," Tom assured her.

After donning forensic suits, he entered the house just behind Nina. No obvious sign of damage, but all internal doors were open, and even from the bottom of the stairs Tom could see lights on upstairs. He strode through the house, checking that Mrs Ives was absent, and returned to the front door.

Marissa leaned against her car, smoking a long, thin cigarette.

"Did you turn those lights on upstairs?" he asked.

"No. I turn no lights on. And all doors were open already, too."

He turned on the spot, glanced up, and stopped.

"Nina!" he shouted.

She emerged a few seconds later, and he pointed up. There was a security camera there, or what remained of one. It had been smashed to pieces, some of which Tom could still see on the driveway.

CHAPTER TWENTY-SIX

"Bloody hell," said Nina. "Better get out and get Stella here."

Tom took down Marissa's contact details and told her she could go, while Nina spoke to the crime scene manager. He could only hear Nina's side of the conversation, but Stella clearly wasn't happy.

"I know you've got a crime scene," Nina said, then stopped. "Yes, I understand, but..."

Nina walked away for a minute, speaking quietly. DS stuff. Stuff a lowly DC like Tom wouldn't understand. Or, more likely, Nina being gentle and not wanting him to hear it. She walked back with half a smile on her face.

"Thanks," she said, just as a grey Lexus rolled into the driveway and stopped behind Nina's car.

A man got out and scowled at them. "Who the hell are you people?"

Tom recognised him from the photo – the one with Ives, Carter and Conway. The good-looking man with his arm draped over Ives' shoulder. A few days' growth had replaced the carefully-tended stubble from the photo, and his clothes were crumpled, but it was definitely him.

Tom stepped forward, but Nina moved faster, warrant card out. The sight of it stopped the man in his tracks.

"The police?" He looked from Nina to Tom, and then at Marissa, who hadn't managed to leave. "What's going on? Why are you here?"

"Who are you, precisely?" Nina asked.

"My name," the man said, enunciating each word, "is Gustavo Arroyo. This is my house."

Tom exchanged a puzzled look with Nina.

"I understand that this house belongs to Christian Ives," Tom said.

The man looked... Tom couldn't quite place it. Embarrassed? Or affronted?

"Yes. Christian is my husband. This is his house, but it's my house, too."

Nina blinked. They turned, as one, towards Marissa, who sat in her car, windows rolled up, the radio just audible through the glass.

"We understood there to be a Mrs Ives," Nina said.

The man who claimed to be Christian's husband nodded. "Yes."

"Yes?" echoed Tom.

"Indeed. Mrs Ives. Matilda. She's Christian's mother. Why? Where is she? Where's Christian, for that matter? Do you mind telling me what on earth is going on? It's bad enough that the neighbours see all this..." He gestured towards Nina's car. "But the police? Here? It's unacceptable."

"Do you know where Mrs Ives might be?" asked Nina.

"Where she might be? In there, of course." Gustavo pointed at the house.

"I'm afraid she isn't," replied Nina.

For the first time, the man looked more worried than angry. "What do you mean? She must be there."

"Is there anywhere she likes to go? Walks, maybe? Does she drive? Might she be with friends?"

Gustavo snorted. "Matilda? Not likely. She has no friends. She's eighty-six years old, and she struggles to leave her bedroom. Leaving the house takes quite some planning."

Tom looked at Nina, then up at the house.

Shit.

CHAPTER TWENTY-SEVEN

The fifteen-minute drive to meet Randle felt both endless and instantaneous. Zoe questioned her decision to bring him and Streeting together, but it was too late for doubts now.

She checked the route and clock, realising she'd be early. The first heavy raindrops bounced off her windscreen, prompting her to slow down. The visibility wasn't great, and she knew Randle would get soaked waiting at their meeting spot – no umbrella could stand up to Cumbrian rain. The thought didn't particularly bother her.

She dialled Alistair Freeburn's direct line as the rain intensified.

"DI Finch, an unexpected pleasure. What can I do for you?"

The familiar formalities with Freeburn were oddly comforting, like a favourite radio show. After the pleasantries, she asked about Christian Ives.

"You were in a photo with him," she said. "Him, Myron Carter and Sinead Conway, among others."

"Ives," he muttered. "Ives, Ives, Ives. When was this? Oh. Chives Property Holdings. I remember."

"Chives?"

"Christian Harcourt Ives. Chives. His little joke, I think. He's clean, as far as I know."

"Clean?"

"Not a criminal, DI Finch. I helped him sell the company a couple of years ago. To a little consortium involving our friend from the Port, and our other friend in the property business."

It was strange how Sinead Conway's name kept appearing lately, after being absent from Zoe's radar for over a year. Probably a coincidence.

She ended the call as she rounded the corner. The rain had eased. Randle stood scowling in his usual suit and shirt, his umbrella having failed against the weather.

"You're late," he said, dropping into the passenger seat. His face had a greyish tinge she hadn't noticed before.

"I'm sorry." She turned with a smile. "No accounting for the weather."

They drove in silence until Randle pulled out a blister pack of pills.

"Painkillers." He swallowed them dry, then took out another pack. "Antibiotics."

The bandage on his left hand seemed larger than before. "How's the hand?" she asked.

"It hurts. But so do many things, as you get older. You'll learn that one day, Zoe. Just the two of us, is it?"

"Yes." She paused. "Carl's meeting us there, though. So three of us. And you'll be in a different room."

"I beg your pardon?"

"A different room. It'll be me and Carl putting the questions. You'll have a live feed and comms into us so you can guide the conversation, but it'll be up to us whether we listen to you."

"This isn't what I wanted, Zoe."

She slowed and turned to look at him properly. David Randle. Here. In her car.

The last time this had happened, she'd been busting him out of Birmingham Crown Court.

"It's what we've got." She held his gaze until he nodded.

"Very well. It'll have to do, I suppose."

After another silence, she asked about Olivia Bagsby.

"Still alive," Randle replied. "Unhappy at Myron Carter's continuing liberty. Otherwise, fine."

The facility appeared ahead, high walls concealing what lay within. A plain metal gate slid open as she approached. They were expected.

The long driveway led to an unremarkable centuries-old house. Four men emerged from an outbuilding as they approached. Zoe and Randle endured being searched while two others checked her aging Mini.

Carl was waiting inside, rising from an armchair, in what resembled an expensive private clinic's waiting room. He approached them but stopped short.

"It's true, then." He stared at Randle with clear hatred.

"It is, Carl." Randle stepped forward with an outstretched hand. "Come now. We're on the same side, aren't we?"

Carl just stared.

"Let's get this done." He nodded towards two more guards, waiting to lead them away.

Having Randle in her car had been awkward enough. But Randle and Carl together?

The sooner this was over, the better.

CHAPTER TWENTY-EIGHT

Beyond the waiting area, the facility turned stark and utilitarian. Carl pushed ahead of the others, following two guards down a narrow corridor into what appeared to be a briefing room: one wooden table, five plastic chairs, cheap carpet, no windows.

David Randle.

David fucking Randle.

He'd thought he'd seen the last of that man years ago.

Carl gestured to the chairs, but Randle had already claimed one at the head of the table. Bile rose in Carl's throat, a mixture of anger and disgust. He swallowed hard, physically pushing back his hatred.

They'd hardly spoken, and already he was having to restrain himself.

Randle smiled at each of them in turn like some kindly uncle. "Well then, let's get things started, shall we?"

"Yes." Zoe sat down next to Randle while Carl took the seat beside her. "I think we—"

"You need to tell me what it is you want from this

process," Randle interrupted. "What do you want Streeting to tell you?"

That same patronising tone, like he was explaining something obvious to people too dim to understand. Carl caught Zoe's tiny eye roll – a gesture he might have missed if he didn't know her so well. He smiled to himself. She might have been secretly working with the man, but Zoe hated Randle as much as Carl did.

Fine. As long as he was on the same team as Zoe, Carl could keep smiling and play Randle's game.

"We want him to stand up in court," he said. "We want him to implicate Carter in the multiple murders and other serious crimes he's committed."

"Yes." Randle stroked his chin thoughtfully. "Very good."

Carl maintained his now-painful smile as Randle continued.

"But what about understanding how Carter's empire works? Don't you want to know about Jenson & Marley? Dagon River Samuels? Mills Allen Begbie Alliance? The black box accounts and the offshore directors?" Randle leaned forward. "Aren't you interested in the way the money flows and how Carter intends to get to it, when the game's been played?"

A game? Carl pushed his distaste aside. "Of course. The more we know, the better. But the more important question is how we get Streeting talking. He's not been willing to say a word, and we've got no reason to believe that's changed."

"We go with the threat angle," Zoe said.

"What's that?" asked Randle.

"We remind him of the threat Carter poses to his life. All the other people Carter's taken out. The bomb in his car."

"Haven't you tried all that already?"

"Yes," Carl began, "but we—"

"Does Streeting know about Mulligan's death?" Randle cut in.

"No. And I don't think he should."

"Explain."

Bloody hell. The man really did think he was still running the show.

Carl took a breath. "Our working hypothesis is that Mulligan's murder was a warning to Streeting. A message to keep his mouth shut."

"Agreed," said Zoe.

"If we tell him about it, I'm concerned it'll have precisely the effect Carter was aiming for."

Randle stroked his chin again. "What do you think, Zoe?"

"I agree with Carl. Maybe if we get nowhere this time, we can think about it later. But for now, I don't want to rock the boat any further."

Randle laughed. "That sums you up to perfection, Zoe. Both of you. You don't want to rock the boat." He shook his head. "And you're wrong. Ralph Streeting's got comfortable. He's dragging out the investigation, using his contacts, keeping you busy, keeping your eyes off the ball. He knows about the threat – you've been through that with him, and he still wouldn't talk. He sits here, disrupting things without lifting a finger. You need to hit back. Do your own disruption. Tell him about Mulligan."

"No," said Carl.

Randle raised an eyebrow.

"No," Carl repeated. "Not now. We're not doing it. Maybe in the future. But let's work with what we've got."

Zoe remained silent.

"You and your boyfriend are in full agreement on this, are you?" Randle asked.

Carl realised he was clenching his fists so hard his nails were cutting into his palms.

Zoe nodded.

Randle shrugged. "Fine. So be it. Will he know I'm listening?"

Carl considered the unobtrusive headsets they'd be wearing. Streeting was observant enough to notice them. "If he asks, we'll tell him. Right. Let's get started."

He stood, so keen to escape David Randle's presence he'd almost forgotten how much he despised the man he was about to meet.

But it was the job. He'd faced down David Randle, back in Birmingham, and he'd won.

It was time to do the same with Ralph Streeting.

CHAPTER TWENTY-NINE

"Is that Detective Sergeant Keyes?"

"Speaking." Aaron sat alone in the team room, sorting through phone data on Mulligan and arranging analysis of Ives' phone, clothes and hair. Ives had given them his phone willingly, even unlocked it for them. This suggested there would be little of value on it, but then, Ives wasn't your usual suspect.

Not really a suspect at all, if it weren't for his insistence that he was Mulligan's killer.

"I understand you're looking into the death of DS Mulligan," said the woman on the phone.

"Yes, I am." He assumed it was someone from Stella's team – there were people in the lab he'd never spoken to.

"This is DCI Carnegie."

"Really?" Aaron caught himself. "I'm sorry. I just wasn't expecting to hear from you."

"You left a message for me to call, didn't you?"

"Oh. Yes. Yes, I did do that."

The call wasn't going well. Aaron felt... starstruck. That was the word.

"How's the investigation going?" she asked, and suddenly he was on firmer ground. Just two police officers, discussing a case.

"It's an odd one. The forensics aren't looking promising, but there's an obvious avenue of investigation—"

"The Streeting connection?"

"Yes. There was something... A sort of message, delivered with Kieran's body. On his shirt. Implying someone should keep their mouth shut. Given the location of the body, and the fact that all the cameras were conveniently out of action... Did I mention that?"

"No, you didn't, but I'm sure everything pertinent's on HOLMES."

"Yes, yes, of course."

"Good. That'll make things easier. Go on."

Aaron explained their line of enquiry – that Mulligan's death had been carried out on Carter's orders.

"Makes sense," she said. "Have you got an actual suspect in mind?"

"We didn't. We still don't, really. But we do have a man who's walked in off the street and insisted that he's the killer."

"And is he?"

"I don't think so, no." He frowned. She'd said something earlier that hadn't registered properly.

"Tell me about this man," she said.

Aaron explained what they knew about Christian Ives: his connections with Carter, his missing mother, his knowledge of the murder's background – which suggested someone involved had briefed him.

CHAPTER TWENTY-NINE

"Why not him, then?" she asked.

"No real motive. He came up with some nonsense about not liking Mulligan, about arranging to meet him at three in the morning at the Port, to have a row about something."

That earlier comment still nagged at him.

"Go on. Anything more on this Ives?"

"He claimed that he'd drawn on Mulligan's shirt as his way of telling him to shut up, but agreed it had been done after Mulligan was dead. And he was terrified. He bore all the signs of someone being forced to confess to something he hadn't done, under duress, and with his mother now missing..."

It hit him. *That'll make things easier*. What had she meant?

"Yes," DCI Carnegie said. "That all makes sense. We'll see what we can find out from here about Mulligan's movements, and we'll keep you informed of any progress we make. For now. But," she continued, "I expect to be taking over the investigation fairly soon."

He frowned. "I'm sorry?"

"I'll be SIO. Me or one of my team. I'm sure you and DI Finch and your colleagues have been doing an excellent job, and I'm sure you'd find out who killed Kieran if we gave you the time, but I'm afraid it's not going to work out that way."

"It isn't?"

"I can't have the investigation into the death of one of my team being led by a different unit, however competent."

Aaron found his voice. "I can assure you we're conducting a—"

"Save it, DS Keyes. I understand this isn't ideal, from your point of view. Believe me, it's far worse from ours. We'll be coming in later today to look over where you've got to, and we'll be bringing it all back to Durranhill with us. Including your suspect."

"He's not really a suspect."

"Yes, you've explained. I'll be seeing you in due course."

Aaron sat holding the dead phone for nearly a minute before shaking himself and dialling the boss. She had to know about this.

Where was she? She'd gone up to see the super ages ago, with no sign of her since.

And now, she wasn't answering her phone. They were about to lose the investigation, and although he knew he'd fight to keep it, the heaviness in his gut told him there was absolutely nothing he could do about it.

CHAPTER THIRTY

NINA STRUGGLED to maintain her patience with the man before her.

"Arroyo," he repeated for the third time. "You're not pronouncing it correctly."

"I really am sorry." Nina smiled at him.

He stepped back, colliding with his open Lexus door and wincing as it hit his spine.

"Sorry," she said again, reminding herself to work on her smile. It seemed to unsettle people rather than put them at ease.

"Gustavo Arroyo." He rubbed his back.

They'd been standing in the driveway under dark clouds for nearly five minutes, still stuck on his name. Nina understood his confusion – from what she'd overheard of his conversation with Marissa, he knew the cleaner hadn't called the police. He'd asked repeatedly who had.

He kept trying Christian's phone number, each attempt met with silence. Nina couldn't explain why until she had his statement.

"I've literally just got back," he said.

"Where from?"

The first raindrops began to fall.

Gustavo stepped towards the house.

Nina grabbed his arm, stopping him. He stared at her hand on his jacket as if it were contaminated.

"We need to get inside," he said, gesturing upward.

"I'm sorry, but you can't go in the house yet. We'll need to speak in the car."

"But this is my house," he protested.

"It needs..."

Nina broke off at the sound of an approaching vehicle. Caroline Deane's Citroën pulled into the driveway. Tom appeared at the driver's door to brief the crime scene investigator.

"Let's talk in the car," Nina said, turning towards her vehicle.

Gustavo caught her arm. Nina glanced down at his hand in surprise.

"Maybe my car?" His attempt to hide his distaste for her Nissan was half-hearted at best.

"Fine."

Inside the Lexus, Nina admired the luxurious interior while Gustavo answered her earlier question.

"Argentina," he said.

The car was nicer than her house. Add a bar and decent speakers...

"Sorry. Argentina?"

"Yes. A business trip. I've just got back. You saw me drive in. I need to call Christian."

She waited as he tried his husband's number again.

"He always answers his phone." Concern creased his

CHAPTER THIRTY

face. "I have no idea where he is. I have no idea where Matilda is. You need to find them."

His worry seemed genuine. Nina decided to drop her bombshell.

"Do you know a man called Myron Carter?"

Gustavo snorted. "Carter? Yes, but really, we don't associate with Carter and his friends."

"No?"

"The man's a lowlife. A criminal. Not the sort of person Christian and I would wish to be seen with, in general."

Tom appeared at the front door in his forensic suit, gesturing to Nina. She asked Gustavo to wait and stepped out into the rain.

"It's not just the camera," Tom said. "There's an extensive security system throughout the house. But it looks like someone's gone at the main unit with a hammer."

"Bloody hell," Nina muttered as Tom went back inside. She tried calling Aaron but got no answer. Then she remembered – she was a DS now. She could make these decisions herself.

Inspector Keane picked up immediately, first asking about her promotion. But Nina didn't have time for small talk.

"Sorry, but we've got something here. I need you to organise a search."

After explaining the situation, she agreed to send photos and details of Matilda Ives.

"I'll get on it right away," he said before hanging up.

The rain eased as Nina looked back at the Lexus. Gustavo sat staring at his phone, likely wondering yet again why Christian wasn't responding.

She took a deep breath and walked down the driveway. Time to tell him his husband had just confessed to murder.

CHAPTER THIRTY-ONE

"No lawyer?" Carl asked. They'd agreed he'd kick things off, but Zoe looked surprised to see Streeting sitting alone when they entered the interview room.

The space was small and stark. Cameras and mirrors lined the walls, with no windows and a heavy, soundproofed door. He hoped there was no mobile signal – Zoe's phone had been buzzing constantly until they walked in. At least that had stopped.

Streeting shrugged. "Not sure it's me that needs the lawyer."

"Meaning?"

"Meaning you," Streeting grinned at Carl, "and you, possibly even more," he turned to Zoe, "are in more than enough trouble yourselves to be worrying about me. Dodgy cops, incompetent cops, cops on the verge of a nervous breakdown. You shouldn't feel ashamed that you haven't managed to pin Bobby Silver's murder on me. Given what you have to work with, I'd be impressed if you managed to bring in a shoplifter."

Carl watched Zoe fight back her exasperation. Streeting had agreed to see them, but clearly just to wind them up. To disrupt things, as Randle had said.

"How's DS Gaskill?" Streeting asked.

Carl's jaw tightened as he bit back a retort. Denise had nearly died in a car bomb meant for Streeting. She claimed she was better, but Carl still worried. He focused on controlling his breathing, his chest rising and falling steadily.

"She's recovering well," Zoe cut in. "She was lucky, really. She wasn't in the car when it exploded. If you'd been behind the wheel, as intended, you'd be dead."

Streeting shrugged.

"Dead like Bobby Silver," she said. "Like Victor Parlick. Like Dean Somerville, nearly. All people Myron Carter considered a threat."

"Change the record, Zoe."

"No lawyer, then," she observed.

"We've been through that."

"Yes, true. But last time we saw you, Trevor Singleton was with you. Isn't he your lawyer any more?"

A frown crossed Streeting's face, and Carl noticed Zoe's slight smile.

"I don't need a lawyer," Streeting said.

"The thing is, Ralph," Carl leaned forward, "we know Trevor Singleton is Carter's pet. He acts for Carter's friends. If he's not acting for you, does that mean you're off Carter's friend list?"

Carl watched Streeting control his breathing, just as he'd done himself moments before. The man had to know he was a target. Had to see that Carter would get to him eventually.

His only path to survival was taking down Carter first.

CHAPTER THIRTY-ONE

"What's all this about?" Streeting pointed at Zoe's left ear, then Carl's. "Someone listening in?"

The bastard seemed to have recovered his composure.

"David Randle's listening in," Zoe said.

A smile broke across Streeting's face. "Bloody hell. The trouble we went to, trying to find that man, and... Well, you don't need to hear about that. Randle, then. He can hear me?"

"Yes."

"Why are you here, David? What do you bring to the mix?"

After a pause, Randle's voice came through their earpieces. "Tell him I was in his position once. Maybe I can help."

Zoe relayed the message.

Streeting's grin turned lopsided. "I doubt it. Things are different, here. And now."

"Tell him about Mulligan," Randle's voice instructed.

Carl shook his head.

"You have to tell him, Zoe," Randle said. "He can play this game as long as he wants."

"I'm sorry," Zoe said.

Carl's mouth dropped open. She was addressing him, not Streeting.

"Mulligan's dead," she said.

"For Christ's sake," Carl muttered.

"What?" Streeting's lopsided grin wavered.

"Kieran Mulligan. Your old DS. Seemed a decent cop. Tom spoke highly of him."

"What about him?"

Streeting leaned forward, urgency in his expression. Zoe spoke deliberately, each word landing like a hammer blow.

"Kieran Mulligan was brutally murdered. By the man you insist on protecting."

Streeting shook his head. "I don't believe you."

But his face showed horror, not doubt. He looked from Zoe to Carl, finding no comfort there.

"No," he said, grief replacing horror. He looked on the verge of tears. "Take me back to my cell."

"Ralph—" Zoe began.

Streeting jumped to his feet. "I don't want to talk to these people," he shouted. "Take me back to my cell!"

CHAPTER THIRTY-TWO

Tom thanked Rob Collins for the lift and headed upstairs. Nina had asked him to go back to the Hub when Uniform arrived – suggested it, really, rather than ordered it.

He'd only said, "Yes, sure," at the time, but it didn't matter if he agreed. She was the DS; he was the DC. The hierarchy was clear, and he was fine with that. They could still be friends outside work. Inside, too. Maybe even keep up those ridiculous bets with her mum's antimacassar.

He pushed open the door to the team room. The sarge sat alone, frowning at his phone and shaking his head.

"Everything OK?" Tom asked.

"No, not really. I've just been on with DCI Carnegie, over at Durranhill."

"Got anything useful for us?"

The sarge shook his head. "The opposite. She wants to take the investigation off us."

Tom dropped into his chair while DS Keyes explained the DCI's reasoning.

"Shit," Tom said when he finished. "What do we do now?"

Finding Matilda Ives remained a priority. But if they were losing the Mulligan investigation, was there any point in progressing it?

Yes. Of course there was. Their job was finding killers and putting them away. If someone else got the credit, so be it.

"I've been trying to get the Port lot down here," the sarge said. "Miles and the team. They need to go over their statements. Can you look into Ives' vehicle? See if there's anything that puts him near the Port at the time of the murder?"

Tom nodded and turned to his screen, typing automatically as his brain processed what he needed to find.

Politics was for the others. For Tom, this was the job.

Christian Ives drove an electric Nissan – like Nina's, Tom noted briefly, before remembering electric cars were everywhere now, even in Cumbria. Ives' was newer, bigger, more powerful, with better range. Probably better maintained, too. Still, for a multimillionaire whose husband drove an appropriately flashy car, it seemed modest.

Tom submitted the data request for any camera hits. He opened the forensics updates window – Stella's team were making progress with Ives' phone. The visible data was one thing, but the lab could find hidden information, location data, anything that might prove Ives was lying.

He reluctantly pulled up the phone company request form. The data might match what was on the phone. Any differences would suggest Ives was hiding something.

He'd likely chase that data for days. But that was the job.

"Come on."

CHAPTER THIRTY-TWO

Tom looked up. The sarge stood beside him, determination etched on his face.

"Where are we going?"

"Downstairs. I'd like to have another chat with Christian Ives, while we still can."

CHAPTER THIRTY-THREE

Carl stood in the briefing room, his mind foggy with anger. He must have walked there from the interview room, though he couldn't remember the journey through his red mist of rage. Zoe and Randle sat in the same chairs as before.

"I don't—" he began.

"Now come on, Carl," Randle said. "You were getting nowhere."

Carl stared at him before turning to Zoe. She frowned, holding her phone to her ear.

Had they planned this together? His chest tightened at the thought.

No. She wouldn't do that to him.

"Zoe?"

She turned away, focused on her call.

They'd agreed not to tell Streeting about Mulligan's death. At least, he thought they had.

"Zoe? What the hell just happened in there?"

She shook her head and stood, walking to the corner, phone still pressed to her ear.

CHAPTER THIRTY-THREE

Carl leaned across the empty space between him and Randle, lowering his voice. "I know you've managed to convince Zoe you're on the level. But you don't fool me. I know you're up to something."

"You're wrong," Randle said quietly.

"What? Are you saying I should trust you?"

"Well, yes, but then, I would say that, wouldn't I?" A smile played across Randle's face.

Carl waited.

"No," Randle continued. "You're wrong about Zoe. I haven't convinced her. She doesn't trust me at all. She's not stupid. You of all people should know that. The only reason I'm here is because I have expertise she can use. And you're wrong about Streeting, too. It worked."

"Worked? He walked out of the bloody interview! He was talking, and then he stopped and walked out!"

"He was talking, yes, but he wasn't saying anything. He was comfortable. Now he isn't."

Zoe slumped into the chair between them, her face pale.

"What?" Carl asked. "What is it?"

"That's... That was Aaron. We're about to lose the investigation."

"Which investigation?"

"Mulligan. DCI Carnegie wants it, and apparently that means she's going to get it."

"Can she do that?"

"Separate reporting structure, apparently, so Fiona can't stop her, even though they shouldn't be investigating the death of one of their own. Looks like the IOPC report's weakened her position more than I thought. And yes, they can investigate murders up at Durranhill. It's in their remit. I have to head back now. See if I can limit the damage."

"No," Randle interjected. "I need to sit down with you and go through Carter's financial affairs. We have to get to the bottom of this mass of companies and bank accounts."

"Why?" Carl demanded.

"Because that's the key. Yes, we can get Streeting talking, but we need more than that. You know we do. It might be boring, but it's always the paperwork that brings these people down in the end."

"Maybe," Zoe said. "But not now. I don't have time for that."

Randle's expression shifted to confusion. "Why not? So someone else investigates a murder. Doesn't mean it's not going to be solved. Why is this such a problem?"

Zoe remained silent. Carl fought back a smile. After all their time in Birmingham, Randle still didn't understand her. How could he not see how much losing an investigation would hurt her?

"I'm sorry," Carl said. "Let me know if there's anything I can do."

"Zoe," Randle pressed. "The business angle is our best way in. You need to talk me through it."

"No," she said. "Wait."

She tapped at her phone for a minute before standing. "You can find your own way back, yes?"

Carl exchanged a glance with Randle.

"Yes, sure," Randle replied. "But—"

"I've just sent you the complete report from Zhang Chen, the forensic accountant we had looking into Carter's businesses. Go through it yourself."

She walked out, leaving Carl staring at the empty space.

Randle was wrong. She did trust him enough to follow

his advice on interviewing suspects, but that was just a difference of opinion. A judgement call.

This was different. This was trusting Randle with sensitive information he had no right to know.

She was wrong. Carl was sure of it. And one way or another, he was going to prove it.

CHAPTER THIRTY-FOUR

"Going back to our previous conversation." Aaron leaned forward. "You claim that DS Mulligan was 'mouthy', yes?"

Ives nodded.

"Do you mind speaking?" Tom asked. "This interview is being recorded on video, but it's always clearer when you can hear the words."

"Yes," Ives said.

It was about as much as he'd said in the last ten minutes. There was still nothing more than they'd come in with: a vague dislike, an arrangement to meet at the Port, in the middle of the night, a row. A death. Nothing more about the actual killing.

There was no real motive, and time was running out. Sooner or later, Kiki Carnegie would be here to take over.

And where the bloody hell was Matilda Ives?

"Do you know where your mother is?" Aaron asked, wincing as he realised how much it sounded like the start of a seventies comedy act.

CHAPTER THIRTY-FOUR

Ives shrugged.

"Mr Ives has shrugged," Tom said for the recording.

"She's missing, Christian." Aaron leaned closer. "Our working assumption is that she's been taken by someone, and that this is how you've been pressured into confessing to a murder you had no involvement with at all. Is that right?"

"No," Ives said.

"We're doing everything we can to find her, Christian. But the more you can tell us – the truth, this time – the better chance we have. And it won't help if we're stuck here wasting time investigating you for a crime you didn't commit."

A knock on the door interrupted Ives' silence. Aaron paused the interview and sighed in exasperation.

Two PCs stood outside, one male, one female, both wearing apologetic looks.

"Yes?" Aaron's irritation showed in his voice.

"PCs Will Parton and Marie Stones," the man said.

"Yes?" Aaron repeated.

"I'm afraid you're going to have to stop talking to the suspect." PC Stones shifted uncomfortably. Aaron had seen her before, had heard good things from Harriett.

"Why?" Aaron asked.

Parton looked pained but said nothing.

"Why?" Aaron's voice rose.

"It's... It's DCI Carnegie," Parton finally said.

Clive Moor appeared in the corridor, walking slowly ahead of two more people, as if that might delay their arrival.

"Sorry, Aaron," Clive said as he approached.

"DS Keyes?" The woman behind him stepped forward.

"Yes, Ma'am," Aaron said, straightening up.

Kiki Carnegie was taller than expected. He'd only seen

her once before, receiving an award. She wore a black trouser suit and wire-framed glasses, frowning as she studied him.

"Good. This is Sammy." She gestured to the man beside her.

"Sammy Knight." The man extended his hand. "DS Knight."

"We've met," Aaron said, taking his hand.

"Have we?" Knight replied.

"Yes." Aaron's tone was flat. They'd met several times, even been out in groups together. Neither had been drunk enough to forget. Aaron hadn't thought much of Knight then, and nothing was improving that opinion.

"Sorry, mate." Knight smirked. "And sorry about all this."

"This?" Aaron prompted.

Tom emerged from the interview room, eyeing the group with confusion.

"Yes, we'll be taking over from here," DCI Carnegie said.

"But..." Aaron was certain there were grounds for objection, but unsure what they were.

"But what?" DCI Carnegie asked.

"But we're in the middle of interviewing the suspect."

"Yes." She smiled. "And thank you for that. I'll expect full notes, but we'll review the recording in case you've managed to get anything useful out of the man. Have you managed to get anything useful out of the man?"

"The man?" Aaron echoed.

DCI Carnegie turned to Knight.

"Ives," he supplied.

She'd come here to do this publicly and didn't even know the suspect's name?

"I need to speak with the super." Aaron strode past DCI

Carnegie, Knight, Clive Moor, and the two PCs, with Tom following behind.

CHAPTER THIRTY-FIVE

"Mr Arroyo, you need to calm down." Nina kept her voice level.

"No." His face darkened to match the clouds outside. "No. I need to go to bed. And you need to stop this nonsense about Christian."

"I'm sorry, Mr Arroyo—"

"Oh, you will be, you can be sure of it."

He'd persisted in trying to contact Christian Ives, even after her assurances that his husband was at the Hub being interviewed.

"He's confessed to murder," Nina said.

"Yes, so you keep saying. Some chap called Molligan."

"Mulligan."

"Whatever. I've never heard of him, and I doubt Christian has, either. It's nonsense. Has Christian actually been arrested?"

"Not as far as I'm aware."

"So you have no right to keep him there." Arroyo's voice carried a note of triumph.

"Yes. He can leave. But he's chosen not to."

For all she knew, Ives had walked out an hour ago, or been arrested after all. But she could only work with what she knew.

"I'm calling our lawyers."

"That's fine. In the meantime, I'd suggest you come back with me to the police station. Maybe if you're there too, we can clear all this up."

"Nonsense." It seemed to be his favourite word. "I'm not going anywhere with you. I've had a long flight, and I'm tired, and you're throwing all this..." He searched for a different word. "...all this *nonsense* at me, and I just want to go to bed."

He reached for the car door handle. Nina placed her hand on his arm.

He stared at her hand as if it might bite him.

"I'm sorry, Mr Arroyo, but regardless of Christian's situation, your mother-in-law is still missing, and the security system in your house has been deliberately damaged. We have to treat the house as a crime scene."

"And?"

"And that means you can't go in there."

"This is just *too* awful!" Arroyo muttered.

Nina thought 'awful' better described Arroyo himself.

"I suppose I'm going to have to stay in some dreadful hotel again." He turned to face Nina with a pointed look and nodded at the door beside her.

"Are you sure you don't want to come with—"

"I'll be leaving now."

"Fine. I'll need your contact details."

He gave her his phone number with a dry laugh. "I

wouldn't worry about that. You can be sure you'll be hearing from me. And from our lawyers."

The rain had intensified, forcing Nina to wait in her car for the windscreen to clear. Arroyo's Lexus remained stationary; clearly waiting for her to leave.

She picked up her phone to text Elena about being late and saw a message from Aaron about DCI Carnegie. Mulligan's boss's boss. Perhaps she had information for them.

There was another text from her mother: *Have some bloody manners, young lady*.

She rolled her eyes and looked up. Through the windscreen, she could see Arroyo in his Lexus, phone to ear, expression grim.

She knew when she wasn't wanted. Time to get back to the Hub.

CHAPTER THIRTY-SIX

"You can't let them do this to us!"

The voice echoed down the corridor as Zoe pushed open the door from the stairwell. She'd left Carl and Randle at the secure facility, trying not to dwell on whether she'd betrayed Carl's trust by breaking the news of Mulligan's death. The drive back had been quick, followed by a dash across the car park and up the stairs.

Now she broke into a run.

People shouting in a police station was nothing unusual. Aaron Keyes shouting in a police station had to be unprecedented.

She pushed open the door to the team room and stopped dead. The only people inside were Aaron, Tom and the super.

And Aaron wasn't shouting at Tom.

"I've already told you!" Fiona's voice matched Aaron's in volume, the two of them standing close enough to touch. "There. Was. Nothing. I. Could. Do. About. It."

"What's going on?" Zoe asked.

The three turned to look at her. Tom's face showed relief, while Aaron's blazed with anger.

Fiona's expression was harder to read.

"Boss, she's handed over the Mulligan investigation to Kiki Carnegie," Aaron said.

"Yes, I got your message."

"I thought we'd have more time. DCI Carnegie's already here. She booted us out while we were questioning Ives."

That didn't sound right. Or professional.

But then, nor was shouting at a senior officer.

"Aaron," Zoe said, "I know this isn't ideal. I'm probably angrier about it than you are. But you can't go shouting at the super like this. You need to apologise."

Aaron's mouth fell open. The look of betrayal on his face reminded her of Carl's expression earlier.

"No," Fiona said, waving her hand dismissively.

"No?"

"No, he doesn't need to apologise. It's good to see an officer with fire in him. And anyway, he's right." Fiona slumped into Kay's old chair, shaking her head slowly. "Kiki Carnegie shouldn't be investigating the death of one of her own people. And I outrank her, anyway. I should be able to stop these people walking all over us."

"Then why didn't you?" Aaron's voice still held anger.

"She doesn't report to me. I can't overrule her own senior officer. And it seems my stock has sunk so low, my word doesn't actually count for much these days."

Zoe took a step towards the super. Fiona stared at nothing, still shaking her head.

"What's this—"

Zoe stopped herself. The IOPC report. She hadn't read it yet. If Fiona was like this, perhaps it was worse than expected. But hours ago, she'd managed to overrule PSD and get Randle into the secure facility.

Zoe had seen the super down before, but never admitting defeat like this.

"Tell me what's happened," Zoe said to Aaron.

He summarised their progress. Ives, it seemed, had an unpleasant husband and a missing mother, but still no clear motive to kill Mulligan.

"This is rubbish," Zoe said, turning away. "I'll see you later."

"Where are you going?" Fiona asked as Zoe reached the door.

"I'm going downstairs to have a little chat with Kiki Carnegie."

CHAPTER THIRTY-SEVEN

THE LIFT DOOR OPENED. Nina spotted DI Finch ahead, taking two steps before vanishing into the stairwell with determined strides.

"Boss?" Nina called, but DI Finch was already gone.

As Nina approached the team room, the superintendent emerged, heading for the stairs at a slower pace. She walked past without acknowledging Nina.

Something wasn't right.

Inside the team room, Aaron – yes, she'd managed to use his first name, even if only mentally – and Tom explained the situation.

DCI Carnegie had taken control of everything – not just the murder investigation, but also Matilda Ives' disappearance, which she'd only learned about through Nina's discovery.

"Shit," Nina said.

"It's not so bad." Tom raised his eyebrows.

Nina gave him one of her withering looks, watching him fight back a smile.

CHAPTER THIRTY-SEVEN

"No, I mean it. They knew Kieran better than we did. They'll have more insight. They might even—"

"Save it." Nina sat at her desk and unlocked her screen. "They shouldn't be investigating the death of one of their own. They're too close. Look – this Gustavo Arroyo. I don't trust him."

"Why not?" Aaron asked.

"He... I don't know. Nothing specific. He seemed appropriately surprised about everything. But... I just don't like him, Sarge."

"Aaron," he corrected.

"Whatever. I think we should look into him. Tom, can you dig around?"

"On it." Tom turned to his keyboard. "Are you bloody kidding me?"

Nina wheeled her chair over. "What have you got?"

"Nothing. And what we did have is gone."

Aaron walked over to stand by the desk. "What?"

"Bloody Kiki Carnegie." Tom pointed at his screen. "Look."

Nina studied the table of information requests, each marked with a black cross.

"What does that mean?" she asked.

"All my data requests. Christian's car info. The phone data from his provider."

"And?"

"It's been denied. Overridden. The phone forensics, Mulligan's phone data we were reviewing, even the arrangements for Miles and his team to give statements. It's all been stripped and sent to her team."

"Isn't it on HOLMES?" Aaron asked.

"Probably. But my access is revoked. Want to bet yours is, too?"

Nina returned to her desk as Aaron checked his own access. Both entered their credentials and case reference numbers.

"Bloody hell," Aaron muttered.

Nina saw the same screen of black crosses.

"So DCI Carnegie's getting territorial," Nina said. "Doesn't mean we can't investigate things she doesn't know about yet."

"What do you mean?" Tom asked.

"Gustavo Arroyo."

Aaron sighed. "You don't like him. That's not grounds for a secret investigation. If you have real suspicions, tell DCI Carnegie."

"Yeah, right." Nina turned back to Tom. "Go on. See what you can find."

Tom glanced at Aaron, who shrugged.

"Can't hurt, I suppose. You'll probably be locked out. But if you find something..."

"We'll tell Kiki's team. Yeah. Sure."

Tom entered the generic Port of Workington code for his search. Using the Mulligan case reference number would have blocked him completely. This was connected to the Port – the body had been found there, and despite Christian Ives' claims, Myron Carter remained the prime suspect.

"He claims he just got back from Argentina," Nina said. "Check Ports records. And financial information. Nothing too obvious."

She watched Tom type, expecting more black crosses, but the requests went through.

At her desk, Nina stared at her blank screen, trying to

pinpoint what bothered her about Arroyo. Surely it wasn't just his unpleasant manner. She dealt with unpleasant people daily.

Two minutes later, Tom spoke up. "He's not lying."

"Who?"

"Your Gustavo Arroyo. Airline database shows return tickets to Buenos Aires."

Nina felt deflated. "Right." Arroyo had an alibi.

"I'll keep digging," Tom offered.

"Yeah. Thanks."

It was kind of him, but pointless. Being a DS didn't stop the same old doors slamming in your face.

CHAPTER THIRTY-EIGHT

"I don't know how long they'll be," said PC Stones.

"No," Zoe agreed. "I suppose not."

The custody suite's waiting area wasn't designed for comfort. She'd been here five minutes already, precious time she could use reading the IOPC report Fiona had just sent through.

DCI Carnegie and her DS were interviewing Christian Ives. Unless he'd changed his story, they had to finish soon.

Within a minute, voices echoed down the corridor. A fair-haired man in his thirties appeared, unremarkable except for his self-satisfied walk – DS Knight, she presumed. Beside him strode a tall Black woman in a dark trouser suit, her short hair and glasses giving an impression of utmost seriousness.

Kiki Carnegie looked like someone who rarely smiled.

Zoe stood to introduce herself.

"Pleased to meet you," DCI Carnegie said, her expression contradicting her words. "This is Sammy Knight, my DS. He'll be taking point on this, so please have your team contact him with any new information."

CHAPTER THIRTY-EIGHT

"Yes, I was wondering—"

"I assume the case notes are all in HOLMES?"

Carnegie had started walking, forcing Zoe to keep pace.

"Yes, I'll have a word with—"

"Good. We've arranged the suspect's transport to Durranhill. Nice meeting you, DI Finch."

Carnegie and Knight disappeared into the rainy car park under darkening skies.

If Carnegie wouldn't answer her questions, maybe Christian Ives would. Zoe passed the custody desk where PC Stones watched her curiously. Down the corridor, she encountered Clive Moor and another PC approaching.

"Sorry, Zoe," Clive said.

"What for?"

"You can't see him."

"Why not?"

Clive lowered his voice. "This isn't my call. DCI Carnegie's given clear instructions: no one talks to the suspect. I've got to station Will here outside the bloody cell."

"We brought him in," Zoe protested. "He's our suspect."

"He *was* your suspect. He's hers now." Clive glanced down the corridor before meeting her eyes again. "If I could get you in there, I would. But I can't."

Zoe watched them split up – the young PC to the cell, Clive back to the custody desk. Shaking her head, she headed for her car.

The Anchor Vaults was busy but welcoming. Her friend Jake Frimpton sat at their usual corner table with two glasses of something non-alcoholic. They'd started surprising each other with drinks – anything but Diet Coke. Some were awful, but finding the good ones made it worthwhile.

She sipped the orange-brown liquid and grimaced. "Not this time, Jake."

"Agreed." He reached for their backup Diet Cokes from the shelf.

"How are things?" she asked.

Jake shrugged and told her the latest news of his father's decline. Solomon hadn't recognised her during her recent visit, or even Jake at first. Each visit required more prompting for recognition.

She scanned the pub, noting the regulars, the drunks, those on their way there.

"You're distracted," Jake said.

"What?"

"Something's on your mind. You're trying not to think about it."

She smiled. "You should be a therapist. Yeah, it's been a day."

"IOPC report?"

"How did you know?"

"Can't reveal my sources. But I heard their initial findings aren't pleasant."

Zoe kept her expression neutral. Jake was a local journalist; sometimes he knew things before she did.

"Is that true?" he asked.

She sighed. "Off the record, yes. Haven't read it all yet, but Fiona's not happy."

"I'm sorry."

She raised an eyebrow. "You are?"

"Yes."

Jake's reporting had partly led to the IOPC investigation, though the corrupt officers deserved the lion's share of the blame.

CHAPTER THIRTY-EIGHT

"For what it's worth," he continued, "I never meant to cause trouble. I'm not fond of your super, but she's good at her job."

"She is. Though right now she doesn't believe it. She's taking the fall for everything."

"You can't be surprised. Someone always has to be blamed."

"Yeah, probably."

Jake frowned. "There's something else."

"What?"

"The IOPC report isn't what's bothering you. You're not engaging. What is it?"

She closed her eyes and took a long drink.

"It's something from the past," she said. "And it's back."

"Something?" Jake asked. "Or someone?"

She opened her eyes. "What do you know?"

"I don't know anything, Zoe. I just know you. And I can tell you're not yourself."

She nodded.

"There's someone I used to work with. He's back, and I'm letting him get involved with my professional life," she added as his eyebrows rose. "I don't know if I should. If I should trust him."

"Why don't you talk to Carl about it?"

She laughed. "That's the problem. I can't. Carl hates him, thinks I'm wrong. And everyone else who knows him... Christ, if I told Lesley or Mo, they'd think I'd lost my mind. I can't talk to anyone. It feels like I'm letting everyone down by working with him, but I don't have a choice. And the more I work with him, the further apart..."

She shook her head.

"The further apart what?" Jake prompted.

"It doesn't matter."
Because she couldn't talk to anyone about Randle.
Not even Jake.

CHAPTER THIRTY-NINE

Carl had drunk three beers by the time Zoe got home. She went upstairs to change and stayed there for half an hour until he followed her up.

"What's going on?" he asked.

Zoe sat cross-legged on the bed, her eyes fixed on her laptop screen. "It's this report. The IOPC. Fiona sent it to me." She looked up at him. "It's not good."

"It lays into the Hub?"

"Yes. They've asked for responses." She spoke as if today's events hadn't happened. "But I don't think it'll make a difference. They've hit Fiona pretty hard."

"Does she deserve it?"

"No." Zoe shook her head. The cat arched its back beside her, annoyed at the movement. "She's not perfect, but she's good, and she's definitely the best they've got. Not that it matters. It's obvious they're going to recommend a change in leadership, however Fiona responds. Do you know Kiki Carnegie?"

The change of topic threw him. He stepped backwards. "David Randle."

Zoe closed her eyes, opened them, put the laptop aside, and met his gaze. "Are we having this conversation now?"

"Don't you think you owe me it? After what happened with Streeting?"

"I'm sorry."

"So you admit you—"

"I'm not sorry I told Streeting about Mulligan's death. I'm sorry I changed my mind, sorry you didn't get the chance to talk me out of it, sorry if it looked like I was going back on an agreed position."

Carl stepped back into the bedroom. "You *were* going back on an agreed position. And it's not just that. How can you trust Randle?"

"I don't trust him."

"Really? You trust him enough to send him the forensic accountant's report into Carter's businesses. You trust him enough to discuss all that, to listen to his advice when it comes to interviewing suspects—"

"I don't trust him." She sighed as he sat beside her. "I just wish you could see the bigger picture."

He gritted his teeth. "What bigger picture?"

"Yes, Randle's a liar. He's a bad person. You don't like him, I don't like him, his own mother probably didn't like him. But there isn't enough in the information I've given him for him to do any damage."

"How can you be sure?"

"Don't you think I know how to do my job?" Her voice was sharp, but she softened and stroked his arm. "Look, it must have been a shock, I get that. What happened earlier. But really, what do we stand to lose from getting informed advice from David Randle? If we don't like it, we can ignore it."

"You didn't ignore it in the interview, though. It's not as clear-cut as you seem to think it is. It's not all black and white, Zoe."

She turned to him, eyes wide. "You're telling me things aren't black and white? Bloody hell."

"I don't mean that. I still think a dirty cop is a dirty cop and there's no changing that, however much we'd like to. No, I mean this stuff about advice. Yes, it all seems very simple. You can listen to him, or you can ignore him. But it doesn't work like that. Not in the real world. He's cleverer than you give him credit, Zoe."

"He'd have to be seriously clever to convince me to do something I thought was wrong."

"He gets inside your head, though."

"Mind control?" She gave him a half-smile. "Is that what you want me to worry about?"

Carl didn't return the smile. "That's not what I mean, and you know it. Randle's a loose cannon. He can damage your investigation. Your career. You can't let yourself get sucked in by him again."

"Look, OK, I get it. He's dangerous. I'll... I don't know. I'll be careful. I—"

Her phone buzzed, and she reached for it with an apologetic shrug. After a brief conversation, she turned to him, smiling.

"I don't know what did it, but maybe Randle was right."

"Why?"

"That was Streeting's new lawyer. He's willing to talk. He wants to see us first thing tomorrow."

CHAPTER FORTY

Tom sat at his desk, scowling at the same screen full of black crosses that had been there yesterday. He'd arrived before eight, not expecting any changes, but already fed up with people keeping things from him.

Harriett had been up at six, heading to Durranhill for something she couldn't discuss. She hadn't said it was important, but it had to be for such an early start.

If they were going to stick together, he'd need to get used to that. The boss must have dealt with the same thing over the years, having a partner in PSD. Maybe he could discuss it with her.

He laughed at the thought of having a serious personal conversation with the boss. It was the least likely scenario he could imagine.

Checking the hunt for Mrs Ives – Matilda – he saw they hadn't found her yet. At least he wasn't locked out of that search. It was a live hunt for a vulnerable person, and every pair of eyes helped.

He returned to yesterday's searches. Black cross after

CHAPTER FORTY

black cross. It wasn't their investigation, but he'd promised Nina he'd keep digging. While they'd blocked the Ives and Mulligan data, nobody had thought to block his work on Ives' husband, Gustavo Arroyo.

Arroyo had dual nationality: British and Argentinian. For the first time in nearly five years of frequent travel, he'd used his Argentinian passport. It didn't matter though – entering or leaving British territory meant you could be found regardless of passport origin. Most countries had reciprocal arrangements for sharing information.

The door opened, and the sarge walked in. Tom started to minimise his screen, then remembered the row between DS Keyes and the super.

"Look," he said as DS Keyes approached.

"Morning, Tom."

Tom ignored the greeting, pointing at the screen. "Look. Gustavo Arroyo. He flew to Madrid. On his Argentinian passport."

"I thought he was going to Argentina?" Nina's voice came from the doorway.

"Connecting flight," Tom explained. "Can't see if he took it yet since he didn't use his British passport, but I've got a request in. Looks like Gustavo was on the level."

He watched Nina's face for disappointment as she walked to her desk and sat down heavily.

"Maybe not, though," Tom said brightly. "Maybe he stayed in Madrid. In which case—"

The sarge's phone interrupted him.

"Boss..." DS Keyes answered. "Yes, we're all here. I'll put you on speaker."

"I've got news." The boss's voice was breaking up with interference. She was in the car.

"Yes?" asked the sarge.

"I won't be in for a bit. I'm on the way to talk to Streeting."

"Is he—"

"Yes. Apparently, he's got himself a new lawyer and he's willing to talk. It'll probably be nothing, but..."

"But nothing's happened for months," Nina cut in. "And now this. It has to be something."

"Yes." The line cleared as DI Finch's voice strengthened. "Listen. I don't want you crossing any lines."

"No," said the sarge, exchanging confused looks with the others.

"Or disobeying any orders."

"Of course not," Tom said, mystified.

"But if you happened to spend a little time looking quietly into this Christian Ives stuff, that wouldn't be the worst thing in the world."

"We can't," Tom told her. "We've been locked out."

After a moment of static-filled silence, she responded, "I know about that. You'll have to be creative. Aaron, see if they'll let you interview Ives again."

"But—" the sarge began.

"You can say his name's come up in connection with something else."

"Oh," said the sarge.

Nina grinned, mouthing 'be creative' to herself.

"We've spoken to Ives," the boss continued. "You've been to his house. From what we've seen, it seems obvious DCI Carnegie has the wrong man."

"Agreed," said Nina.

"And the last people who should be investigating a

murder are the people who worked with the victim every day. Yes?"

"Yes," they chorused. Tom felt purpose surge through the room like electricity.

They'd find out who'd really killed Kieran Mulligan, even if Mulligan's colleagues were trying to stop them.

CHAPTER FORTY-ONE

Zoe did a double-take as she entered the room. She turned to Carl. "You didn't tell me—"

"I didn't know," he replied.

Ralph Streeting sat beside his lawyer, Paula Vernon, a specialist in PSD investigations. She was the same lawyer who'd sat with Huz during his confession and with Cummings during his attempts to dodge responsibility.

The tension in Zoe's shoulders eased. Paula Vernon was skilled, which could make things harder, but she played fair. Unlike Stan Basham's games or Clarissa Bexley's vendetta, Vernon was straightforward. Zoe preferred that.

Streeting looked less confident than during their previous meeting. He leaned forward, watching them as they took their seats. Carl went through the formalities and explained their headsets to Paula.

In the other room, Randle listened. He'd been quiet when Zoe had picked him up earlier, not even trying to provoke Carl. If she didn't despise him, if she had fewer pressing concerns, she might have worried. But she attributed it to his injured hand.

Carl cleared his throat. "I just want to make something clear."

They'd planned this strategy with Randle. Set out their position, then let Streeting lead.

"You're not getting some kind of special deal, Ralph."

"No?" Streeting asked.

"No. Our intention is to prosecute you for Bobby Silver's murder. You know the sentence. We'll inform the judge about your assistance regarding the tariff, but your crimes won't be forgotten."

"I don't think—" Paula Vernon began.

"Fair enough," Streeting cut in.

Zoe suppressed a smile. This was promising.

"Look," Streeting continued. "I get it. I've had things checked out. I understand it's true."

"What's true?" Zoe asked.

"What you told me yesterday. Kieran."

Zoe studied his expression. Something new flickered in his eyes.

"Yes," she said. "I'm sorry."

Streeting nodded. "You've made your position clear. Now I'll do the same. You need to know I'm not afraid of Myron Carter. I'm not doing this because I'm scared he'll have me killed."

"Doing what?" Carl asked.

Streeting ignored him. "The only reason I'm doing this is because of what happened to Kieran. To..."

His gaze dropped to the corner of the room. Carl started to speak, but Zoe's knee nudged his.

Wait.

"He was a good lad," Streeting said, his voice different now. "He didn't deserve this."

The realisation hit Zoe. It wasn't anger in his eyes and voice. It was grief.

This, from the man who'd murdered Bobby Silver. Who'd ordered Victor Parlick's death. Who'd have killed Olivia Bagsby, given the chance.

A man who killed without remorse, guilty and innocent alike.

But Kieran Mulligan's death had crossed a line.

Zoe glanced at Carl, seeing her own surprise mirrored in his face. He opened his mouth but closed it again without prompting.

The reason didn't matter. The strangeness didn't matter. Streeting was about to turn.

Neither Zoe nor Carl would question their good fortune.

CHAPTER FORTY-TWO

Be creative, the boss had said.

Aaron took a look around the room. Tom tapped on his keyboard, eyes narrowed at his screen, digging up whatever he could on Gustavo Arroyo. The man had been out of the country when his mother-in-law went missing and Mulligan was killed, but it didn't mean he wasn't involved.

To Tom's left, Nina was on the phone, talking quietly, getting an update from Uniform on the search for Matilda Ives.

Under the radar, all of it.

Aaron pulled up the database of unsolved crimes and began to scan through them.

Half an hour later, he was still scanning. He'd forgotten, working murders, how many other crimes there were, and how rarely perpetrators got caught. It was a question of resources. You could solve a murder and leave the shoplifters and muggers to get away with it. Or you could let the killer walk free and stop a few of the others – just a handful, really, a drop in an ocean of crime that might be low-level but could still ruin lives.

A zero-sum game, they called it. There were only so many police to go round. It was up to the senior officers to make that sort of decision. Not for the likes of Aaron.

Which was a good thing, he thought.

He added filters. Narrowed the region, made sure the crimes involved a high degree of violence.

It was funny, but not in a laughing sort of way. He'd been talking about just this the previous night with Serge, who'd asked why he wasn't looking into promotion yet. Serge didn't understand it. Aaron had explained that he was worried about the impact it would have on the family.

The truth was, Aaron could face down a killer, or a corrupt cop, or even a senior cop. He'd shouted in the super's face just a day ago. But he didn't like the idea of facing the consequences of his own decisions, and the higher you rose, the more serious those consequences got.

Be creative.

A great idea, in theory. But finding something he could use was...

Hello. What was this?

He picked up the phone and dialled the number he'd been given for Sammy Knight.

"Yup," said Knight.

"Sammy? It's Aaron."

There was a pause.

"Aaron Keyes," Aaron said.

The pause went on.

Bloody hell.

"DS Keyes from the Hub," he added.

"Oh, yeah. Sorry. What can I do for you, Aaron?"

"It's..." Aaron stopped, realising he hadn't thought this through. "Well, it's... I've found..."

"Is there an intermission in this performance?" Knight asked.

Tosser, thought Aaron.

"You know the Cranshaw attack?" he said.

"No, can't say I do."

"Oh. Really?" Aaron replied, as if this showed an unexpected lack of diligence.

"What are you on about, Aaron?"

"I'm surprised, that's all. Near fatal attack, in Workington, back in June."

"What's it got to do with me?"

"Well, it has certain features in common with the Mulligan investigation. Fits the same profile. And it's unsolved."

"What... How... What do you want..."

"I was hoping I could speak to Christian Ives about it."

"Ives?"

"Yes. Like I said, same profile."

"We've arrested him, you know. In connection with Mulligan's murder."

"You have?" Aaron asked, genuinely surprised. "Can I speak to him about this other attack, though?"

"I don't know about that. I'll have to clear it with DCI Carnegie."

"It's just that I was chatting to the super about it."

"You were?" Knight said, sounding bored.

"I was, yes. And she'd heard from the ACC's office. Apparently, he considers this a priority."

"He does?" Knight's voice perked up.

"He's been getting heat about violent attacks in the

Workington area, and he wants things like this dealt with as a matter of urgency. Obviously, it's been unsolved for months, but if it came out that we had a lead, after all this time, and wasted time before following it up..."

He stopped himself. *Don't go too far.*

"Fine," Knight said after a few seconds. "You can come over this afternoon. You know where we are."

"I do," replied Aaron, but the line was already dead.

He smiled as he put down the phone. He couldn't quite believe the extent of the lies he'd just told, but it might just have worked.

And he'd certainly been creative.

CHAPTER FORTY-THREE

"Can you say that again, please?" Carl watched as Zoe leaned forward.

Streeting nodded. "There are four of them. Directors based in the Caymans and Jersey. If Myron says 'Jump', they ask 'How high?' And they control another six companies that aren't on the list you've just been through."

Zoe sat back, processing this new information. Not just the accounts they knew about. Not just Jenson & Marley and the others. Six more companies under Carter's control.

Randle's voice came through Carl's earpiece. "Who are the shareholders?"

Zoe repeated the question.

"Each other, mostly," Streeting said. "Or nominees. More people and businesses that you can't tie directly to Carter, but which operate according to his instructions."

"We need their details too," Randle said through the device.

Carl swallowed back his disgust at Randle's voice. "Names, please."

Streeting turned cold blue eyes towards him, surprised at the interruption. "Names?"

"These nominees. The ones who do Carter's bidding."

"You can't touch them, you know. Most of them are in different jurisdictions where the finance laws are so opaque you could never prove a thing. And those who aren't, well, they've got the best lawyers and accountants money can buy, Carl."

"Just give us the names, Ralph." Carl didn't like using the man's first name, but that seemed to be where they were.

"I just don't see the point."

Carl exchanged looks with Zoe before leaning in and lowering his voice. "You know about Canary. The investigation that got Zoe her promotion, back in Birmingham. Yes?"

"Yes."

"And you know everyone involved in that got brought down in the end." Including the man listening on the feed.

"So I've heard." Streeting frowned, clearly uncertain where this was heading.

"And you know about Trevor Hamm. The man who ran organised crime down there."

"I met Hamm a couple of times." Streeting's missing grin returned. "With Myron, way back. Forton Services."

"You met him?" Zoe asked.

"Burger, chips, discussions about mutual opportunities in the field of organised crime. Didn't come to much, but he seemed OK. Dead now, isn't he?"

"Yes," Carl said. "But before he died, Zoe put him away and brought everyone down with him. Because this is the point, Mr Streeting."

Streeting flinched at the formal address. Stripped of his rank months ago, alongside everything else associated with the job, that 'Mr' would sting after years of being something more.

"When Zoe Finch brings down an organisation," Carl continued, "she doesn't just cut off the head and leave it to sprout another one. She takes all the limbs with her. That's why we need to know everything. Everything and everyone."

"Thanks." Zoe smiled at Carl with a warmth he hadn't seen in weeks. He nodded. "And it's also about sewing every last detail up. Just like these nominees of yours, Carter will have the best lawyers money can buy. If there's a loophole, he'll squeeze through it. The more rope we can find to tie him up with, the harder that'll be."

"OK," Streeting said, addressing Zoe rather than Carl. "That's fair enough."

They continued for several minutes before Streeting stopped. "That's it. That's all I know about the business side."

Carl nodded. "Ralph, are you willing to stand up in court and give evidence against Myron Carter?"

Streeting considered the question. His face creased in a grimace. "No."

Carl stood.

"What are you doing?" Paula Vernon asked.

He'd almost forgotten the solicitor was there.

"I'm ending this interview and recommending we continue with the prosecution of your client without any further delay. He hasn't given us what we want."

"I've just sat here and listened to him answer your questions for an hour," she replied.

"It's good, but it's not enough. I'm sorry. This interview is—"

"I hadn't finished," Streeting said.

"What?"

"I said no, but I hadn't finished. What I was going to say was, no, unless certain conditions are met."

Carl sat back down.

CHAPTER FORTY-FOUR

"Still nothing on Matilda," Nina said, blowing out her cheeks in frustration.

Tom shrugged in sympathy.

Aaron's demeanour caught Nina's attention. There was a nervous tension about him, different from his struggles the previous year. She detected excitement in his manner, and something else she couldn't quite place. Guilt?

That was it. Excitement mixed with guilt – that feeling when you know you should feel bad about something, but you're too buzzed to care. It reminded her of her teenage friends' faces after they'd nicked sweets from the corner shop. She'd worn that expression herself, no doubt.

What was the sarge up to?

Before she could ask, her phone rang. She snatched it up, hoping for news about Matilda Ives.

"Nina?" A familiar voice came through.

"Dr Robertson. Everything OK?"

"You tell me. Where were you?"

She blinked. "Where was I?"

"Any of you. I put an email out about doing the PM this morning, and no one showed up. Had to go ahead without you. I don't like doing it that way, but it couldn't wait, not with everything else piling up."

"Hang on." Nina turned to her keyboard, tapped out a command, and looked up at her screen to see another black cross. "Look, this shouldn't have happened."

"You're telling me—"

"But it's not us you should be talking to. It's not our investigation any more. All the files and system access have been switched to DCI Carnegie's team at Durranhill. DS Sammy Knight should be dealing with it."

"They didn't get in touch at all."

Arseholes. "They should have done. They would've received your note. We didn't even get it. I'm sorry. You'll have to give your findings to Sammy Knight. Want his details?"

"Knight? No, it's OK. I've come across him before." The pathologist's tone suggested it hadn't been a pleasant experience. "I've got his contact info here somewhere. Thanks, Nina."

"But while you're on..."

"Yes?"

Nina glanced around the room. "I was wondering if you could give me the lowdown. In brief."

"The lowdown?"

"Yeah. The PM findings. How Mulligan died."

"I thought it wasn't your investigation any more."

"No-oh," she stretched the word. "But let's just say it should be. And it won't surprise me if it lands back on our desk when Knight and his friends can't solve it."

CHAPTER FORTY-FOUR

"You know I shouldn't be telling you this sort of thing, Nina."

She waited.

"But since it's you... I found splinters in and around the head wounds."

"Splinters? Like wood?"

"That's what you'd expect, isn't it? But no. Metal splinters. My best guess is that he was attacked with a blunt metal object."

Nina winced. Roddy Chen had been attacked with a metal object in Whitehaven over a year ago. He'd nearly died but recovered.

Mulligan hadn't been so lucky.

"What about time of death? Could you put a number on that for me?"

"You know we don't usually do that, Nina."

She waited again. Some people couldn't stand silence, would say anything to break it. Nina wasn't one of those people, but she hoped Chris Robertson was.

"But informally," he said, "between you and me, I might be able to take a stab. I reckon we're looking at some time between midnight and four. Definitely no later, given the state of the body when I found it. And probably no earlier, either. OK?"

Nina thanked him and ended the call. Between midnight and four, he'd said.

And Christian Ives claimed he'd killed Mulligan at around three in the morning. He might have been lying about who'd done the killing, but it sounded like he was spot on with the time.

CHAPTER FORTY-FIVE

"Conditions?" Carl asked.

Zoe fought back a surge of excitement. She'd been worried when he'd gone in for the kill, insisting that without Streeting's evidence it was over. Someone had reminded her recently that the police could still use information they couldn't present in court. If that was all they got from Streeting, it would be better than nothing.

Who had told her that? Her old boss, Lesley, probably. It didn't matter.

When Carl stood up, she'd worried he was moving too soon, ending things before they got everything they could.

But perhaps Carl had read Streeting's mood perfectly.

"There's more evidence," Streeting said.

"What sort of evidence?" Carl asked.

"I'm coming to that." Streeting seemed to have regained control, which made Zoe uneasy. But if he gave them what they needed, it would be worth it. "I'm not scared of Carter, but I'm not stupid either. I won't give evidence against him unless I'm certain he's going down, and the only way I'll be certain is if you get hold of that evidence."

Zoe glanced sideways at Carl, noting his narrowed eyes. She recognised that look. He didn't trust Streeting, and she couldn't blame him.

Then it hit her – where she'd got that advice about using information to guide an investigation, even if it couldn't be used in court.

Not Lesley. David Randle. Without realising it, she was taking advice from David Randle.

Shit.

"I've always known it might come to this," Streeting continued, clearly enjoying his position of power. "So I concealed recording devices in some of Carter's offices."

Zoe looked at Carl again. His mouth hung open.

Recording devices? If they could get something with Carter's voice on it, get experts to verify it...

"Where are these devices?" Carl asked. "We searched your office and home. We didn't find anything like that."

Streeting shook his head with a rueful smile. "They're still in his offices."

"But what about the recordings?" Zoe asked. "Don't your devices transmit data?"

"Sadly, no." Streeting turned to her, still smiling. "If I'd used transmitting bugs he'd have found them within hours. I used Empress SE400s."

Zoe glanced at Carl, who looked as confused as she felt.

"They use local storage," Streeting said. "The recordings are still on the devices themselves. Which means they need to be recovered physically."

"How many of them?" Carl asked.

"Three," Streeting replied.

Carl pulled out a sheet of blank paper and a pen from his document holder and slid them across the table. "Here. I want precise details. Where they are, how the security in the locations works, how we can recover them. I want..."

Streeting was shaking his head again.

"What?" Carl demanded.

"They're tiny, these things. Very well hidden, too." Streeting's smile shifted from rueful to smug. "And as for the locations, well, I could try to describe exactly where they are, but it's difficult. Very easy for Carter's people to destroy them. Or even for you lot to damage them by accident."

"So?" Carl said.

Zoe knew what was coming.

Of course she knew what was bloody coming.

"If you want to get them," Streeting said, "you're going to have to take me with you."

CHAPTER FORTY-SIX

Tom glared at his screen, his hatred for those black crosses growing with each failed search attempt.

He kept forgetting and logging in, desperate to find connections between Mulligan and Ives. Each time he typed in the Mulligan case reference number, his screen filled with those same crosses.

This covert work felt wrong. As a police officer, he believed in transparency. What was the point if he couldn't do his job openly?

Behind him, Nina muttered curses under her breath. The absence of DCI Carnegie's team at Mulligan's post mortem had rattled her.

Maybe she was right to be bothered. The sarge had just confessed to lying to DS Knight to get an interview with Ives, mixing shame with pride as he told them.

"Which investigation did you use?" Tom asked.

The sarge looked up. "What do you mean?"

"When you told DS Knight you were looking into one of DI Markin's unsolveds. Which one?"

"Oh, right. Cranshaw. Alec Cranshaw. Stabbed in the leg back in June."

"I thought you said it was the same MO as Mulligan."

"Knight's not going to look that far into it."

Tom shook his head, surprised. The sarge was probably right, but it wasn't like him to take risks. "Can I use the case reference?"

The sarge read it out.

With a live investigation he wasn't barred from, the black crosses appeared less frequently. Still, starting from the suspect end made more sense when it came to finding connections.

Searching for Mulligan would raise flags. Searching for Ives might stay hidden. And there were other databases besides HOLMES that wouldn't trigger alarms. Even regular internet searches might yield results.

But first, he had someone to contact. He dialled the number Nina had taken from Ives' husband.

Gustavo Arroyo didn't answer.

Tom sighed and turned back to his screen. Time to do this the slow way.

CHAPTER FORTY-SEVEN

THE FAREWELL between Zoe and Carl had been less icy this time. Though arguments loomed about Streeting's recording devices, Carl had left the interview room in good spirits, even managing civility with Randle in the briefing room.

Zoe wanted to discuss it further, but they both had other commitments. They'd parted ways to their vehicles, and footsteps from behind reminded her she was meant to give Randle a lift back.

They'd been on the road barely two minutes when Lesley's name flashed up on the dashboard display. Randle glanced at it.

"Aren't you going to answer?"

"Not with you here."

He laughed. "She doesn't know, does she?"

"Doesn't know what?" Zoe asked, though she knew exactly what he meant.

"She doesn't know about me. That we're... That we've been working together. Aren't you going to tell her?"

Zoe remained silent as the phone stopped ringing.

"How do you think she'll react?" Randle's quiet laughter made Zoe's blood run cold.

It was him. Everywhere. In her earpiece during interviews. In her head when least expected. In her home with his messages. At work with his sudden appearances. Now here in her car, laughing at a woman worth ten of him.

She pulled over on an empty stretch of road and turned to him. The laughter stopped.

"I'm sorry," he said.

Too bloody late for that.

"For laughing," he added. "I didn't mean that. I hold DCI Clarke in the highest esteem."

"You spent years lying to her, manipulating her investigations. You worked for the man whose bomb nearly killed her, David." The anger threatened to overwhelm her.

"I wish it hadn't come to this."

"You wish you hadn't been caught," she corrected.

He shook his head. "It's not that. It's all…" He closed his eyes, then opened them, looking out at the farmland and the glinting River Keekle.

"It's more than that," he said. "I got caught up in something. It seemed like the obvious thing to do."

"That's your excuse?"

"You didn't know Bryn Jackson, did you?"

"No," she said. "Not really."

And she'd been glad of it. Bryn Jackson was the West Midlands ACC, whose murder had been her first investigation as a DI. One of the first and only things he'd said to her had been to call her friend and colleague Mo Uddin a 'Muselmann'.

CHAPTER FORTY-SEVEN

She shivered. Yes, Jackson had been bad news. And he'd controlled Randle, by all accounts.

But that wasn't enough. It didn't excuse him.

CHAPTER FORTY-EIGHT

"It's like one minute you're all 'Where's the bloody results, mate?' and next thing I'm in a ghost town, yeah?"

"What?" Nina pulled her phone away from her ear, staring at it. She wondered if there was something wrong with it – something that turned sentences into nonsense. Since Keisha had joined Stella Berry's CSI team, Nina had struggled to understand her at times. But usually the words at least made sense.

"You're going to have to explain what the problem is, Keisha. Imagine you're talking to someone who's, I don't know, forty. OK?"

"Alright, granny. I've done the work on your crime scene. Mulligan. Usually, I've got you lot calling me every five minutes chasing me for what I've found, but this time, it's like you've hit mute with your fat granny fingers."

Nina hoped Keisha didn't speak to her actual grandparents like this. But she understood the woman's frustration. And she was right – just like the pathologist earlier.

Why had no one from DCI Carnegie's team been following up?

"I'm sorry," she said. "It's not our investigation any more. It's being run by DCI Carnegie's team from Durranhill. DS Knight should have been in touch."

"Knight?" Keisha's voice carried a note of distaste. "Sammy Knight?"

"Yes."

"Smug Sammy Knight?"

"That's the one."

"Yeah, that explains it. He'll probably get someone else to call me."

"Why?"

"Because he pinched my bum at a club night in summer."

Nina's shock lasted only a moment. "Was this... Was this unwanted?"

"What do you reckon? He's old enough to be... He's too old for you, Nina, and that's saying something."

Nina pushed back thoughts of her mum's matchmaking. "Did you report him?"

"No."

"Why not?"

"Because I thought kneeing him in the balls would be just as effective and I'd get to see the results first hand."

Nina bit back a laugh. "Ah." She could see why Knight hadn't called for the forensics results.

She'd have given anything to have been at that club night. "Look, while you're on..."

Keisha was happy to relay her findings. "He wasn't killed on the spot. He was moved there. And I'll tell you something else."

"What?"

"That guy whose hair and clothes you had swabbed?"

"Ives?"

"Yeah. Ives. He wasn't involved. If he had been, there'd have been bits of wood all over him. Dust and that."

"And there wasn't any?"

"There's always some. But the sample we analysed contained a statistically irrelevant quantity of wood fragments. Which means he wasn't there. His prints don't show up on anything else at the site, either."

Nina ended the call after thanking her and pulled up the team inbox. Though she had no access to the investigation on HOLMES, they still had copies of Ives' earlier interview notes. She scanned through the documents, growing more convinced that Ives wasn't guilty.

Ives had claimed he'd killed Mulligan on the spot, but Keisha thought otherwise. Ives hadn't even been there. And he'd told them the murder weapon was a log, while the pathologist thought it was metal.

Ives was lying. He knew some details – the message on the shirt, the time of death, the location. He knew the cameras hadn't been working. He knew just enough to mess up the investigation, keep them busy. But not enough to get himself convicted of murder.

Unless that was his plan all along. A double bluff.

Nina's phone buzzed with a WhatsApp from her mum.

The same man. The same photo.

But really, what do you think? said the message.

Nina shook her head and tapped out a reply, then deleted it and typed something less sweary.

Really, Mum? You've just sent me a photo of some bloke.

Yes, he looks very respectable. But I don't know anything about him. You need to stop this.

She read through it, took a breath, and tapped send.

CHAPTER FORTY-NINE

"What's up, working man?" Denise said when Aaron finally answered.

"Who is this... Oh. Yes. OK, I get it."

"So? How's life treating you? I want all the details."

Aaron sighed down the line. She knew he probably didn't have time for this, that it wasn't fair to put him on the spot. But she was bored.

"Well," he said. "We had a murder investigation, and then we lost it."

"What?"

"The Mulligan investigation."

"Ah." Denise pictured Kieran Mulligan. She hadn't known him well, but she had known him. And he'd been clean, as far as she knew.

What a waste.

"We were working on it."

Denise sighed, grimacing at the pain no one could see. Today it was her head. Yesterday, her neck. The day before, her hip. And before that, her head again. No pattern, no way

CHAPTER FORTY-NINE

to predict what would come next. She stared at the two painkillers in her hand, each quadruple the recommended strength. Eight times her prescribed dose.

But what did doctors know?

"I know you were working on it," she said. "You told me. I might be off work still, but I haven't lost my mind. What's happened?"

"It's been taken over by someone else. DCI Carnegie, at Durranhill."

"Why?"

"Don't ask me."

She sensed something else, something he wasn't saying. Her instinct was to push, to find out what he was hiding, to keep going until he broke.

But this wasn't an interview room. And Aaron Keyes wasn't the only one with secrets. The pain peaked behind her right eye, then began to recede.

"What else is new?" she asked.

Aaron launched into a story about a romantic evening with Serge being ruined by Annabel puking everywhere. Denise quietly swallowed one of the pills.

"Sounds miserable," she said. "Hope she's better now."

"She's on the way. How about you?"

"I'm fine." She thought she could feel the pill working already, though it was probably just the placebo effect. "Getting better every day."

"Good to hear," he said.

A short silence fell while she swallowed the other pill. The drawer beside her was running low. Soon she'd need to make another call.

"I'm ready for work," she said. "I've told DI Whaley. I can go back. Doctor's signed me off for light duties."

"Really?"

Nina's voice filtered through in the background, talking to someone else. She'd made DS while Denise had been stuck at home recovering. The world had moved on.

"Really," Denise said. "I'm better now. Well, almost better. Well enough."

As she said goodbye and let him return to whatever crisis was brewing in the Hub, she knew it was true. The doctor had signed her off. As far as anyone knew, she was ready.

The fact that she'd spent two months lying to the doctor about how much fucking pain she was really in – well, that was neither here nor there.

CHAPTER FIFTY

Zoe hesitated to ask favours under the circumstances, but David Randle's presence at the Hub would draw unwanted attention. His last unexpected visit had already raised eyebrows.

"Why do you want a room on the sixth floor?" Carl asked over speakerphone.

The sixth floor housed a semi-secret suite of interview rooms and cells, complete with its own entrance and lift. Usually reserved for PSD, it would be perfect for questioning Randle.

"Because I need to speak to him properly, and I don't want to do it in the car."

"Can't we just find him a cell?" Carl's voice dripped with disdain. "Push him in, lock the door, and forget about it?"

"I am here," Randle said as they emerged onto the main road. "I can hear you, Carl."

"I know." Carl paused. "OK, then. Fine. When will you be there?"

"Ten minutes," Zoe replied.

"I'll have a room waiting."

The room Carl arranged was unfamiliar to Zoe. Smaller, grubbier, rougher than the Hub's usual pristine spaces. This must have been where they put their more inconvenient guests. The ones they wanted to forget about.

Zoe left Randle with a canteen coffee and a seven-foot giant of a guard watching through the open door. She retrieved some printouts from her office and returned to begin their analysis.

For most people, examining bank accounts, companies, directors and shareholders would be mind-numbing. The endless chain of nominee directors and their associated accounts could make anyone's head spin.

But Zoe found it fascinating. She stood beside Randle over a chipped round wooden table covered in papers, with Zhang's forensic accounting report to one side, piecing together the details Streeting had provided.

"What about this?" Randle's bandaged finger hovered over a particularly dense passage.

"I'm not sure," Zoe admitted.

"Let's call him."

"Call who?"

"Your accountant. Zhang."

Zoe frowned, suddenly aware of her situation.

"I don't know about that."

"What are you afraid of, Zoe? I can hardly get to the man down a phone, can I? And why would I bother?"

She considered his point. What was she afraid of?

But this felt like another step down a path she'd stumbled onto without thinking.

"Zoe," Randle prompted. "If you're going to understand—"

CHAPTER FIFTY

"Fine," she snapped, echoing Carl's earlier resignation.

Zhang answered immediately, his round face filling the screen, black hair now falling in waves to his shoulders.

"Zoe Finch!" His Birmingham accent was warm and familiar. "How the hell are you?"

She couldn't help smiling at his friendly face.

"A Brummie?" Randle asked.

"Kings Heath," Zhang replied. "Who's this, then?"

"This is David Randle," Zoe said. "A former colleague."

Zhang fell silent. "Ah." Clearly the name meant something to him.

"Listen, I was hoping you could help us," Zoe said quickly. "And I'd really appreciate it if you'd keep this conversation to yourself."

"Of course." Zhang's grave smile seemed out of place, but Zoe trusted him.

"We were puzzling over this section of your report." She pointed her phone at the printout. "And we've managed to get some more information from one of Carter's former associates. I was hoping you could help us put it all together."

Zhang's usual cheerful expression returned. "Of course. The more information we have, the more we can work out. Tell me what you know."

They spent thirty minutes analysing the data. Occasionally Zoe became so absorbed she almost forgot who she was working with. Almost – but not quite. The discomfort lingered, along with worry about her judgment. Still, she'd achieved her goal: more names, more companies, more directors. Less chance for Carter to escape.

"It's funny you called now," Zhang said finally. "I was thinking of calling you."

"You were?"

"Yes. You see, I still look into the Jenson & Marley bank accounts occasionally. Just to see if anything's changed."

"And has it?"

"Well, as it happens, it has, a little. You remember, Jenson & Marley is the company at the top of the tree, as far as we can tell. It's where all the money gets funnelled, in the end, from all the other companies and bank accounts."

"Yes, we know that," Randle interrupted.

Zoe shot him a pointed look, which he ignored.

"The money continues to flow in," Zhang continued. "Just like it did before. But for the first time, as far as I can tell, there are also significant sums flowing *out* of Jenson & Marley."

"Where to?" Zoe asked.

Zhang's expression turned to one of confusion. "I don't know. If we could find that out, Zoe, if we could show it going to Myron Carter personally, then maybe we could bring it all down."

After thanking Zhang and ending the call, she turned to Randle, who looked thoughtful.

"This feels like something significant, Zoe."

"True," she said. "But when doesn't it?"

CHAPTER FIFTY-ONE

"Christian Ives?" said the man.

"Yes." Tom paused. "Christian Ives, or Gustavo Arroyo."

"Sorry. Names don't ring a bell. Were they... Were they involved?"

"I can't tell you that, I'm afraid. We're at an early stage."

Tom considered his words. Were they really at an early stage? Or were they just motoring down a dead end? This was the second time in five minutes he'd given that response to one of Mulligan's friends – names he remembered from their brief time working together, names that matched numbers in the phone data backed up to the team inbox before his access was revoked.

Neither Chloe Gaines nor Grant Turing had heard of Christian Ives or Gustavo Arroyo. Tom was about to end the call when another thought struck him.

"Sorry," he said. "Just one more question. Have any of my colleagues been in touch?"

"Nope." Turing's voice was flat. "We heard about Kieran,

couldn't really believe it. We thought, given where he worked, someone would give us a call. But until you called, I hadn't heard a thing. Nor has anyone else, far as I know."

Tom collected a list of Mulligan's other friends and their numbers before offering condolences and ending the call. He'd contact the others later, but Gaines and Turing were the names Mulligan had mentioned personally, and they were his most frequent contacts.

And the Durranhill team hadn't even contacted them.

Thinking of Durranhill, he pulled up the internal directory for two more names and numbers.

"Yes?" DS Sharon Virgil's voice carried tension, like she was too busy or too troubled to talk.

"I'm sorry." Tom introduced himself, though they'd met once, briefly, in the team room with Mulligan. She and Mulligan had been friends, he thought. Or at least friendly colleagues.

"I remember you, Tom. Working undercover, weren't you?"

So she knew about that. Everyone at Durranhill probably did – his stint working under Streeting, monitoring him to prevent evidence being hidden about Bobby Silver's death.

"Yes," he admitted.

"I still can't believe it. Kieran. I just..."

Her breathing was slow, controlled, like she was suppressing her emotions.

"Have the investigating team spoken to you?" he asked.

"I thought you *were* the investigating team," she said, confusion in her voice.

Tom felt frustration rise but kept it contained. He didn't correct her assumption. Instead, he asked about Kieran's personal and professional life. She knew little.

CHAPTER FIFTY-ONE

"I didn't work that closely with him, to be honest. No one did, really, except DI Streeting. And... well, the last few months, it's just been Kieran on his own."

Since Streeting's arrest.

His next call was to DC Shaw, the other officer he'd met in the team room.

"Shaw," came the clipped response.

"Nigel, it's Tom Willis. DC Willis from the Hub. We met—"

"I remember you. What's up?"

"I was hoping to talk to you about Kieran, see if you had any insight into—"

"You were hoping to talk to me?"

"Yes," Tom replied, uncertain.

"Let me get this straight. You were involved in some of the weirder stuff Kieran was caught up in, and then Kieran got himself killed, and instead of coming forward to offer your information to the investigating team, you're sniffing around for intel?"

Tom's stomach dropped.

"It's not like that," he protested.

"It sounds like that. You know who I work for?"

Tom's unease grew as realisation hit.

"DCI Carnegie?"

"That's right. You shouldn't be coming to me, asking questions. I'm part of the team that's going to get to the bottom of this, and we will, and we don't need you sticking your nose in stirring things up."

Shit. "It's just—"

"Although by the sound of it, we already have the killer in custody."

"Not Ives?" Tom asked.

"I'm not at liberty to say. Listen, DC Willis. Tom. Friendly word of advice, from one DC to another. You need to drop it."

The call ended.

Tom stared at his screen, wondering if anyone knew anything useful about Mulligan. His eyes caught another name in the Durranhill personnel list.

He barely knew DI Song Hae-Won, but then he'd hardly known Virgil or Shaw, either. Calling a DI out of the blue was different, he supposed. But she'd seemed approachable enough. Tough, even intimidating, but someone he could work with.

She answered professionally, giving her name and rank. He introduced himself and waited for her to say she had no idea who he was.

"Tom Willis? You're the one in the car park, aren't you? Got Ralph Streeting arrested and swore at me when you thought I'd nicked your parking space."

He grimaced. "Yes," he said. "I'm sorry about that."

"What can I do for you, then, Tom Willis?"

He explained, and heard her sharp intake of breath.

"What did that other one tell you? Nigel Shaw?"

"He said to drop it."

"Look," she said, "I didn't know Kieran. I mean, I didn't know him at all, and I wasn't involved in any of his investigations, so I don't have any information for you. If I did, given what you've just told me, I'd probably give it to you, under the radar, and then route it through the proper channels. But Shaw was right."

"He was?"

"Oh, I don't know about this Ives, or the investigation, or

any of that. But he was right about dropping it. I've been working at Durranhill for seven years, and if there's one thing I've learned, it's that you don't cross Kiki Carnegie. Not if you know what's good for you."

CHAPTER FIFTY-TWO

Aaron stood in the reception area at Durranhill, waiting. He'd signed himself in and messaged Sammy Knight to say he'd arrived. Ten minutes had passed. The receptionist had offered him a seat, but both chairs were occupied by what looked like journalists or lawyers – they had that hungry look, sizing up the place.

The station was surprisingly quiet. Just a low hum of activity, less bustling than he'd expected for a place this size. Maybe they kept stricter shift patterns here than at the Hub.

"This way."

DS Knight strode towards him at such speed that Aaron had to step back to avoid a collision. Knight pulled up inches from him.

"Come on, then. This way. Haven't got all day."

"Are we—"

"Christ's sake, Aaron, yes. I'm taking you to see Ives. It's what you wanted, isn't it?"

Not the friendliest welcome, but Aaron would take it if he got what he needed. He hurried after Knight through a

CHAPTER FIFTY-TWO

door that nearly hit him, down a corridor and a flight of stairs to a custody suite. Another sign-in and search followed.

The search felt unnecessary – clearly Knight's way of showing how unwelcome Aaron was.

"In here." Knight led him to a door guarded by a man nearly as large as Roddy Chen. "Out of the way."

The guard stepped aside, and they entered.

Aaron gasped.

"What?" Knight asked.

"Nothing."

Ives sat across a metal table, cuffed to a bar with shackled legs. Fresh bruises marked one side of his face.

"Right, then." Knight gestured towards Ives. "You've met this chap, right?"

Ives raised bloodshot eyes to Aaron's, nodded, then looked down again.

"You still don't want a lawyer?" Knight asked.

Ives shook his head. Aaron noticed there was no tape running.

"What happened to you?" Aaron couldn't help asking.

"The transport was a bit bumpy, wasn't it, Christian?" Knight's tone made it clear what had really happened. Someone here had beaten Ives – maybe Knight himself.

Another Tel Cummings.

Aaron looked meaningfully between the door and Knight.

Knight laughed. "I don't think so, mate. I'll be here the whole time. In case anything pertaining to the Mulligan investigation comes up."

Aaron had expected this, but it still hit hard. How could he ask what he needed to with Knight watching?

"You ready to go then?" Knight asked. "Let's get recording."

Ives suddenly leaned forward, eyes desperate. "Have you spoken to Gustavo?"

"You'll have to speak to DS Knight here about that," Aaron said.

"What about my mother? Have you found her yet?"

Aaron turned to Knight.

"Not yet," Knight said. "No sign of her."

Ives looked close to tears. "I don't understand. Why haven't they let her go?"

What?

"Start recording," Aaron said.

"Easy now," Knight warned.

"Remind him he's under caution and start recording. There's something—"

A bang interrupted him. Ives looked past him towards the door. Knight turned, too. Another bang followed, then a familiar voice.

"Open this door," DCI Carnegie shouted. "Open this door right now, Aaron Keyes, or you'll wish you'd never been born."

CHAPTER FIFTY-THREE

"Empress what-was-that?" The voice came through the speakerphone.

Zoe glanced at her notes. "Empress SE400."

"Never heard of it," said Superintendent Singer.

"Neither had I." Zoe leaned forward in her chair. "But I'm not an expert in bugging devices. Are you?"

Inspector Morris Keane, beside her, tried to hide his smile. Across the desk, Fiona maintained her stony expression. It had been months since Zoe had seen warmth in the super's face.

"Fair point," Singer conceded. As Superintendent Ops Command, he'd be taking the Silver Command role if they recovered these devices.

"What do you think?" Fiona's gaze was fixed on the speakerphone.

"Three locations?" Singer said. "I take it we'll need armed support?"

"I think so," said Zoe.

Morris nodded. "I wouldn't like to send my people in without it."

"Three simultaneous raids, all armed." Singer's voice was tight. "Let's hope no one decides to rob a bank that day."

Fiona's face twisted. After sending Randle away, Zoe had gone straight to brief them all together. The super had waited, reluctant but patient, while Morris made his way upstairs and Singer was tracked down. This was their first time hearing any of it.

And there was worse to come.

"There's one further complication." Zoe straightened her shoulders. "Ralph Streeting needs to come with."

"What?" Three voices spoke in unison.

"He won't describe the locations of the devices. Says it's too complicated. Insists it'll be too easy for them to be damaged or destroyed."

"Is he bullshitting you?" Morris asked.

"I don't think so."

"Don't think so?" Singer's tone sharpened. "I'm not sure that's good enough, DI Finch."

"I know it's not ideal." Zoe studied the faces before her. Morris wore an expression of deep concentration. Fiona's usual cloud of depression had lifted, replaced by determination and focus.

"That's the understatement of the year," Singer replied. "We've got to make sure he doesn't use this to escape."

"My people can keep an eye on him," said Morris.

"Yes, I'm sure they can," Singer replied. "But even if he is genuine, we've got to assume he'll be a target for Carter's people."

"Which is why we need your AFOs," Fiona said with a slow nod.

CHAPTER FIFTY-THREE

Silence filled the room.

Zoe knew that Singer could end it all with one word. If he deemed it too dangerous or unlikely to succeed, the whole plan would die here.

"OK," he said at last. "Leave it with me."

CHAPTER FIFTY-FOUR

"What on earth do you think you're doing, Aaron Keyes?" DCI Carnegie's eyes flashed with anger.

"What do you mean?" Aaron asked, though he had a fair idea.

She looked around the tiny room, taking in Sammy Knight, and Ives with his cuffs. A younger man with a crew cut stood beside her, but Aaron didn't recognise him, and DCI Carnegie wasn't in the mood for introductions.

"Have you started this interview? Are you recording?"

"No, Ma'am," Knight said.

She nodded, satisfied. "Good. Nigel, get him out and back to his cell."

The other man stepped forward to unshackle Christian Ives.

She turned back to Aaron. "And you can explain what the bloody hell is going on here."

"I'm really not sure—"

"Save it. I've just heard your lot at the Hub are snooping around the Mulligan investigation. Is that right?"

CHAPTER FIFTY-FOUR

Aaron remained silent.

"DC Willis has been making calls to DC Shaw here. Among others. So I asked Nigel to look at this case you claim fits the profile. Cranshaw, was it?"

DC Shaw looked up from the chains where he and Knight were struggling with a lock. "Yes, Ma'am."

"Cranshaw. Nothing in common with this investigation. The victim was a known drug dealer, and the only reason we don't have the offender in custody is that he fled the country."

Aaron swallowed. "Is that right, Ma'am?"

A clanking noise drew his attention. Ives was finally free from the table, rubbing his wrists where the cuffs had bitten into them. Shaw yanked him to his feet and led him from the room.

"You know it is," she snapped.

Ives stumbled against the wall as he left. The bruises on his face looked stark under the overhead lights. Aaron decided DCI Carnegie wasn't the one with cause to be angry.

"What happened to Ives?" he said.

She narrowed her eyes. "What?"

"Ives. Your suspect. Beaten up, was he?"

She stepped towards him, eyes widening. Knight remained by the table, his gaze darting between them.

"What did you say?"

Aaron met the DCI's gaze. "Have you made any effort with this investigation at all? I know you haven't followed up with forensics or the post mortem. I know you haven't contacted the victim's friends or colleagues. So what exactly have you done?"

Her mouth opened and closed. She wouldn't be used to

this from a detective sergeant. Aaron could hardly believe his own words.

"Christian Ives wasn't anywhere near those logs," he continued. "No prints. Insufficient wood fragments. And despite what he says, the crime wasn't even committed there. What did his phone data say?"

DCI Carnegie blinked. She shot a look at Knight, who looked even more nervous than before.

Nervous was better than smug.

"DS Keyes." She smiled. "Thanks for your input. But it's up to me how I run my investigations."

Something lurked behind that smile. Surprise, perhaps shock. Aaron's thoughts shifted from *what* to *why*.

Why hadn't her team followed up? Was someone deliberately stalling? Were they hiding things from their own DCI?

"I think—" he began.

Carnegie waved him silent. "Have you actually asked Christian Ives where he was?"

"Well..." Aaron frowned. Of course they had. Ives still claimed he'd done it. And Ives was lying.

"Because I can tell you he has no alibi, from midnight until he walked into your Hub. His phone was conveniently switched off. And his car was pinged heading towards Workington shortly before three, matching his statement about the timeframe."

"What about—"

"I hadn't finished. Ives' prints aren't on the logs because he wore gloves, and the wood doesn't show up because he managed to shower and change before turning himself in."

"That's all possible," Aaron said. "Just about. Only it's a

lot of effort for someone who's going to head straight to the nearest police station and confess."

She shook her head. "People do strange things. Otherwise we wouldn't have jobs. Now bugger off back to the Hub."

Aaron nodded. With Ives back in his cell and no cooperation likely from Durranhill, there wasn't much point staying.

"Goodbye, Ma'am." He smiled as he passed her, wondering all the way to the car park whether he'd just ruined his career or shown the backbone a DI needed.

CHAPTER FIFTY-FIVE

That expression was back on Aaron's face, a curious mixture of guilt and glee, of shock at the thing he'd done, and delight that he'd done it.

Nina had seen that look elsewhere. *Where was it?*

Aaron pulled the team room door shut behind him. "Better go home."

"Why?" Nina asked. He'd been gone a couple of hours, hadn't called in the meantime, and it wasn't like she was his mum, but still...

"We've been warned off the Mulligan investigation." Aaron turned to Tom. "You spoke to someone at Durranhill, right?"

Tom nodded. "That'll be Shaw. He's part of the investigating team, apparently. I didn't realise."

"Well, now they know we've been snooping around. And they've told us not to."

Nina felt heat rising in her face. "That's it then, is it? They've told us not to, so we have to stop?"

"Well, technically, yes." Aaron's smile widened. "I didn't

CHAPTER FIFTY-FIVE

take it lying down, mind. I may have just had a blazing row with DCI Carnegie in public."

"You what?"

"I told her that her team weren't doing much of a job."

His eyes were wide, and now she had it.

Arsonists. When they came in and confessed, that was what they looked like. Excited, guilty, shocked, delighted at what they'd done.

Aaron might just have set fire to his own career, but he wasn't worrying about it.

"OK," Tom said. "That's great. But where does it leave us? Because you're right. They're not really doing anything."

"Agreed. So we carry on, but be subtler." A shadow passed across Aaron's face. "And..."

"And what?" Nina asked.

"It's nothing."

"It's not, Aaron. What's worrying you?"

Aaron turned, checked the door was still shut, and sat at his desk. "I just don't know *why* they were so incompetent. I mean, not even bothering to follow up on the forensics and the pathology? They've still got Ives there, they've beaten him up a bit, and he looks..."

"Maybe someone should have a quiet word with PSD about that." Nina turned to Tom, who was staring at his screen.

Tom looked up, saw her staring at him, and stared blankly back, then past her at Aaron, then back to her. He frowned in confusion. "What?"

Christ, Nina thought.

"Maybe *someone* should have a quiet word with PSD about that," she repeated.

"Oh, yeah." Tom nodded. "I'll talk to Harriett. But the

Ports information I asked for has just turned up. I'm... Oh. Blimey."

Nina laughed. "Blimey?"

"Yeah. Gustavo Arroyo. He didn't go to Buenos Aires."

Aaron stood and walked to Tom's desk. "I thought you said he'd left the country."

"I did. He did. Went to Madrid for his connecting flight, but he never took it."

"What?" Nina said.

"He just stayed in Madrid for two nights and came straight back. He said he'd just arrived, when we saw him at the house, right?"

Nina thought back to the conversation in Arroyo's Lexus. *I've just got back. You saw me drive in.*

"Yes," she said.

"Well, he was lying. He'd been in the country around forty-eight hours by then." Tom turned back to his screen, tapped a box, and continued. "Yes. Two days before he said he was back." He swung his chair around to face them both. "Before Mulligan was killed."

"We need to pick him up." Nina hadn't liked Arroyo from the start, but he'd had an alibi.

Now, he didn't.

"We don't even know where he is," Tom replied. "And he's not answering his phone. I tried him earlier."

Aaron coughed. "We couldn't pick him up even if we knew where he was. Not unless we want to bring Carnegie into it."

"Fuck's sake," Nina muttered.

"Indeed," Aaron agreed. "In the meantime, the best thing we can do is carry on working quietly. Find out what we can. OK?"

CHAPTER FIFTY-FIVE

"OK," Tom and Nina said in unison.

CHAPTER FIFTY-SIX

It had been so long since Zoe had been to the lighthouse.

The wind was gentler than she remembered, the sea lapping instead of raging. As dusk fell and her shadow lengthened behind her, she stepped away from her car and strode towards the lighthouse, trying to project a confidence she didn't feel.

Would Olivia really be here? Here, where they'd met that one time? Here, where she'd taken the photos that had condemned her to more than two years in hiding? David Randle had agreed to set this meeting up, reluctantly, but Zoe had insisted, and in the end he'd conceded. But it was the same old question.

Could she trust Randle?

Her phone rang, breaking the calm. Zoe pulled it from her pocket, ready to ignore it, then saw Fiona's name on the display. The super never called in the evening.

She turned back to the almost deserted car park. "Hello?"

"Zoe. Where are you?"

CHAPTER FIFTY-SIX

"I'm meeting a source. I'll explain when I can. Is everything OK?"

"I've been talking to a source of my own. I've got some information for you."

Zoe pulled open the door of her Mini and slid back into the driver's seat. "Yes?"

"I can't tell you where I'm hearing this from, but there are whispers Carter knows about your visits to Streeting."

"But..." Zoe closed her eyes.

"I know. It means someone's been passing him information. It also means he knows that killing Mulligan has backfired on him. And it's possible he knows about..."

Shit. If Carter knew about Streeting's recording devices, they'd lost their advantage.

"Where did you hear this?" Zoe asked.

"I can't—"

"Fiona, this is important. Could be critical. Where did you hear this?"

"I can't say," Fiona replied firmly. "Let's just say it comes from within the police. In an administrative capacity."

Luke. Fiona's assistant. Luke knew people everywhere.

Zoe looked at the phone display. "I've got to go, Fiona. Thanks for letting me know."

The wind had picked up in the few minutes she'd been in the car. Zoe wrapped her jacket around herself as she walked along the sea wall to the tiny lighthouse. Lights moved about on the upper level, and as she approached, she heard voices that stilled at her footsteps.

She stepped onto the metal stairs and made her way up, gripped by cold and darkness and sudden foreboding.

Could she trust Randle? Mulligan had been murdered not far from here, just to send someone a message. Would they do the same to her? Could she get help in time if they did?

"Zoe," said a voice she recognised.

She took a deep, ragged breath of relief.

"Olivia," she replied.

At the top of the steps stood Olivia Bagsby by the railings at the far end of the small square structure. Beside her was David Randle.

Olivia faced the Port, the same direction she'd faced to sketch her sunrises and take those photographs. She turned now, and Zoe took a step towards her, then stopped as Olivia flinched away, her back pressing into the railings.

"It's OK," said Zoe.

"Is it?" Olivia directed the question more at Randle than Zoe.

Randle nodded.

"Thank you for coming to meet me," Zoe said. "It's been too long."

"Would have been sooner if you'd arrested Myron Carter."

"You know..."

Zoe stopped herself. It was an old argument. Olivia wasn't safe without Carter locked up, but they couldn't lock up Carter without Olivia's evidence.

"I'm happy to see you," she said. "You're looking well."

"Am I?" Olivia frowned. "I don't even remember what I used to look like. I had long hair. Now..." She pushed a hand through her hair. "It was important I didn't look like me."

Zoe had never seen Olivia's hair. The artist had worn a headscarf to complement her dungarees and apron. Now she had short blonde spikes that looked fine, good even, but didn't suit the woman Zoe knew Olivia to be.

CHAPTER FIFTY-SIX

She'd been fighting to stay alive for so long, burying everything that made her who she was.

Sudden, desperate sadness filled Zoe for everything Olivia had endured.

"I'm so sorry all this has happened," she said.

Olivia shrugged. "I didn't want to come, you know. Not tonight. Not here. But David said... What have you been up to, the two of you? He won't tell me."

Zoe opened her mouth to reply.

"It's best she doesn't know," Randle said, shaking his head. "Safer for her."

Was that true? It could be, Zoe supposed. Which meant she couldn't tell Randle what she'd just learned from Fiona.

Strange. She wanted to tell him. She wanted his advice about Carter possibly being onto them, wanted his opinions.

She hated him. But what he'd said in the car about his past, his regrets...

She still didn't know if she trusted him. But Olivia clearly did.

"We're close," she said.

Olivia looked unconvinced. "You've been telling me that for so long now, I can't take it seriously."

"This time it's real," said Randle.

Olivia looked from one of them to the other, searching their faces. "Really?"

"Really," replied Zoe, and saw something she'd hoped against hope to see again but hadn't truly believed she would.

She saw Olivia Bagsby smile.

CHAPTER FIFTY-SEVEN

"Top-up?"

"Yes, please." Nina held out her glass. Elena poured as the TV played quietly in the background, and Nina couldn't help smiling to herself.

"What?"

Nina looked at her housemate. "What do you mean?"

"What are you smiling for, Nina Kapoor?" Elena raised one eyebrow.

Nina's smile broadened. "Just that if you'd asked me a couple of years ago what I'd be doing on a night off, the whole town at my feet, all its bars and clubs... Don't look at me like that, Elena. Whitehaven has a glittering nightlife, and I won't hear a word against it. It's just... I've passed my exams, and now I spend my nights off sipping wine on the sofa with my housemate."

"And this disappoints you?"

"Far from it." Nina raised the glass to her lips and drank.

They fell silent, both women's attention on the screen,

where a pair of dancers had just scored close to maximum points and the audience had gone wild.

"Oh!" Nina set the glass down on the coaster on the table beside her. Was she middle-aged already? "I forget to tell you. Probably shouldn't, to be honest. But Ralph Streeting's talking."

Elena turned to her, her eyes wide. "Talking? You mean he is telling you things? About the... the business?"

The 'business' was people-trafficking, among other things, and Elena had been one of its victims.

"Not me personally, but yes. We're getting closer."

"Closer to what?"

Nina shook her head and smiled. Elena was involved and had helped them a great deal. But she shouldn't know things like this. She *couldn't* know things like this.

Elena returned her smile, then frowned. "Wait, he is not going to get away with it, is he?"

"What do you mean?"

"That man. Streeting. He is a killer and a..." Her voice changed suddenly, a jumble of what Nina could only assume were Romanian swear words falling from her lips, before she returned to English. "You're not going to give him a deal, are you?"

"If he helps us, he might get a slightly shorter minimum term. But he's going to prison, Elena. There's no doubt about that."

There wasn't any doubt, was there?

Nina closed her eyes and wondered whether there was any way Streeting could wriggle out of the justice he deserved.

Surely not. The boss wouldn't let that happen. Nor

would the super. Or PSD. DI Whaley. Harriett. Denise Gaskill.

The names and faces flickered through her mind. She was onto her third glass of wine now, and the room was warm, the darkness welcoming. She could feel things closing in around her and was ready to surrender when her phone rang.

Bugger.

Her eyes snapped open, and she answered before checking the display.

"Nina?" said her mum.

Double bugger.

"Yes," mumbled Nina.

"Are you OK, Nina? You sound like you're half asleep."

"I'm fine, Mum. Are you OK?"

"Yes. Well, no, actually."

Nina forced herself to sit up, blinking. Elena watched her, concern in her big grey eyes.

"What is it?" Nina asked.

"What exactly do you mean, I 'need to stop this'?"

"What?" *That didn't make sense. Did it?*

"You know very well what, young lady."

Did she? The words sounded familiar. Something she'd heard, or read. Yes, read. No, not read. A message she'd sent. About that man, from the art class. The photos. Her mother's 'eligible young man'.

"Hang on," Nina said, but her mum was still talking.

"All I am trying to do is stay in touch with my daughter. Is that too much to ask?"

"No, of course not. But you can't just take over my life."

"I have no intention of taking over your life, Nina Kapoor." There was a sharpness to her mother's voice that

CHAPTER FIFTY-SEVEN

blew a cold wind through the fuzz of Nina's mind. "You made it clear a long time ago that you wouldn't allow that, and I've always respected it."

"Mum—"

"Don't interrupt me while I'm speaking to you. I have to say, I'm upset. I understand I can't tell you what to do. But now it's like you want to have nothing to do with me at all."

"Mum—" Nina said, but there was nothing, just silence, and then the steady tone of a dead line.

Her mum had hung up on her.

She reached for her wine glass and was surprised to find it almost empty.

"More?" Elena's voice held a note of concern.

"God, yes," Nina replied.

She sipped, then sipped again, then took a gulp. As the warmth of the wine spread through her, her feelings subtly shifted.

Of course she felt a little guilty. She didn't want to hurt her mum. She wasn't cruel. But this wasn't fair.

It was her life, not her mum's. And she had no interest in being set up with strange men. Particularly strange men who looked three decades too old.

CHAPTER FIFTY-EIGHT

How could Zoe trust that man?

Carl sat in his car at the back of the car park, watching through binoculars. Three figures stood before him.

He recognised Randle straight away, and Zoe would be impossible to miss. But the other woman was a stranger to him.

Olivia Bagsby. The woman who'd started all this two years ago. Who'd been so close to death she'd turned to David Randle for help.

Zoe moved towards the other two. She'd done this earlier and Olivia had backed away, but now she stepped forward. The two women shook hands.

Randle stood to one side, observing. The meeting was over, and Olivia Bagsby was alive and back in Cumbria.

At least Zoe had told him about this meeting. He'd tried to talk her out of it, warning of the dangers, but she'd insisted. She'd agreed to let him watch, though.

Small comfort. If they'd attacked her, if someone had been lying in wait, what could he have done?

CHAPTER FIFTY-EIGHT

What could he do now?

He watched her descend the steps. Earlier, she'd walked away from her car and back again to take a call. She knew he was there. But even now, leaving the lighthouse, she was more than a hundred yards away. If someone was hidden in the shadows...

Don't imagine things. Just keep watching.

His eyes followed her as she drew nearer, as she unlocked her Mini and climbed in. Her gaze swept over his car, acknowledging his presence without giving it away. He watched as she started the engine and drove away towards Whitehaven.

Then he waited.

Twenty minutes passed before Randle and Olivia Bagsby emerged. They headed up the road past the car park on foot. He resisted the urge to drive after them – they'd hear his engine in the still evening air. Instead, he got out quietly and kept his binoculars trained on them until they stopped by a grey Vauxhall Astra, nearly a quarter of a mile up the road.

He forced himself to wait longer, risking losing them.

Finally, he got back into his car and followed, keeping his lights off until they reached Workington's outskirts. He tracked them into the hills, praying they wouldn't spot him and that Zoe wouldn't call asking why he hadn't followed her home.

He didn't want to lie to her. She'd known he'd watch the meeting. But he hadn't mentioned his plans to follow Randle.

He'd read Zoe's notes. No transcript – Randle hadn't allowed recording. But she'd been confident she'd remembered his exact words.

If I get the merest hint of Whaley sniffing around, I'll tell Olivia to get out. And if I tell her to, she will.

Well, here he was, sniffing around. Following them out of Workington, heading southeast on a road busy enough to risk his lights. They turned onto a steep, narrow road south of Lamplugh. He killed his lights as they passed a new housing estate and a caravan park. The roads grew narrower. They slowed beside a terrace of three cottages with a newer one attached, but continued past, taking more turns until they reached a track little wider than a footpath, heading up towards Cogra Moss.

He couldn't follow them up there. But he could see their destination. The Astra's lights were on, and thin clouds let pale moonlight illuminate the hills. He stopped and watched as David Randle and Olivia Bagsby made their way slowly up the track, towards the narrow, single-storey building at its end.

CHAPTER FIFTY-NINE

"Here." Tom pointed at his screen.

The sarge leaned in to look where Tom was pointing.

"Madrid to Manchester," Tom said

"He was on that flight? You're sure?"

"Unless someone else was using his passport." Tom paused, considering the possibility. But there was no point dwelling on it. Anything could be faked — passports, videos, biometric data. You had to take some things on trust.

His conversation with Harriett that morning came back to him. He'd told her about Durranhill, about DCI Carnegie's failure to follow up on the Mulligan investigation. Really, DS Knight's failure, but things flowed both ways in the police.

Harriett had said she'd look into it. She hadn't sounded surprised, but that was PSD for you. Tom only got through the day because he'd decided to take most things at face value. Harriett didn't trust anyone.

"And after that?" The sarge scanned further down Tom's screen.

"Hang on. Here it is." Tom tapped on another icon, bringing up Gustavo Arroyo's airport parking booking. He frowned at the details. "That's not the Lexus." He typed in the registration of the vehicle that had sat in a Manchester Airport car park for two days – a Range Rover.

"He's got a Range Rover as well?"

"No." Tom shifted the display to show more information. "Looks like a hire car. And... yes. He's handed it back already."

"Hang on, he hired a Range Rover to drive to the airport, leave it there, and then drive back again?"

"Looks like it. Want me to see if I can track its movements?"

Aaron grinned. "Go on, then."

"Why would he do that?" Tom tapped away at his keyboard. "Seems like a serious waste of money. Even if the Lexus was out of action. Hiring an expensive car like that, just to drive it to the airport."

"Wealthy people, aren't they?"

"Yes, from the look of their house. Well off, but not that rich. Why would anyone do that?"

The sarge nodded slowly, his eyes narrowed with realisation. "The same reason he flew on his Argentinian passport."

"What reason is that?"

"Because he thought it would make it harder for us to trace his movements."

Tom shrugged. "He's not wrong. It held us up, didn't it?"

The sarge grinned and put a hand on his shoulder. "You got there in the end. Ah, now." He pointed at Tom's screen. "Is that it?"

"Yes. Vehicle movement data."

The Range Rover had pinged numerous ANPR cameras

on the motorway, heading first west from Manchester, then north on the M6.

"All the way to Penrith," Tom noted. "Looks like he was heading back this way."

"Nothing else?"

"Not here, no. I'll have to request it."

DS Keyes nodded his approval. Tom entered the Cranshaw case reference, then stopped. "They know about Cranshaw, don't they?"

The sarge looked blankly at him.

"That it wasn't real. No actual connection with Ives and Mulligan."

"Oh. Yes. Good point. Can't use that."

Tom switched back to the generic Ports case reference and entered the search parameters for the Range Rover Ives' husband had hired, and the general area west of Penrith – all of Cumbria. He paused over the 'enter' button, then went back to add the details of Christian Ives' own vehicle, the electric Nissan.

He'd probably be blocked anyway. But Kiki Carnegie had told the sarge that Ives' car had been pinged around three in the morning, on the way to Workington.

They only had her word for that. It would be good to know whether that word could be trusted.

CHAPTER SIXTY

"Sit down, Carl."

Carl took the seat opposite Branthwaite's desk. The DCI leaned back and studied him.

"I've seen your surveillance request."

"Yes, Sir. I was going to speak to you about that." Carl shifted in his seat.

"You were, were you?"

"Yes, of course." Carl smiled. "I wouldn't expect you to sign off without knowing what or why."

Branthwaite returned the smile. "House in the middle of nowhere. Surveillance possible from nearby structures. Up Cogra Moss, is it?"

Carl nodded.

"So these nearby structures of yours, we're not talking five-star accommodation, are we?"

"No, Sir. I saw an old shepherd's hut. Some derelict barns."

"And your grounds for this surveillance?"

CHAPTER SIXTY

Carl drew in a breath. "I have reason to believe that a former police officer might be planning something, Sir."

"Planning something?"

"Yes, Sir."

"And does this 'former police officer' pose a threat to the public?"

"Possibly, Sir. Without surveillance, I can't be sure."

Branthwaite nodded. Carl glanced around the office. It could have been anywhere, this room, and Branthwaite any senior employee in some industrial park. A couple of family photos, two rugby trophies and a signed rugby shirt. Branthwaite had played until recently and was still involved in the local club.

"It's David Randle, is it?" the DCI said.

Carl had known this was coming. "Yes, Sir."

"You have history with Randle."

"Well, yes, but I don't think that's relevant—"

"Look, Carl, I understand where you're coming from." Branthwaite leaned across the table, his gaze intense. "You know Randle's dodgy, I know Randle's dodgy, my blooming milkman probably knows Randle's dodgy. And yes, he breached his Protection conditions. But as far as I understand it, the man's being cooperative now. Isn't he?"

"He claims he is, Sir. I just don't trust him."

"And I don't trust the blooming milkman, but I can't put surveillance on him, can I?"

"It's hardly the same, Sir."

"No, it isn't, but really, lad. You should know better."

Carl shrugged. He'd known it was a long shot.

He thought back to his conversation with Zoe the night before. She really believed in Randle. She believed he regretted his past, that his actions were some kind of atonement. She'd worked under him, been instrumental in unmasking him as the criminal he'd been all along. And yet she believed him.

"I should really be telling you just to let it go," Branthwaite said. "But I like you, so I'll put something in place."

Carl blinked and looked up. "You will?"

"Yes. It won't be twenty-four-seven, Carl. We can't afford that, we're not Elon bloody Musk. But we'll get some people to stop by, from time to time. Put electronics there and cameras for when we can't have human eyes on the place. That good enough for you?"

Carl smiled. It was better than he'd hoped for. "Thank you, Sir." He stood to leave.

"One more thing," said Branthwaite.

Carl sat back down. "Yes?"

"Denise. She wants in. Says you're being too slow."

"Oh."

She'd gone over his head, then. Direct to the DCI.

"I'm surprised she hasn't been in touch with me," he said, then stopped.

Branthwaite fixed him with a stare. "She says she has. Says you've had her requests and done nothing about them. Says you've been sitting on your hands waiting for God knows what."

"I've replied to her, Sir. I have been in touch."

"Oh, I don't doubt that. You're not heartless. You're just not getting on with it."

"I'm not sure, Sir. I'm not confident that she's ready."

"Do you have any specific grounds to be concerned about her health?" asked Branthwaite.

"Well, no, but—"

"Good. Well, the doc's signed her off, and we can't really

CHAPTER SIXTY

argue with him, can we? One day per week or its equivalent in hours, light duties only. Agreed?"

Carl frowned.

"Come on, lad. Best place for her. If she's in a little, you can keep an eye on her and actually see if you've got reason to worry."

"OK, Sir."

It seemed fair. And it wasn't as if Branthwaite needed his consent anyway.

CHAPTER SIXTY-ONE

DENISE'S HEAD pounded as she stood, nearly tripping over something by the bed.

She bent down, feeling around in the dark until her fingers found a whisky tumbler. She lifted it to her nose. Whisky, certainly, but she couldn't remember drinking it. Or why.

That would explain the headache.

In the bathroom, she filled the glass with cold water and took two painkillers, tasting last night's scotch as she swallowed.

Just two, these days. She'd be back at work soon. Had to watch the dose.

Her phone rang before she could return to bed, the sound piercing through her skull.

"'Lo." Her voice came out like gravel.

"Denise? Are you OK?" Harriett sounded surprised.

"Yeah, yeah. Fine. Getting better every day."

She didn't feel better. But that was how recovery worked, wasn't it? If it didn't kill you, you got better. Bad, better, best.

CHAPTER SIXTY-ONE

She was nowhere near best.

"Are you sure?" Harriett's voice carried that earnest enthusiasm that seemed unnatural. Denise had thought it was part of her cover at the Hub, but no, it was just Harriett.

"Yes. Back to work soon, Harriett. Light duties, but the doc thinks I'm ready and I feel ready, so there's no need to push it. OK?"

"OK."

"Is that why you were calling me? At..." She looked for her bedside clock, frowning when she couldn't find it. She checked her phone instead.

Nearly ten. How long had she slept? How late had she been drinking?

"No, sorry," Harriett said. "I was wondering if I could have a chat with you about one of the teams at Durranhill."

Denise smiled. Weird and earnest, yes, but Harriett could be direct when needed.

"Which one?"

"DCI Carnegie's team. They've taken over an investigation from DI Finch's team. The Mulligan murder."

"I'd heard."

"Yes. There are questions about how they're conducting the investigation. The man they've arrested seems to have no connection with it at all."

"Why have they arrested him, then?"

"He came in and confessed." Harriett gave an embarrassed laugh.

Denise grunted. "Hardly no connection then, is it?"

"Yes, but that's it. No other connection. The forensics and pathology don't add up and his mum's missing. We're thinking he's being forced to do this."

Denise spotted her clock on the floor, almost under the

bed. She must have knocked it over in the night. The green numbers showed 9:58.

"They didn't follow up on the forensics or the post mortem," Harriett continued, "and they haven't been in touch with Mulligan's friends and colleagues. There's definitely something going on here, but I don't know if it's simple incompetence or maybe something more sinister."

Denise squeezed her eyes shut. The clock numbers burned behind her eyelids.

Why had she been drinking? Why had she poured whisky down her throat on top of the painkillers?

"Could be something else." Her throat felt raw.

"What?"

"It's a cop who's been killed, Harriett. Don't forget that. Doesn't matter if they worked with him or not, he's one of us. They'll be keen to get a result. Even keener than usual. Maybe overly eager to arrest."

"So not actual corruption. But still a PSD matter."

"Indeed. But if you're asking what I know about them, the answer's not very much, I'm afraid. Obviously Streeting reported to Carnegie, but he's a separate matter. The rest of them... Sammy Knight, is it?"

"Yes."

"I've seen him about. Not been impressed, but it takes a lot to impress me. And Harriett?"

"Yes?"

"Why me?"

"What do you mean?"

"I mean, why have you called me at home instead of just nipping down the corridor and asking the boss in person?"

"He's... He's busy."

CHAPTER SIXTY-ONE

Alarm bells rang in Denise's head. Or maybe the painkillers weren't working.

"Too busy to deal with something like this? What's going on, Harriett?"

Harriett sighed, the sound of a decision being made.

"It's Streeting. He's been talking. To DI Finch's team, but DI Whaley's involved. They've even got that old bent cop from Birmingham in on the conversation."

"What?" Denise squeezed her eyes shut again, trying to make sense of it all. Aaron hadn't mentioned any of this. Not about Streeting, not about this other one. And this involved her – she was the one who'd been blown up, after all.

The name came to her.

"This other cop. Is it David Randle?"

"That's the one."

Fuck. Were they really trusting a man who'd lied and cheated and got caught and ratted out his own bosses to save his skin? And what were they talking to Streeting about?

If he gave them Carter, would they cut him a deal?

She bloody hoped not.

"I hope they get what they're after," she said, and then she saw it.

On the floor, on the other side of the bed, lay the remains of what must have been an expensive vase, green and brown glass, now in pieces. Water had soaked into the carpet. The flowers – lilies – were dumped in one spot, as if she'd pulled them out and let them fall. No card was visible, but she didn't need one to know who they were from.

At least now she knew why she'd been drinking last night.

CHAPTER SIXTY-TWO

Zoe noted the name on the display as she answered the phone. "Checking up on me?" she said.

"Well, you weren't exactly a barrel of laughs the other night," Jake replied.

She frowned.

"But you already seem better now," he continued. "Come to a decision?"

"A decision about what?" She paused. "Oh."

"Oh indeed. So have you? Are you still working with this negative influence of yours?"

"Yes," she took a breath. "And he's still a negative influence, and everyone else still thinks I'm insane. But the good news is, I'm not."

"You're not?"

"He's sorry. He screwed up, did some terrible things, and he regrets them."

Jake laughed.

"Really," Zoe insisted.

"Really? You're a cop, and you're working with someone

CHAPTER SIXTY-TWO

who's done something so bad that you can't discuss it with your former boss, or the DS who worked for you, or your partner, who's a DI in PSD. Christ, Zoe. It doesn't take a genius to work it out. You're working with a bent cop from Birmingham, and last I heard, Ian Osman was still in prison, so it's David Randle, isn't it?"

She clenched her fist. "I forgot. Never say a word to a bloody journalist."

"Ah, but I'm not just any bloody journalist. And I'm right, aren't I?"

"I can't say. Not officially."

"And if, unofficially, it is David Randle, you really believe he regrets what he did?"

Zoe closed her eyes. She pictured Randle in her car. His eyes. His earnestness.

"Yes," she said. "I don't trust him. But I believe that, at least."

Her phone beeped, and she checked the display. "Listen, Jake, thanks for calling. But there's another call coming through and I really have to take it."

"Go. Follow your instincts, Zoe. They're usually good."

Let's hope you're right. She ended the call and answered the next one.

"DI Finch," said a familiar voice.

"Mr Freeburn." Alistair Freeburn wasn't a married man, but if he had been, he'd probably have insisted he and his wife refer to each other that way. Mr and Mrs Freeburn. In the home. In private. "How have you been?"

"Very well, but busy."

"How can I help you?"

"I've been hearing things. Things I thought you ought to know."

Something positive, at last? "Yes?"

"Things about a certain gentleman at the Port of Workington."

Why did people always have to speak this way? It was always 'a certain gentleman' or 'our mutual friend' or 'my former associate'. Why couldn't they just say 'Myron Carter'?

If he was bugging their phones, he wouldn't have to work hard to figure out who that 'certain gentleman' was.

"What have you heard?" she asked.

A sudden gust slammed a volley of raindrops against her window, and she looked up, momentarily alarmed.

All was clear. The clouds were already parting, the sun playing on the distant fells. Things could change so quickly here.

"I'm sorry," she said. "You'll have to repeat that."

"I said, I gather he's been making cash available."

"We'd heard the same thing. Removing sums from Jenson & Marley."

"Yes, and he's been liquidating legitimate business assets and sending the proceeds through the same route, to that same bank account. I don't know what it means, Zoe, but I... Well, it just sounded like it might be important."

"It might well be, thanks." She ended the call.

It wasn't until she'd picked up the phone again that she realised what he'd said.

Zoe. He'd called her Zoe.

It had taken long enough.

Still smiling, she dialled.

Randle picked up almost immediately. "News?" he said.

"Nothing." She corrected herself. "Well, maybe something." She related what she'd just heard from Freeburn.

CHAPTER SIXTY-TWO

"On top of what our friend Zhang told us," Randle observed.

"Yes. And..."

"And what?"

She turned again to the sun falling in shifting patterns on the fells, and the clouds, gathering and breaking and gathering and breaking again. Would she ever know, for certain, what sort of person David Randle really was, and whether she could trust him?

He was different, though. She was sure of that. Not good. Possibly not even better than he had been. But different.

And it was Randle she'd chosen to call. Before Carl, or Fiona, or Aaron, or anyone else, she'd turned to David Randle.

What did that say about her?

"I've heard other things," she said. "I understand that Carter knows Streeting's talking."

"How do you know that?" Randle paused. "Sorry. I know you can't tell me that. But if it's a reliable source, then it all adds up to the same thing, doesn't it?"

"It does," she said.

Neither of them needed to spell it out.

Carter was getting ready to run.

CHAPTER SIXTY-THREE

Tom hadn't heard back about Arroyo's temporary Range Rover. Nina stumbled in late, and Aaron shot her a look.

"Yeah, I get it. You're a DS now. Act like one. Sorry." Nina slumped into her chair.

There was no real defence there, and not much of an attack by Nina's standards. Aaron turned to his desk, catching her reflection in the silver photo frame where Serge and Annabel beamed at him. She rolled her bloodshot eyes at his back.

Never change, Nina.

His phone rang. He checked the display, mindful of his recent run-ins with senior officers.

One of them was calling.

"Come upstairs please, Aaron," said Detective Superintendent Kendrick.

"Certainly."

Less than a minute later, he sat opposite her, trying to read her expression before deciding it was pointless. He'd never been able to gauge the super. Her smile meant nothing.

CHAPTER SIXTY-THREE

"Thanks for coming up, Aaron."

He smiled back, though it wasn't as if he'd had a choice.

"I've received a complaint about you."

He pulled in a breath. "DCI Carnegie?"

"One and the same. Want to give me your side?"

It felt like being invited to rant about a bad driver without consequences. Of course he wanted to give his side.

He nodded. "She's really messing up the Mulligan investigation."

He laid it all out: the lack of contact with the victim's colleagues or friends, the failure to follow up on forensics or pathology, the fact that both indicated the man they'd arrested wasn't guilty. The super sat quietly, taking it in, prompting occasionally, her frown deepening.

"DCI Carnegie is perfectly entitled to complain," he said finally. "It's her investigation. But I have doubts, and I'll ensure those doubts are passed on to PSD. With respect, Ma'am, you don't need to involve yourself in this."

She grinned – not just smiled, but grinned.

"It's nice to see you can stand up for yourself against other people. Not just me."

Before he could respond to her reference to their argument, DI Finch burst in.

"Sorry to interrupt."

"I assume this is important," the super said.

"Yes." The boss gave him a glance as she dropped into the seat beside him. "There have been some developments."

Aaron stood to leave, but DI Finch waved him back down. "You can stay. You need to be involved in this."

"In what?"

She held her gaze on him. "I've now heard from two sources that Carter's liquidating assets and drawing money out. It's not something he's done before, and it's a big risk for him to take."

"This, on top of what I told you on the phone last night," said the super, her expression troubled.

The boss nodded. Aaron didn't know what they'd discussed, but clearly it was significant.

"I'm not a betting woman," said the DI. "But if I was, I'd put a lot of money on Carter getting ready to disappear."

"I think you're right," agreed the super. "Think you've got enough for an arrest?"

An arrest? Myron Carter? *An actual arrest?*

"Yes," she said. "With what we have, we can bring him in under the same trafficking charges we used for Streeting."

The super raised an eyebrow. "Enough for a charge?"

"If I had that, I'd have arrested him months ago. With the emails we got from Ryan Tobin, I think we have enough to make the CPS think. But not enough to convince a jury against an expensive defence lawyer's doubts."

"Get him into custody," Aaron ventured, "and maybe we'll get what we need while he's out of action."

Both women turned to stare at him. He felt himself redden. Had he spoken out of turn?

"That's fair," said the super. "OK." She turned to DI Finch. "Bring him in."

The boss stood and walked to the door, then stopped. "You want in on this, Aaron?"

He examined the super's face.

"We're done, Aaron." She nodded. "You can go."

The DI tapped her hand against the door impatiently. "Well?"

Arresting Myron Carter? Arresting *Myron Carter?*

"Hell, yes." He stood and followed her out of the room.

CHAPTER SIXTY-FOUR

"Well, that's..." Tom scratched his head and turned to look at Nina, frowning.

"That's what?" she asked. Aaron had been summoned to see the super, so it looked like the role of prompting Tom had fallen to her.

"I don't know whether to say unexpected, or totally unexpected. Look."

She peered at his screen, then squinted. Everything was just that little bit harder this morning, and it didn't seem fair. She hadn't drunk that much last night, had she?

"What is it, then?" she asked.

"Gustavo Arroyo's car. The ANPR data I asked for has come back."

"That's good, isn't it?"

"I suppose so. But it looks like he just headed back towards Cleator Moor. Where he lives. He doesn't need an excuse for that."

"So why lie about it?" Nina said, realisation dawning.

"Exactly. Why lie about how long he was away?" Tom

tapped the screen. "He's back here two days before he says he is. Midday."

"And that's..." Nina squinted again as the digits turned over in her head. "Ten hours before we have our last firm location on his husband's phone."

"Twelve hours," Tom corrected. "And around fifteen before Ives claims to have killed Mulligan. I've put in a request for Arroyo's mobile data. Cell tower info might tell us where else he's been."

"What a mess." Nina rubbed her temples. "Any data on Ives' car?"

Tom tapped another icon and his display changed, black crosses everywhere. "There's a link here. You can ask for permission to access investigation data. Gets sent to the SIO for verification."

"Kiki Carnegie?" she said. "We won't be clicking that. So we don't actually know whether the ping on his car she claims to have is real or not."

Tom turned to look at her, his mouth open in surprise. "You don't think she's lying, do you?"

"I'm not sure. I doubt she is. But someone on her team might be lying to her. Either that, or they're so incompetent you've got to suspect something, haven't you?"

"Promotion's made you paranoid." Tom tapped again, and the display changed once more. "The financial information I asked for has come back."

Nina groaned inwardly. *More numbers*. Just what she needed. "Anything interesting?" She wasn't even going to squint this time. It would just make the headache worse.

"I asked for everything on Gustavo Arroyo. Didn't even try Christian Ives."

"Fair enough." She nodded.

CHAPTER SIXTY-FOUR

"And there's a joint account, both their names, so it's the usual screen full of black crosses and a link to ask DCI Carnegie for access."

"Again, we won't be clicking that."

"No. But we might not need to." Tom's expression had changed to one of triumph.

"Why not?"

"Because Arroyo has his own bank account, and DCI Carnegie doesn't seem to have bothered putting that behind the information firewall. We can see everything."

Nina edged closer, despite the headache, and leaned towards his screen, reading down the columns of numbers and across to the descriptions.

She whistled.

"Big spender," said Tom.

He wasn't wrong. Gustavo Arroyo seemed to be shedding money like oil from Nina's old Fiesta, and like the Fiesta, everywhere he went, he left an obvious trail. Hotels, flights, food, bars, clothes: famous names, expensive brands.

"Where does he get that kind of money?" asked Tom.

"I guess Ives made a lot of money when he sold up," she replied.

"Maybe. But not enough. Look."

She followed his finger to the end of the row, and then down the column marked *Account Balance*.

There was a lot of red in there.

"He's got a two hundred grand overdraft," she said. "Imagine asking for that at the bank?"

"Imagine finding a branch with someone in it you could ask. But he hasn't."

"Hasn't what?"

"Hasn't got a two hundred grand overdraft. Look. He's paid it all off."

She looked at the bottom of the screen, and sure enough, the red had turned black. Her eyes flicked left, looking for the deposit, and there it was.

"A quarter mill," said Tom. "Two hundred and fifty grand, in one transaction, put into his bank account."

Nina whistled.

"It's a lot, right?" Tom said. "Imagine that."

But it wasn't the numbers that had her attention. It was where the money had come from. She leaned further forward and touched the screen. Tom flinched with annoyance – he didn't like people touching his tech. Not even her.

But he didn't say anything, because he'd just seen the same thing she had.

The money that had been deposited in Gustavo Arroyo's account had come from a corporate bank account, in the name of a business they were both familiar with.

Jenson & Marley Offshore Services.

CHAPTER SIXTY-FIVE

"DI Finch and DS Keyes to see Myron Carter," Aaron said through the open window.

Zoe watched the guard, her fingers drumming against her thigh. Carter could be leaving, even now. He could be gone already.

"Don't think so," said the man at the entry kiosk.

Zoe leaned across Aaron. "It's not really up to you. Open the gate, please."

The guard tilted his head. It was the same man who'd been there when they'd come for Mulligan's body. "I can't just go letting people in, even if they ask nicely. And you've not asked nicely, have you?"

Zoe waved a hand through the open window.

Roddy Chen emerged from the passenger door of the car behind them. The guard turned to look at him, eyes widening as he stepped back.

The barrier lifted.

Aaron drove forward, then stopped and waited until the

car behind was through. Martinez and Chen probably wouldn't be needed, but their presence was reassuring.

"There." Zoe pointed in the direction they'd taken last time.

Aaron pulled up beside a row of forklifts in front of shipping containers, and Zoe stepped out.

The wind had dropped. Where cranes and containers had stood days ago, there was just empty space stretching to the sea. She could make out the white-capped waves, but barely heard them. She'd never known it so still.

She turned in a slow circle. She'd spent so much time working this investigation, focusing on this one man, and she'd hardly spent any time here, in his domain.

And now it was almost over. If Carter hadn't fled already.

She stopped, recognising a location from Olivia's photos – where the women had walked from the ships to the minibuses that took them to the warehouses. Where they were kept, waiting to be sold to Carter's customers.

And not far from that spot was where Mulligan's body had been found.

Zoe completed her turn, and there he was, standing outside one of the long, single-storey buildings dotting the Port. Five others stood with him – the same big men who'd been there the other day.

Roddy Chen emerged from the other car, and suddenly the men didn't seem quite so imposing.

Carter walked towards her, his entourage trailing behind. She waited in silence as he approached, watching his smile waver then return.

Myron Carter was nervous.

CHAPTER SIXTY-FIVE

"DI Finch. Lovely to see you here. Any news on the unfortunate young man you found here the other day?"

Roddy Chen took a step forward.

Zoe gave a tiny shake of her head, and Roddy stopped.

"Myron Carter," she said.

"Yes."

"Myron Carter."

"Still me." His smile was fixed now.

He had to know what was coming.

"Myron Carter," she said a final time, and continued before he could interrupt. "I'm arresting you in connection with offences under section two of the Modern Slavery Act."

CHAPTER SIXTY-SIX

"You know her?"

Nina pointed at the uniformed PC standing outside Christian Ives' front door.

Tom tapped the brakes and turned as they passed the driveway. He quickly looked away when the woman glanced in their direction.

"Nope," he said. "Not one of ours."

A patrol car was parked in the street with one of Stella's white vans behind it. Nothing in the driveway. He parked further along the road, out of view of the house.

"We could just go in, couldn't we?"

Nina shook her head. "She'd make us sign in."

"So? We'd still be in."

"For about five minutes. And then we'd have our arses kicked halfway across the Irish Sea by Kiki Carnegie."

This cautious approach wasn't like Nina at all.

"You afraid of her?"

Nina rolled her eyes. "Nope. But if we don't tread carefully, we won't get anywhere. And don't look at me like that,

CHAPTER SIXTY-SIX

Tom Willis. I'm a DS now and I've got to be a bit more circumspect."

"Swallowed a dictionary?"

"Careful, then. Sensible. Alert to the consequences of my actions. Sometimes—"

"Hang on." Tom had been watching the rear-view mirror as they spoke. Someone in a white forensic suit had just walked out of the driveway towards the white van.

He reversed slowly, stopping as the figure reached the van. Rolling down his window, he saw them smile behind their mask.

"Tom? What are you doing here?"

"Caroline," he said, keeping his voice low. "Can we have a quiet word?"

She glanced around, then shrugged. "Don't see why not." Without invitation, she pulled open the rear door and climbed in. Tom drove forward again, avoiding the PC's gaze.

When he'd parked around the corner, Caroline Deane pulled down her mask. "What's going on?"

"Is anyone from DCI Carnegie's team there?" Nina asked.

"No. I thought there would be. Not really been briefed or anything. I just turned up, and that PC was there. I don't know her. She didn't seem to know what was going on either. Are you on this investigation?"

"We've been taken off it," Nina replied. "And frankly, we don't believe DCI Carnegie's team are running it effectively." Her phone buzzed, but she ignored it.

Caroline nodded. "DI Finch would have had one of you here with me, at least at the start."

"Can you tell us what you've found?" Nina asked.

Caroline hesitated.

Tom decided to be more direct. "They've arrested the man who lives here, Christian Ives. You know that?"

Caroline nodded. Tom's phone buzzed, but he pressed on.

"We don't think he was really involved. His mother's missing, and nobody seems to be trying too hard to find her. Meanwhile, his husband has lied to us about where he was at the time of the murder, and we've just discovered he was recently paid a quarter of a million pounds."

"By who?" Caroline leaned forward, intrigued.

Tom felt Nina tense beside him, but continued. Caroline Deane had proven herself reliable. "By one of Myron Carter's companies." Her mouth dropped open. "So you can see why we might be interested in following up every aspect of—"

"It's OK." Caroline waved a gloved hand. "I didn't find much, but I'll tell you. You know the security system was smashed up, right?"

"Yes."

"But there's no sign of forced entry. Apart from the security system, there's hardly anything unusual about the place at all."

"Has Gustavo Arroyo turned up?" Nina asked. "We don't know where he is."

"No, no one's been here except me and the PC."

"Hardly anything, you said," Tom prompted. "That means there was something?"

"Yes. Mrs Ives. The missing woman. There are big gaps in her wardrobe, and in the cabinet in her bathroom. And in the attic, there's a pattern of lines in the dust. Suggestive of a large rectangular object, that's been there a long time and has recently been removed."

CHAPTER SIXTY-SIX

"A suitcase?" Nina asked.

"Looks like it. Mrs Ives had time to pack, or someone who knew the place packed for her. And that's—"

Nina's phone buzzed again. This time she checked it.

"Shit," she said. "It's the boss."

She answered, apologised, and listened, her eyes widening.

She turned to Tom. "We need to head back. There's news."

"What, have they found Arroyo?"

"Bigger news than that, Tom."

Caroline leaned forward, hanging on every word. Tom could see the excitement building on Nina's face.

Nina smiled. Not smiled, grinned.

"Myron Carter's just been arrested."

CHAPTER SIXTY-SEVEN

"That really just happened, didn't it?"

Zoe looked over her desk at Aaron, who was rubbing his hands together like someone who'd just found the biggest cookie in the jar. Or arrested the most dangerous criminal in Cumbria.

Why didn't she feel the same excitement?

All that time she'd waited for this moment, and now it was here, she felt... What?

There was excitement, yes. But more fear than anything else. This might have been what she wanted, but not *when* she wanted it. Carter's own actions had set the agenda – the rumours from Freeburn, the movement of money from his accounts.

She couldn't help worrying they were playing into his hands.

She'd watched him carefully after the arrest, examining his expression. The nerves behind that fixed smile had vanished the moment she'd delivered those critical words.

CHAPTER SIXTY-SEVEN

She'd arrested the man. His top lieutenant was still in custody, and Carter had failed to kill him.

So why was Carter so relaxed?

Either he was faking it, or he knew something she didn't. She hoped it was the former.

"Who do you reckon?" Aaron asked.

"What?"

He shook his head with a smile. She must have missed something.

"What?" she repeated.

"Who do you reckon Carter's lawyer will be?"

"Not Stan Basham." Though she wouldn't have minded Basham. He was a horrible man and a horrible lawyer, but she knew all his tricks.

"Trevor Singleton, I reckon," Aaron said.

"It won't be Singleton."

"Why not?"

"Because Singleton acts for his people. Not the man himself. Whoever Myron Carter has up his sleeve, they're a step up from Trevor Singleton."

"Who, then?"

"I don't know, Aaron. No point worrying about it in advance."

But she was worried. The more she knew, the better prepared she'd be. Everything was at stake over the coming hours. Years' worth of work. She found herself running through the interview checklist she'd written as a new CID officer.

Keep calm. Don't be emotional. Don't waste an opportunity. Don't follow a dead end.

It had been years since she'd needed these reminders. They'd become second nature through all those hours in windowless rooms with lawyers and suspects. Angry ones, frightened ones, clever ones, cold ones.

Know as much as you can. Watch their eyes. Watch their hands.

"You OK, boss?" Aaron asked.

Zoe blinked, realising she was staring at a blank stretch of desk. "Yes." She forced a smile. "Yes, Aaron. We've done all the hard work. We're close now. Just the last few pieces of the puzzle. If we can get Streeting's recording devices..."

If they could get their hands on those, maybe it wouldn't matter. Maybe Carter would be right there on tape, saying words he couldn't take back.

But they couldn't count on it. Couldn't count on recovering the devices, on the evidence being there, on the devices even existing.

Know the time, but don't watch the clock.

Every minute would count in there, but even more outside. Every second until they had enough evidence to charge him, or they had to let him go. And if they let Myron Carter go, he'd head for open water, and they wouldn't get a second chance.

Don't play your hand too soon.

She'd judge every sentence, weigh every word. Going in too hard might get an early hit, but it could give him too much time to recover.

Be smarter than they are.

But was she?

Her phone buzzed: a message from Clive Moor in the custody suite. She read it, looked up, and fixed Aaron with what she hoped was a confident smile.

"The lawyer's here. They're ready for us."

"Who's the lawyer? Someone we know?"

CHAPTER SIXTY-SEVEN

"Oh, yes." She kept her tone breezy.

It had been a while since they'd faced each other across the table.

Be smarter than they are. The most important element.

Between her and Aaron, they were smarter than Myron Carter. But were they smarter than Carter and his lawyer?

"It's Clarissa Bexley." She stood, picked up her jacket from the back of her chair, and made for the door. "Let's show these bastards who Cumbria CID really are."

CHAPTER SIXTY-EIGHT

"You've done well here, in the last year or two." Clarissa Bexley settled into her chair in Interview Room Four.

Zoe studied the lawyer. Some highlights in her hair, a shorter cut and new glasses. But otherwise, the same woman. "Thank you."

"I mean it, DI Finch. When I first saw you... Well, you've done well. And I think that, for the most part, you've been a credit to a constabulary that needs your sort of robust, honest policing."

Robust? Zoe's muscles tensed. What did Bexley mean by that?

"Which is why I feel I really should warn you, for your own sake, that you're making a terrible mistake."

"I am?"

"With this arrest." Bexley gestured towards Carter beside her. "It's not just that Mr Carter will be walking out of here soon enough, with apologies from you and your colleagues and your bosses and *their* bosses. It's the compensation claims we'll be making. It's the light we'll be shining on the darker corners of this station of yours. It might have seemed like a good idea at the time, a nice bit of publicity after all the recent unfortunate incidents, but really, DI Finch, it's going to backfire. And it'll backfire so badly you'll—"

"Interview with Myron Carter," Aaron cut in. "Present is his solicitor Clarissa Bexley, DI Zoe Finch and DS Aaron Keyes."

Bexley fixed Aaron with a basilisk glare as he continued with the formalities. Carter sat there, looking as relaxed as any man could be in a police interview room.

"I'm producing a series of photographs marked A through to D." Zoe handed copies across the table to Carter and his lawyer, giving them a moment to take in what they were seeing.

Watch their eyes. Watch their hands.

Carter looked surprised. Moderately surprised, she'd have said, if she'd had to grade it. Not dismayed.

But then, people like Carter were rarely dismayed on the outside. His hands remained perfectly still.

Probably good at poker.

"For the benefit of the recording," Aaron said, "the photographs show a group of people. The important individuals here are Ralph Streeting, Victor Parlick and Mr Carter, each of whom are circled and labelled within the photographs. Can you confirm you can see these individuals and that the labels are correct?"

"Yup," Carter said. "Least, I think so. I didn't really know Victor Parlick well."

Zoe ignored the last comment. "It's our contention that these photographs show you, Myron Carter, giving instructions to Ralph Streeting to have Victor Parlick killed. As you can see in the final photograph, Mr Parlick is clearly the subject of your discussion with Streeting."

"Clearly?" Bexley scoffed. "I don't think a jury would agree."

"And even if they did," Carter added, "this idea of an instruction to have a man killed, it's a bit of a stretch, isn't it? Far as I know, Parlick's death was an accident."

Zoe produced an extract from Parlick's post mortem and read it out loud, for the recording.

"Hardly conclusive, is it?" Bexley said.

It wasn't. Not on its own.

"Me and Ralph," Carter said, returning to the photographs. "We were discussing shift patterns at the Port. That's why I'm gesturing to Parlick. Might have been anyone. Just whoever was on duty at that point, in that place."

"Why would you discuss your shift patterns with a serving detective inspector?" Aaron asked.

Carter smiled as if the very idea were ridiculous. "Because he suspected the influence of organised crime on my operation. Thought people had infiltrated my businesses. Wanted to know who was working where, when, that sort of thing. I was trying to set his mind at ease."

"There are women who will give evidence that they were trafficked at the Port," Zoe said.

"Women?" Carter asked.

Now it was Zoe's turn to smile. "Three, at the last count." She produced the other set of photos. "Two of them can even identify themselves in these images."

Bexley peered at the photos, making a show of removing her glasses for closer examination. "I don't see my client in these images."

CHAPTER SIXTY-EIGHT

"No," Zoe admitted. "Ralph Streeting is—"

"Has Ralph said anything?" Carter asked.

Zoe let the silence hang for a minute. She knew Carter wouldn't show it, but he had to be feeling something, didn't he?

Don't play your hand too soon.

"Let's take a break," she said.

Carter shrugged, as relaxed as ever.

"When we return, we'll look through your finances."

She stood and left the room without looking back.

CHAPTER SIXTY-NINE

Nina hadn't visited this room recently, not since the secure network upgrade had allowed them to watch interviews live on the big screen in the team room.

But the secure network was down while Jeff from IT crawled around the space beneath the floor, reconnecting and fixing things. For now, they were back to the old way: squeezed into a narrow room three doors down from Interview Room Four, with its bank of screens, overly loud speaker system, and excessive heating.

Nina, Tom, and DI Whaley were crammed into the space. Two people were a squeeze. Three was ridiculous.

She tried to shut it all out: the heat, the others breathing. Focus on Carter. Focus on Bexley.

Focus on getting the bastards.

But they both looked too relaxed. The boss was showing Olivia Bagsby's photos. She hadn't mentioned Olivia herself, and neither had Bexley. Nina wondered if Carter knew the woman was back in Cumbria.

If he did, he showed no sign of concern.

CHAPTER SIXTY-NINE

They moved on to Victor Parlick. Nina watched Aaron, sitting beside the boss, occasionally firing questions across the table. He appeared composed, but she knew better. He'd liked Victor, felt responsible for his death. Sometimes you couldn't reason with Aaron Keyes.

"We were discussing shift patterns at the Port," Carter said.

Nina felt DI Whaley stiffen beside her.

The whole thing was bloody ridiculous. But with the right lawyer, it would work. Plant doubt in one juror's mind and they'd infect the rest. They needed more evidence.

The boss produced photos of the women at the Port. Carter and his lawyer examined them.

Nina's attention drifted in the stifling heat. She snapped back to focus.

Nothing. Clarissa Bexley had removed her glasses and held a photograph almost against her nose.

The argument with her mum last night was playing on Nina's mind. They hadn't spoken since. Her mum had hung up on her – something that had never happened before. Usually it was the other way around, as it should be. You hung up on your mum, not the reverse.

"I don't see my client in these images," Clarissa Bexley said.

Nina felt her phone weighing heavy in her pocket. She wanted to check her messages, to send one.

The heat was unbearable.

A noise came from the side. Light flooded the room briefly before darkness returned. Air moved around them.

Someone had opened the door. Nina turned, trying to make out shapes in the layers of darkness.

"Hello?" she said.

"Budge up, you lot," Denise Gaskill said. "Plenty of room for one more."

CHAPTER SEVENTY

"It's good to see you." Zoe's gaze settled on Denise Gaskill. "And I'm sorry, but we don't have time for the appropriate celebrations."

Denise nodded. "Agreed. Let's get the job done and then we can get hammered. Those of us who want to, at least."

The team room was well-populated. Carl and Denise were there, along with Tom, Nina and Aaron. Even the super had come down from her office to hear the latest. No Branthwaite or Harriett – someone had to keep things rolling in Durranhill. But there was enough police brainpower in the room to make them ten times smarter than Myron Carter and his lawyer.

Hopefully.

"For those of you who weren't there," she said. "I can tell you that after the first stage of the interview, we haven't exactly broken Carter. Not yet. But we didn't expect to."

"No." Fiona's voice was dry. "But tell me, Zoe, what *did* you expect?"

The cynicism in the super's voice caught Zoe off guard. "I'm sorry?"

"What was the point of this first stage, as you call it?"

"Setting the scene. Ground rules. Get them comfortable."

"And then hit them when they're least expecting it?" Fiona arched an eyebrow.

"That's the plan."

"Good. Well, I hope it works, Zoe. I've already had Becca bloody Grey from the ACC's office onto me."

"What?" Aaron turned to face the super.

Behind him, Carl and Denise exchanged glances. Zoe made a mental note to ask about that later.

"You heard me," Fiona said, her tone characteristically unhappy. "Apparently, we've pulled in an important pillar of the business community on the flimsiest of pretexts."

"But why would we do that?" Zoe asked. *What the hell?*

"To distract from our *problems*." Fiona inclined her head meaningfully. "Although, to be fair to Becca Grey, she was less of an arsehole about it than usual. I've put in a call to the Chief Constable's office, see if I can get some backup there."

"And?" Carl asked.

"Big Jo's away. Some international policing conference."

"I believe it's in the Bahamas," Carl said. "I'm sure they're getting a lot of important work done."

Gentle laughter rippled through the room, lightening the mood enough for Zoe to move forward.

"Mulligan," she said. "What's the latest?"

"I don't think we need to hear about that," Fiona said.

Zoe turned to her. "I'm sorry, but you're going to want to hear this."

Fiona shrugged and listened as Nina outlined the situa-

CHAPTER SEVENTY

tion: the same complaints about Durranhill – no follow-up on friends, family, forensics or pathology. Plus an additional failure: no one to brief Caroline Deane on what she was looking for at the Ives house.

"She was there by herself, checking on literally everything," Nina said. "Just one PC on the door. No briefing, no background knowledge other than what she'd already picked up through us."

"Did she find anything?" Despite herself, Fiona showed interest.

"Yes. It's not forensics, really, but it looks like whoever took Mrs Ives made sure she was going to be comfortable."

Zoe hadn't heard this before. "Go on."

"Half her stuff's gone," Nina continued. "Either they gave her time to pack, or they knew her well enough to pack for her. And there's more. Gustavo Arroyo."

"Ives' husband," Zoe explained for those who weren't familiar.

"He's been lying," Nina continued. "Said he was in Argentina when he was only in Spain. Said he'd just got back when he was around two days earlier, including on the day of the murder. Hired a car and used his Argentinian passport to muddy the waters. He's got a major spending habit, no clear source of income, and until last week, an overdraft of two hundred thousand pounds."

"What happened last week?" Zoe asked.

Nina smiled. "Someone put a quarter of a million quid in his bank account."

Zoe let out a sharp breath. She wasn't the only one.

"Who?" Aaron asked.

Nina looked at him. "A company you might be familiar with. Jenson & Marley Offshore Services."

The sound of another collective intake of breath filled the room. Zoe turned to explain to Fiona, but the super shook her head.

"I know who Jenson & Marley are," she said. "You spent long enough trying to convince me to pay for that forensic accountant, remember?"

Zoe nodded.

"OK," Fiona said. "This is good work, all of you. But there's more work to be done. I'm not going to ask you about Mulligan. It's not your investigation. Now we know about this Jenson & Marley link, there has to be a connection between Carter and Ives. So we focus on Carter, right?"

Heads nodded around the room. Fiona clapped her hands together once and headed for the door, then turned back.

"Let's pin that bastard down once and for all."

She turned and walked away.

CHAPTER SEVENTY-ONE

"You're... Oh." Tom stared at the team room door swinging shut.

Thirty seconds ago, the place had bustled with activity. The super had left for her office, followed by the PSD pair and the boss. The sarge had taken Clive Moor aside for a word. Nina had declared that her headache could only be cured by pickled onion Monster Munch and headed for the canteen.

Tom had tried to warn her about the broken machine, but she'd already gone.

He turned back to his screen. The phone data from Gustavo Arroyo had arrived.

The records showed minimal calls and texts, mostly between the same few numbers. Heavy mobile data usage, but no details of what for.

He could dig deeper, given time. But without the phone itself and its search history, it could take weeks. Even then, Arroyo might have covered his tracks.

Tom could waste hours trying to crack Arroyo's internet

habits. And even if he succeeded, odds were Ives' husband had just been downloading episodes of *The Traitors* for his next flight.

Better to focus on location data. Cell towers would tell him where Arroyo had been.

Starting with the day of Arroyo's return: first ping on Manchester's outskirts, then a trail of hits moving from the airport, west, then north.

The detail thinned past Lancaster. Fewer towers up here. North of the motorway, west of Ambleside and Windermere, you could cover twenty miles on one tower's signal.

Still, it was enough to track him towards the Hub and beyond, to his home.

Yes – he'd stopped. Then moved again. West to Whitehaven, where the tower coverage improved.

Tom's pulse quickened. If Arroyo had taken Matilda Ives there, keeping his phone on, they could pinpoint him within hundreds of yards.

But Arroyo hadn't stopped in Whitehaven. He'd gone south, where towers were sparse. Weak pings between Mirehouse and Woodhouse, consistent with driving towards Sandwith.

Then nothing.

Tom scanned empty column after empty column.

The door swung open. Nina walked in, crunching.

"You could have told me the machine was broken." She brushed crumbs from her shirt. "Had to beg some salt and vinegar off Rob Collins. And he charges interest when you borrow crisps."

"I did." Tom turned back to his screen.

"Arroyo's cell tower data?" Nina asked through her mouthful.

CHAPTER SEVENTY-ONE

"Yep. He came this way, stopped at home, headed to Whitehaven, then south, and then we lost him. Probably did it on purpose."

"Did what?"

"Kept his phone on, moving somewhere traceable. Then turned it off and went wherever he—"

"What's this?" Nina sprayed his screen with crisp debris. "Sorry."

She reached forward.

Tom winced, then followed her pointing finger.

At the bottom of the page sat an entry he'd missed. Another ping. Faint, but within range of the nearest tower.

The tower stood in St Bees, five miles south of Whitehaven. For the phone to hit that tower and no others, it had to be west, maybe slightly north. Not east – that would have triggered the Egremont tower.

Arroyo had switched his phone off, dropping off the grid. But he'd turned it back on briefly. Checking messages, maybe.

And wherever he was when he did, it wasn't far from home.

CHAPTER SEVENTY-TWO

THERE WAS ONLY one chair in the room they'd been offered, just down the corridor from Zoe's office. Carl stood back and pointed to it.

"You think I can't stand up, boss?" Denise walked past him to lean against the wall and folded her arms.

God, that woman could be exasperating.

"No. But you're back on light duties after recovering from major injuries, so I'd like you to sit."

"The key word there is recovering." Denise shook her head.

Carl stared at her until she walked over and lowered herself onto the chair. Her sullen look turned to surprise and then alarm as it sank under her weight, continuing downward until her knees couldn't take it any further and she tumbled forward. She pushed herself against the floor and rose to her feet before Carl could help.

"Trying to injure me again, boss?"

"It's a disused office," he said. "Guess it's a chair grave-

CHAPTER SEVENTY-TWO

yard, too. Maybe we'll both stand, then. I just wanted to ask how you're doing."

She smiled. "I was fine until about twenty seconds ago."

He laughed, but he'd been watching her. He'd seen the occasional grimace when she thought no one was looking. Heard a gentle groan as she squeezed her way out of the viewing room after the Carter interview.

There was a tap on the door, and Zoe walked in.

"Mind if I have a word, Carl?"

"Sure."

"In private, please. We can go to my office."

"I'm not standing around here by myself." Denise leaned back against the wall. "And if this is about Streeting, or David Randle, then I should know about it."

Zoe's eyes seemed to be asking for something. Asking Carl to intervene, maybe.

He wasn't going to do that.

"Denise is right, Zoe. And we could do with someone else's view. Someone who hasn't been involved in the same conversations for the last few months."

Zoe looked from him to Denise and back again, then nodded. "In that case, we might as well stay here. It won't take long. I've just spoken to David Randle."

Carl nodded.

Keep it calm.

"He wants to talk to Carter," she said.

"What?" Denise and Carl said simultaneously.

"That's insane," Carl added.

At least he and Denise seemed to be on the same page.

"Look, we don't have enough on Carter," Zoe said. "You know we don't."

"What about the financial stuff?" Denise pushed herself

forward from the wall. "Your forensic accounting report. Haven't you got decent material there? With the emails you got from the Jenson & Marley server, too. It must be enough to implicate him."

Zoe shook her head. She looked tired, Carl realised. "It should be. But it's not watertight. And as for the emails, you know how we got them. I can't guarantee we'll be able to use them. His lawyers will put up a fight, that's for sure. But David thinks he can get more."

"Sure he does." Denise's sarcasm was sharp enough to cut.

"Look, I get it. He was bent. He—"

"Not 'was', Zoe," said Carl. "He 'is' bent. People like that don't just change."

"Fine. He's bent. You don't trust him. Frankly, I don't trust him. But Olivia Bagsby does, and without Olivia, we can't—"

"Can't what, DI Finch?" Denise pushed herself away from the wall and stood closer to Zoe than she appeared comfortable with. "I keep hearing this, how indispensable Olivia is to the prosecution of Carter, or Streeting, or both, but apparently even she's not enough to charge him, so what use is she?"

Zoe held her ground, though Carl could see the tension in her muscles.

"Without Olivia, we can't produce the photos. Without the photos, the evidence from Elena and Maria and Alexandra is that much easier to discredit. Without the photos, we can't tie Carter to Parlick's death."

"And yet you still need more."

"Yes. And we need Randle to get it. It was Randle who got Streeting talking. He's got more knowledge of the way

CHAPTER SEVENTY-TWO

organised crime operates than the rest of us put together, and yes, that might be from the wrong side of the line, but we can't ignore that sort of expertise."

Denise snorted. "I can do a pretty good job of it."

"He has a plan, too. You remember Trevor Hamm?"

Carl felt a shiver run through him. He could hardly forget Hamm. Randle's paymaster, back in Birmingham, before his pet copper had turned against him, and he'd been arrested, charged, and convicted. Before he'd been busted out of prison, then killed. He nodded.

"Randle wants to use Hamm as an example," Zoe said. "Tell Carter he needs to come clean and help the police dismantle his operation. Explain that we'll have Carter anyway, but if he leaves everything intact, his successors will fight over the scraps, and he'll end up getting caught in the crossfire."

"Like Hamm was," said Carl.

He wanted to hate the idea, but he couldn't, because it was smart. It might even work. He just hated the man whose idea it was.

"That's crazy," said Denise. "All of it."

"No." Carl turned to her. "I think we can make this work." He turned back to Zoe. "As long as I can be in the room with him."

"That's not going to work," said Zoe.

"Not a chance," added Denise.

Carl looked at Zoe. "Can you give us a minute?"

Zoe nodded and stepped out of the room, closing the door behind her.

"Denise," he said.

"Yeah, yeah. I know. I'm being too... Too what, exactly? Too me?"

He laughed. It would be good to have her back, properly. But not now. Not like this.

"Whatever you want to call it, it's not what we need at the moment."

"For the record..." she began, but he was shaking his head, and she stopped.

He pushed open the door. Zoe stood four doors down, past her team room. She'd made sure to give them privacy. She made her way back, and they started again.

"Randle says it has to be just the two of them," Zoe said. "Him and Carter. Cameras on, but sound muted. He needs to be able to talk in confidence. Needs Carter to be able to say whatever he wants."

Carl heard a noise to the side and turned to see Denise's face twisted in a painful rictus. There it was again: the sort of noise a gagged kidnap victim makes when the kidnapper brings out the chainsaw.

"I don't like it," he said.

"Nor do I," replied Zoe. "But I still say it's the best route to go."

He sighed. "I'll have to run it past Branthwaite."

Zoe shook her head. "Last time I checked, this wasn't a PSD investigation, Carl. Unless you want to report Randle for breaching his conditions, and blow up the entire case in the process, then I'll note your concerns and move on."

It was a good thing there was only the one unreliable chair in the room because it meant there was nothing for Carl to fall down into, and he forced his legs to keep him upright.

Zoe had never spoken to him like that before. Not in private. Certainly not in public. He felt his face redden, and opened his mouth to say something, but he couldn't think what.

Zoe must have seen it, though. Her expression softened.

"I'm sorry. Look, let's try Carter one more time, with everything we've got. The emails, the financial stuff, the lot. I don't like it, Carl. But I don't think we've got any choice."

He nodded, dumbfounded, thinking back to the woman she'd been years earlier, when he'd first seen her. When he'd met her as part of his assignment to take down David Randle.

I don't like it, she'd said, and he thought that was probably true. She hated it. Maybe not as much as he did, but enough.

But he'd learned a few things about Zoe Finch in those years, in Birmingham and Cumbria. He'd learned she was a brilliant cop, and most of the time, when they disagreed about something, she was the one who turned out to be right.

He'd learned she cared, even when it looked like she didn't. She cared about bringing in criminals, and she cared about the people who got caught in the crossfire. People like Victor Parlick. People like Denise.

He'd learned that she took a problem and worked it until it unravelled.

And he'd learned that if she could only see one way through that problem, she'd take it.

CHAPTER SEVENTY-THREE

"Are you nearby?" Caroline Deane asked.

"Nearby where?" Nina paced the floor of the team room, shedding bits of salt and vinegar crisp as she went.

"Ives' house. Are you still around?"

Nina suppressed her irritation. As if she could spend all day hanging around Cleator Moor when there were murders across Cumbria and their prime suspect was just two floors below. Tom shot a disgusted look at the crisp crumbs, which she ignored.

"No," she said. "Back at the Hub. They arrested Myron Carter."

"Oh, yes. Of course."

Nina reflected on Caroline's odd position – part of the investigation, but removed enough to switch off from it. Though not entirely removed – Carter's people had rammed her van months ago while she transported evidence from Bobby Silver's house. She could have died if she hadn't been such a skilled driver. Yet somehow Caroline had disconnected from the bigger picture – the phone data, photos, documents, bank accounts and forensics – all aimed at finally nailing Carter.

"Anyway," Caroline said. "Results are in from the house."

"That was quick."

"There wasn't much to examine. Christian Ives and his husband don't entertain much. We found prints for Ives and the cleaner. Two other sets – likely Matilda Ives and Gustavo Arroyo, given where we found them. If anyone else was there recently, they were careful."

"So no home invasion by masked thugs?"

"Sorry. I don't think so."

Nina ended the call and turned to Tom, who'd been following her side of the conversation.

"So we're in agreement," he said. "Gustavo Arroyo took his mother-in-law?"

"Right. But we can't find them if our hands are tied. I'm going to speak to Kiki Carnegie."

She dialled before Tom could stop her, relieved when she learned DCI Carnegie would call back later.

"Did you have it out with her?" Tom asked as she set down her phone.

"With DCI Carnegie?"

"No. With your mum. That bloke she was trying to set you up with."

"Ah. Well, yes. It didn't go well." Nina recalled the argument. "She hung up on me, Tom. My own mother."

Tom's mouth was tight, holding back what looked like both amusement and something more thoughtful.

"You want my advice?" he asked finally.

"No. Why would I want your advice, you loser?"

He ignored the jibe. "You're right to be annoyed. And it's

good that you've spelled it out for her. But I think you probably owe each other an apology."

"She owes me an apology. If she thinks—"

"And you owe her one, too. She's older and more set in her ways, whereas you're more circumspect."

"I'm what?"

"You're careful and sensible and alert to the consequences of your actions. Right?"

She closed her eyes and nodded slowly. "Right. So the olive branch needs to come from me."

"You want me to write it for you?"

"Bugger off." Nina turned to her phone and spent five minutes composing a message. She passed it to Tom, who made a few changes before returning it.

He was right. This was better.

I'm sorry, it read. *I don't want to argue. I love you very much, and of course I want you to be part of my life. But that's the thing. It's MY life, and I don't know how many times I have to tell you that I'm not interested in you setting me up with strange men.*

Spot on, she thought. An olive branch and her point, wrapped up in a few lines.

Two birds, one stone.

She tapped send.

CHAPTER SEVENTY-FOUR

"What am I supposed to make of this?" Clarissa Bexley stared at the large sheaf of documents in front of her.

Aaron glanced at DI Finch, grateful when she answered instead of him. His potential responses weren't suitable for the interview room.

"It's OK, Miss Bexley. We'll take you through these financial statements, item by item, and ask specific questions relating to specific items."

Aaron almost felt sorry for her. The pages were filled with numbers that even he struggled to understand after multiple reviews. Clarissa Bexley had no chance.

They started with Alistair Freeburn's initial disclosure.

"These came from a local law firm." Bexley's tone carried a hint of superiority that grated on Aaron. Yes, Freeburn had represented questionable people, but he wasn't defending Myron Carter.

"Yes," the boss agreed.

"Well, I assume they're protected by client privilege."

DI Finch tilted her head, her sympathy clearly artificial.

"I'm afraid not. Your client wasn't the client in question. We've been assured by multiple legal sources that these records can be used as evidence."

"Fine," said Bexley. She and Carter proceeded to deny or question every single item presented.

After twenty unproductive minutes, with Aaron's anxiety growing at their lack of progress, the DI introduced the forensic accountant's analysis. This time, Bexley couldn't dismiss it so easily.

"This fellow," she said. "Zhang Chen, is it?"

"Yes," confirmed DI Finch.

"Has all the appropriate qualifications, does he? From the right country?"

Aaron's smile tightened as he recalled their encounter with Bexley two years earlier. Her son had been part of a racist group inadvertently involved in Mick Halfpenny's plot to murder Elena's friend, Daria. Her obvious disdain for Zhang, based solely on his name, suggested that the racism ran in the family.

"Of course," said DI Finch.

"Well, if this is his analysis, then I can hardly question it without preparation, although I can assure you that it will be questioned in detail once my team has had the opportunity to review it. My client is responsible for numerous import and export businesses, in addition to his domestic logistics operations."

"Indeed," Aaron said, breaking his silence.

Bexley raised an eyebrow in his direction. "That being the case, it's absurd to suggest that he can be expected to keep on top of them all. Mr Carter's staff would have dealt with all this." She waved at the report.

Aaron turned to Carter. "Your lawyer seems to be

CHAPTER SEVENTY-FOUR

implying that you don't know what's going on at your own companies, Myron. Is that right?"

Carter grinned. "I don't know *everything*, DS Keyes. No one knows *everything*. I could tell you, for instance, where DI Finch's son hangs out on his way back to his flat in Stirling of an evening. I could tell you which days your lovely daughter Annabel attends her nursery. I know a lot. But I don't know that much."

Every muscle in Aaron's body tensed. DI Finch's foot tapped gently against his leg. The air felt thick with tension, pulsing with his heartbeat.

Stay calm.

It had always been personal between him and Carter, since Victor Parlick, if not before. But this was different.

Carter would pay.

"All I can say is," Bexley's voice barely registered, "Mr Carter is a big picture man. The CEO. The detail is not his domain. This has nothing to do with him. I wonder..."

She frowned, looked at Carter appraisingly, then back across the table.

"What?" said Aaron.

"Well, have you considered the possibility that someone else might have been using Mr Carter's companies for their own purposes? What better way to hide one's misdeeds than to hoodwink an honest businessman like Mr Carter here? To use his very respectability as a smokescreen?"

A brief silence followed, then Aaron felt a strange vibration. He glanced at DI Finch, who was visibly struggling not to laugh. His own control was better, though he felt the same urge.

"Very good," said DI Finch, composing herself. "But if you don't mind turning to the final set of documents I produced earlier, you'll see that there's no real possibility Mr Carter wasn't involved in these arrangements."

"What are these?" asked Bexley, opening the folder.

Carter thumbed through the papers beside her, nodding as he recognised messages he'd sent or received, completely untroubled.

"A set of emails," replied Aaron. "In which your client quite clearly makes a number of arrangements that contravene the Modern Slavery Act."

"I don't know where you got these emails, but you know you can't use them, don't you?"

The legal situation was unclear. One judge might admit the emails; another might exclude them. Ryan Tobin had stolen them, but the boss might have obtained them legitimately.

"Are you prepared to bet your client's liberty on that?" asked DI Finch.

"Are you prepared to bet your career?"

Bexley seemed surprised when DI Finch simply nodded.

People like Bexley didn't understand. For DI Finch, it wasn't about career advancement or maintaining a spotless record. It was about getting results honestly and cleanly.

Aaron had learned that from her – when to take risks and put himself on the line. He'd done it arguing with DCI Carnegie and arresting Marc Langham in Elterwater.

He'd learned from a master, and however good Bexley was, she couldn't beat DI Finch.

CHAPTER SEVENTY-FIVE

"Here we go." Nina picked up her buzzing phone like it might explode at any moment.

Tom turned from his screen, where he'd been compiling a list of roadside cameras within range of the St Bees cell tower. There weren't many, but more than he'd expected, even on the smaller roads. Most probably weren't working, but worth checking. If he could track that Range Rover, he might find Arroyo and Matilda Ives.

Nina answered with "DS Kapoor," confirming it wasn't her mother calling.

Tom watched her listen as DCI Carnegie's voice blasted through the phone, loud enough for him to hear every word. Nina's eyes widened with each passing second.

"Who the hell do you people think you are?"

DCI Carnegie paused for breath. Nina opened her mouth, but Tom shook his head vigorously. She closed it again.

"Yet another idiot DS from the Hub. How are you all so useless? Is it something in the air? Or do they breed you down there? Is it some kind of genetic lab experiment gone wrong?"

Another pause followed before Carnegie continued. "It's like someone took a bag of rags, stuffed them with the crap you find when you clean out your gutters, and gave it a warrant card."

Nina kept silent as Carnegie went on. "Or maybe you've been harvested. Is that it? Scraped off a dunghill somewhere, and given the false impression that you're good for anything other than crawling around in shit?"

The line went quiet. Nina raised her eyebrows at Tom, who shrugged.

"DCI Carnegie," Nina ventured.

"DID I SAY YOU COULD TALK?"

Nina fell silent.

"ANSWER ME!"

"Er, no?"

"Precisely. Now, I'll thank you to keep your big stupid noses out of our investigation. I don't expect to come across you again, but if I do, you'll regret it."

The line went dead with an audible click.

"Bloody hell," Nina muttered.

"Are we going to... How did she put it? Keep our big stupid noses out of her investigation?" Tom asked.

"How are you getting on with the cameras?" Nina nodded toward his screen.

Tom tapped it to show his spreadsheet. "Nineteen cameras so far. I've created a map, too." He brought up an image showing a tangle of intersecting lines.

"What the hell is that?" Nina peered at the screen.

"All the possible routes any vehicle could take past any one of those cameras."

"Well, if Arroyo did that route, he's got more problems than just having us after him. Have you requested the footage?"

Tom nodded.

"Good. Looks like we'll be keeping our big noses right in the middle of DCI Carnegie's investigation for a little longer."

CHAPTER SEVENTY-SIX

"Regardless of their admissibility or otherwise," Bexley said, "this is the first we're seeing of these emails."

"Oh, Mr Carter's seen them before." Aaron leaned forward. "He wrote most of them."

Bexley ignored him and fixed Zoe with her penetrating stare.

Zoe shrugged. "You're seeing them now. Take a few minutes to read them, if you like."

She didn't need to read them herself. These highlights spanned more than twenty pages, and she'd memorised every word. The document contained extracts from Jenson & Marley's email server, downloaded by Ryan Tobin before he'd left the company to become an environmental activist. He'd handed them over as thanks for solving his friend Kevin Downes' murder months earlier. Even without the financial evidence, photos, and testimony from Elena and the other trafficked women, the emails were damning enough.

Carter and Dean Somerville, discussing women like commodities.

CHAPTER SEVENTY-SIX

Romanian and Hungarian units are currently cheaper than Ukrainian and Russian.

She waited. Carter maintained his composure, unruffled. Bexley's frown deepened as she read – though Bexley only had three expressions: frowning, glaring, or that hideous smile of hers.

Bexley snapped the folder shut. "You know they're not admissible."

"We've been through this," Zoe said. "Maybe not. But maybe they are. That'll be for the CPS and the judge to decide, won't it?"

Carter closed his own copy with deliberate care and pushed it away.

"Well?" Zoe asked.

"I don't know what you want me to say." Carter's voice remained steady. "I've never seen these before."

"You wrote them," Aaron said.

"Either they're doctored, or someone has simply hacked my accounts to frame me. Which does rather tally with what my lawyer here has said about using my respectability as a smokescreen."

The same words had been amusing coming from Bexley. From Carter, they chilled Zoe.

"Interview paused," she said. She stopped the recording and walked out; Aaron ran behind her.

Upstairs, she sent Aaron to the team room and retreated to her office. She shut the door and picked up the phone.

Just do it, she told herself. *Don't give yourself time to think about it.*

Could she have done more down there? Could she have tried harder?

No point worrying about it now. She dialled.

"Yes?" David Randle answered.
"How soon can you get here?"
"Why?"
She swallowed. "Because you're on. You and Carter. It's happening."

CHAPTER SEVENTY-SEVEN

Carl marched along the corridor to the stairwell. Halfway down to the next floor, he realised Denise wasn't behind him.

He turned around and marched back up. She stood in the corridor, glaring at him.

"I might be on the mend, but I can't move at that speed. Not on a staircase, anyway."

"Let's take the lift."

They descended to the ground floor and crossed to the secret entrance that probably wasn't as secret as it should have been given its frequent use over the last year. Then back up to the sixth floor, the special custody suite, the offices set aside for PSD.

Offices with chairs, desks and phones.

DCI Branthwaite answered immediately. "Got a confession out of Carter, have they?"

"No, Sir."

"No. Not pigging likely, is it? So what are you calling me for?"

Denise stared at Carl, a bemused frown on her face.

"I..." Carl glanced at Denise and corrected himself. "We're concerned about the direction DI Finch is taking this investigation, Sir."

"We?"

"Me and Denise, Sir. She's here with me."

"Is she indeed? Good stuff. So what's your partner been up to then, Carl?"

He laid it out as succinctly as he could. Zoe's plan to get Randle in the room with Carter. Cameras on, sound off. He'd hoped it would sound more rational when he spelled out the details, but it didn't. It still sounded crazy.

"Pigging hell," said Branthwaite. "Let me have a think."

Denise's frown deepened.

Carl placed his hand over the phone. "He's just had his first grandkid. His daughter says he swears too much. Won't have him do it in front of the baby. This is his way of cutting down."

Denise grunted, clearly understanding the words but not agreeing with them.

"The thing is," said Branthwaite.

Carl's heart sank. Things rarely went well when Branthwaite started a sentence that way.

"It's not like you can actually do anything about it, can you?"

"Well, Sir—"

"You could call me and ask me to do something about it, but it's not a PSD investigation, so the most I can do is piss... is pig off a few people. Make life uncomfortable for you at home. And the thing is, your missus—"

"They're not actually married, Sir," Denise said.

"Objection noted, but it's a figure of speech, Denise. But

CHAPTER SEVENTY-SEVEN

DI Finch knows what she's doing, and if anyone's aware of that, it should be you."

"I suppose so, Sir." Carl knew he was fighting a losing battle, but he wouldn't give up without throwing a punch or two. "But she's still capable of making mistakes. And I think trusting David Randle is one of them."

"But she doesn't actually trust him, does she, Carl? She's just using him. And yes, he's using her, and she knows it, they both know it, half the pigging world knows it. You didn't want Randle in talking to Streeting, did you?"

"No."

"And yet, from what I hear, it was Randle's intervention, via your other half, that got Streeting talking. She was right then, and she's probably right now. You heard anything about your surveillance that suggests otherwise?"

"No." He hadn't heard much about his surveillance at all, but then, he hadn't really expected to. There was someone else in the house, presumably Olivia. That was it. "But it doesn't feel right, Sir."

"And nor does my left b... arm. If you've got something concrete, let me know. If you don't, let DI Finch carry out her investigation her way."

Branthwaite hung up.

Carl turned to Denise. "I think I preferred it when he swore."

"It won't last."

But his mind was elsewhere. Downstairs. Where they were about to put together a combination that would make Randle and Streeting look like orange squash and water.

All he could do was hope it didn't explode.

CHAPTER SEVENTY-EIGHT

Nina heard Tom tapping on his keyboard beside her. She tried to focus on her screen, on deciphering the mess of contradictory information they'd received since Christian Ives had first walked into the Hub and claimed to be a murderer, but she couldn't.

DCI Carnegie's words reverberated through the near-silence of the team room, each a sharp edge or a hard fist as it made contact.

Dunghill? Lab experiment?

She glanced at Tom. He was frowning at his screen, following that mess of black lines until he found some sort of order. If he managed it, what would they do? Who would they tell?

One thing was certain. She wouldn't be getting on the phone to Kiki Carnegie.

Bag of rags with a warrant card?

Nina had weathered plenty of verbal beatings over the years. She couldn't remember many she hadn't responded to. Maybe the first time the super had chewed her out, over the riot down by the mosque. The tongue-lashing from her mum, after the incident on the ice. DCI Carnegie had just joined a very select group of people who could shut Nina Kapoor up.

It wouldn't happen again.

The DCI had put on quite a show. Good range, some imagination. But next time she tried something like that, Nina would be ready.

And it wasn't really fair. All Nina was trying to do was her job. Why get so angry about it?

Unless you had something to hide.

"Look at this." Tom's voice interrupted thoughts that were starting to slide in a worrying direction.

"What?"

"Here." His attention remained fixed on his screen.

Nina sighed and pushed her chair over to see.

His screen was full of lines, but now most were grey, pale, hardly there. It gave her less of a headache, but it didn't tell her anything.

"What am I looking at?"

Tom pointed at the few lines still clear and black above the rest. "You're looking at the route of Gustavo Arroyo's cars during the time he got back from Madrid to when we saw him turn up at home the other day."

"Cars, plural?"

"Yes." Tom tapped an icon in the corner of the screen, and a map of West Cumbria appeared over the lines. "The first bunch of routes are the Range Rover. Then he takes this road here." He indicated a road heading east. "Takes him to Ambleside, where he returns the Range Rover and picks up his Lexus. Then heads back this way again."

"This first point." Nina tapped one of the two main hubs. "This is Cleator Moor, right?"

"Right. That camera's about quarter of a mile from his house."

"And the other point?"

"Well, it's just a camera. I doubt he's actually visiting the camera. But he's driving past it a lot of times in a short period. Six times, three return journeys. So wherever he was going, it has to be important."

"Right," Nina agreed. "And where is this camera?"

"Here." Tom pointed to a chunk of land on the coast, then tapped again, and the map turned into a satellite view. Sea and land. Fields, buildings, beach, and a whole lot of caravans.

"St Bees?" she said.

"St Bees," he agreed. "Whatever Gustavo Arroyo was doing during the two days he claims to have been in Argentina, it was in St Bees."

CHAPTER SEVENTY-NINE

"Once more unto the breach," Zoe whispered to herself as she pushed open the door and walked in.

"On your own?" Clarissa Bexley asked.

Carter looked up, his posture relaxed. Whether it was genuine or a front, Zoe couldn't tell.

"I've asked DS Keyes to sit this one out." Zoe remained standing, meeting Carter's gaze. His expression showed only mild interest, as if watching events unfold from a distance.

Bexley gestured towards the table. "Tick, tock. You can't keep my client here indefinitely, and if you had enough to charge him, you'd have done it already. So let's get on with it, shall we?"

Zoe stayed where she was. Both Carter and his lawyer frowned up at her.

"At least start the recording and ask some bloody questions," Bexley said.

Zoe stepped forward, sat down, and leaned across the table, interlocking her fingers. "I'd like you to talk to someone."

"Who?" Bexley asked.

Carter gazed back at Zoe, unblinking.

"It's up to you, but I think you'll benefit from it."

"If you're bringing a colleague into this, it won't—"

"Let DI Finch talk," Carter interrupted, his eyes fixed on Zoe.

"Any conversation you have won't be under caution," she continued. "You can say what you like. We won't record it. We won't even be listening. No audio. We'll have video on, but solely for your security, and you're welcome to cover your face with your hands if you're worried we'll lipread your conversation."

"I really don't think—" Bexley started.

"Who?" Carter asked.

"David Randle," Zoe said.

Carter's eyes widened.

"I'd like a few minutes with my client," Bexley said. "Mr Carter, we need to discuss this sensibly. You don't know what—"

"David Randle," Carter said, rolling the words around his mouth like he was savouring them.

"Yes," Zoe confirmed.

"That's a man I've been trying to find for a long time," Carter said.

"Mr Carter," Bexley pressed. "We should—"

"I'll do it," Carter said. "Yes. I think this is going to be fun."

CHAPTER EIGHTY

Tom felt relief at finding a lead. Not just because it might help locate Gustavo Arroyo and Matilda Ives, but because it seemed to be taking Nina's mind off her encounter with DCI Carnegie.

She'd been uncharacteristically quiet. In their years working together, they'd handled violent mobs, senior officers barely containing their aggression, football hooligans, the press, and once, three drunk priests who'd forgotten both God and the law. He'd never seen her this silent.

Now they were back to the grunt work – ploughing through maps and camera data, calculating journey times with regular traffic patterns. Even Tom found it tedious. Nina wasn't doing the work, just watching him, but her frustration was palpable, making his fingers work faster on the keyboard.

After ten minutes, he spotted something. "Hotel."

"Yeah?" Nina's tone was sceptical.

"If he went here, stopped for maybe ten to fifteen

minutes each time, then headed back, that would match the movements on the camera."

"Give them a call."

He did. Nina's scepticism proved right. The Willow Guesthouse was closed until next June, according to the recording.

"Arroyo could still be there," Tom said. "Could have stashed his mother-in-law there, too. Empty building, all the amenities. It's possible."

"He could have stashed her in the nearest Butlins."

Tom bit back his response about there being no Butlins within range. He turned back to his keyboard instead.

"Caravan park," he announced five minutes later.

Nina shrugged.

Another recorded message – closed for winter, reopening in May.

Winter? In September? Granted, Cumbria could turn nasty quickly, but this seemed premature.

The next hotel was open but empty, closing in days. The lonely proprietor tried keeping Tom on the line, but Nina's need – and Matilda Ives' – was greater.

Two minutes later, he found another possibility. This one was smaller, more remote – perfect for hiding someone, if it wasn't closed for the season.

"Hello," came another recorded voice through static. "You're through to the Bowen Hotel."

Tom's finger was hovering over the end call button when a live voice cut in.

"Hello?" A male voice, irritated at the interruption.

"Hello, I was wondering if you could help me." Tom put the phone on speaker. Nina shook her head beside him.

"You after a room?" the man asked.

CHAPTER EIGHTY

"No, I'm after a guest. I was wondering if you had a Mrs Ives staying with you."

"No, I don't." The voice turned aggressive. "Who are you, anyway?"

"DC Tom Willis, Cumbria CID."

"Yeah? Well, we don't 'ave no Mrs Ives 'ere, right?"

The accent was London, not local. No wonder he sounded annoyed – probably expected a longer season.

Nina leaned forward. "This is DS Nina Kapoor."

"Yeah? Still ain't got no Mrs Ives."

"Do you have any guests staying there, Mr..."

"Bowen, innit? Bill Bowen. And yeah, I do, as it 'appens."

"Many?"

"Just the one," Bowen admitted.

"I don't suppose the one guest you have staying with you is a woman around the age of eighty-six, either alone, or with a male visitor around thirty years younger?"

Bowen whistled. "'Ow the 'ell you know that, eh? You got cameras on my place?"

"Is she there now?" Nina asked.

"Yeah, she don't really go anywhere."

"Mr Bowen," Nina said. "Please take note of my number and call me if anything happens. My colleague will be with you shortly."

She ended the call, and they exchanged grins.

"Looks like those big noses of ours are about to get busy again," Tom said.

Nina laughed. "Off you go, then. And don't go getting distracted by any dunghills."

CHAPTER EIGHTY-ONE

Zoe spent five minutes with David Randle, watching him swallow pill after pill.

He tossed back three tablets. "Painkillers." The bandage on his hand was smaller now, exposing his thumb and part of his palm. The visible skin was smooth and red, like a burn.

"Still hurting?" she asked. Did she care? She wasn't sure.

"You don't know the half of it. So what have you got from him?"

"Very little." Zoe explained their situation – Carter and his lawyer deflecting every piece of evidence, denying knowledge of emails and cash movements, providing innocent explanations for the photos Carter appeared in.

"What's your plan?"

Randle swallowed three more pills. "Antibiotics. Like I said, I'm going to remind him of Hamm. They have a lot in common, Carter and Hamm. They could almost be each other."

Which makes you Streeting, Zoe thought.

"And?" she prompted.

CHAPTER EIGHTY-ONE

"And you know what happened to Hamm. If you leave something behind, people will fight over it. They won't want the old man waiting in the wings, ready to throw his weight behind a rival, or stir up trouble. Even if he's in prison."

"You think it'll work?"

"You have a better idea?" Randle swallowed two more large green pills.

"What are they?"

"No idea. Doctor's orders. Right. Let's do this."

Zoe led Carter to the prepared room, flanked by PCs Stones and Parton, with Clive Moor following. She retreated to Interview Room Four to observe.

A screen had been set up for Clarissa Bexley to watch, "Just in case," the lawyer had said. Zoe could have watched from her office, but wanted to see Bexley's reactions.

Bexley remained impassive as Carter and Randle stood in the empty room, hands over mouths, speaking for ten minutes with unreadable expressions.

Come on, Zoe thought. *Give me something*. Without results, she'd have wasted time and damaged her relationship with Carl for nothing.

Her phone buzzed with a message from Jake Frimpton: *Is it true? You've got Carter?*

Off the record, yes, she replied.

Movement on the screen caught her attention. Carter emerged first, his escort still in place.

She found Randle in the briefing room, struggling with a pill bottle, shaking his head.

"Nothing?" she asked.

"Nothing. He won't admit a thing. Not even to me."

Zoe helped open the bottle and watched him swallow three more pills. The shooting had aged him considerably.

"I'm sorry," he said. "I tried."

"You used the line about Hamm?"

"Carter thinks he's tougher than Hamm was. Thinks he has more loyalty from his people. I don't know what to say, Zoe. I did everything I could."

She closed her eyes, feeling waves of nausea rise and fall. Carl had been right, and she'd been wrong.

All this, and they had nothing.

CHAPTER EIGHTY-TWO

The Bowen Hotel was a grand name for a semi-detached house overlooking the railway line in the centre of St Bees. Just to the south, Tom could see more impressive dwellings, presumably with better views. He parked a few doors down, past a shallow bend. If the neighbours were in, they'd be wondering why there was a car outside their house. One look was enough to see it was that sort of place.

The patrol car pulled in behind him, almost blocking the neighbour's drive. A large grey Lexus, parked inconsiderately on the bend, took up at least two spots.

Got you.

Bill Bowen answered the doorbell wearing an apron stained with egg spatter. His long grey hair hung loose and was streaked with white.

"Yeah?" His age surprised Tom.

"We spoke earlier."

"Oh, right." Bowen gestured upwards. "Top floor, Room Two."

It was a standard two-storey semi. 'Top floor' seemed redundant.

Tom took the stairs leading straight up from the entrance hall, Martinez behind him, Roddy Chen a few paces back. A narrow corridor stretched ahead, with an open bathroom door at the far end and three other doors, all closed. Two had numbers on them.

One and Two.

Tom tapped on the door marked Two, waited, then raised his fist to bang harder. The door opened.

Gustavo Arroyo stood behind it, his expression shifting from annoyance to alarm. Tom glimpsed an armchair upholstered in worn green fabric, with an elderly lady perched on it, sipping tea.

Arroyo made his move before Tom could react. With surprising strength, he pushed Tom aside and darted past. He was beyond Martinez half a second later, but came to an abrupt halt against Chen's bulk.

People didn't just run past Roddy Chen.

Tom took a moment to consider his options, then settled on false imprisonment. The exact charge could be determined later.

"Well, that was unexpected," said Matilda Ives as Tom led her down the stairs. Ahead, Arroyo continued protesting his innocence between Chen and Martinez.

"Are you OK, Mrs Ives?"

"Well, yes. You're very young, aren't you? Do you work here?"

"No, I don't, Mrs Ives."

He'd already explained he was police. Clearly, he'd need to explain again.

"Are we going to another hotel now?" She stepped out of

CHAPTER EIGHTY-TWO

the front door, missing the sight of her son-in-law being placed in the patrol car. Instead, she turned to Tom with a hesitant smile. "Only, if we are, I hope it's better than this one."

Tom sensed Bill Bowen bristling behind him.

"I wanted to go to the tearoom here, in this one. But Gustavo told me there had been a flood and they couldn't open it, which was a shame. I do so like a hotel tearoom."

"I'm sorry to hear that." Tom noticed Bowen's glower. He'd just lost a paying guest.

"So I've been stuck in my room the whole time eating sandwiches," she said.

"How long has that been?"

Mrs Ives looked confused. "Ooh, I'm not sure, dear. More than a day, certainly. Less than a week, I think."

Tom looked past her at Bowen, standing in the doorway. "Do you know—"

Bowen turned away and slammed the door shut.

CHAPTER EIGHTY-THREE

Zoe looked around the room. Three expectant faces looked back at her.

"Well done on tracking down Arroyo," she said.

Tom grinned. Nina nodded. Aaron shrugged. They were waiting for the important news.

She took a deep breath.

"I'm sorry to have to tell you that we haven't got anywhere with Carter."

A collective slump. A long, slow exhalation.

"Randle didn't help?" asked Aaron.

She shook her head. "Nothing helped. They're denying the emails, twisting the photos, insisting someone else must have been manipulating the bank accounts. It's all exactly what we expected, but still..."

"It's bloody annoying when it actually happens," said Nina.

Zoe nodded. "We've got Carter until just after noon tomorrow. That'll be our twenty-four hours up. I'm not going to ask the super for an extension based on what we have now,

CHAPTER EIGHTY-THREE

so either we find something first thing tomorrow, or we have to let him go."

"He'll run," said Nina.

"I'll see what we can do in terms of surveillance. And maybe Ralph Streeting's recording devices will give us what we need."

Aaron and Tom exchanged glances.

"What?" Zoe said.

"Well, boss..." Tom looked at Aaron, who gave a half-hearted shrug.

"What?" she repeated. "If you have something to say, say it."

Tom licked his lips. "Do you really believe these devices exist?"

She smiled. She could see why they might doubt it. Streeting was hardly trustworthy.

"As it happens, I do, Tom. Now, what's Gustavo Arroyo said?"

"He's denying any involvement with Mulligan and claiming he found Matilda Ives at the hotel," said Nina.

Tom leaned forward in his chair. "I spoke to the guy who owns the hotel just now. He's not happy. Lost his only paying guest. But he's willing to confirm Arroyo's lying."

Zoe nodded. "We'll let him stew. See if he's more cooperative after a night away from his little luxuries." She pulled out her phone. "And now it's time to set the cat among the pigeons."

She found the number she wanted, hit the call button, and set her phone on the spare desk, speakers on.

"Carnegie," said the DCI.

"It's Zoe Finch, from the Hub."

"Christ. Don't you lot give up? How many times do I have to tell you to keep out of our investigation?"

"DCI Carnegie," she said. "We have some information. During the course of an investigation into a missing woman—"

"Matilda Ives?" interrupted the DCI. "That's not your investigation, Finch. I've a good mind to—"

"No," Zoe said, her voice rising. "The search for Matilda Ives wasn't your investigation. I happen to know it wasn't your investigation because I've spoken to Uniform, and you weren't even doing it, were you?"

DCI Carnegie was silent.

"In the course of our work," Zoe continued, "we've found both Matilda Ives, and the man who took her. That's Gustavo Arroyo. Christian Ives' husband."

An involuntary gasp of surprise came from the other end of the phone.

"Given the concerns we already have regarding the arrest of Christian Ives, I'd be grateful if you'd take this into account, alongside all the other exculpatory evidence that's been presented to you."

"I don't believe you're in any position—" began DCI Carnegie.

"And please," Zoe cut in, raising her voice. "Don't threaten or insult my team again."

CHAPTER EIGHTY-FOUR

THE HOUSE WAS in semi-darkness when Aaron pushed open the door.

He paused in the hallway. It wasn't that late – surely Annabel wasn't asleep? And where was Serge?

The scent of garlic and mint wafted through the air, mixed with something meaty – lamb. Following the aroma, he made his way to the kitchen.

Pop music filtered through the door. Not his taste. Not Serge's, either.

Definitely Annabel's.

He pushed open the door to find his husband and daughter in the middle of the kitchen. Annabel bounced from one leg to another, arms moving in a complex pattern. Serge attempted to copy her movements.

Serge spotted Aaron and gave an apologetic shrug. "We saw it on TikTok."

Aaron pulled them both into a hug, feeling their warmth against him, breathing in the cooking smells while the awful music played on. "What is it?"

"One of the Megans," Serge said. "I don't know which one. Now, Annabel's agreed to go to sleep early tonight and leave us in peace for a nice meal together, haven't you, sweetheart?"

Annabel's lower lip jutted out in a pout.

"I don't mind—" Aaron began.

"But I suppose she can join us for a little lamb, eh?" Serge said.

"Yuck!" Annabel wrinkled her nose. "I want hummus."

"Very well." Serge adopted his French waiter's voice. "Supermarket hummus and white bread for Mademoiselle. Navarin of lamb printanier for Messieurs."

The meal was delicious. Annabel dozed off before they'd finished and was tucked up in bed before they moved on to coffee and cognac.

"What's the occasion?" Aaron asked when they settled on the living room sofa.

"You've been stressed. I thought you could do with it."

Aaron shook his head, overwhelmed by his good fortune. "I've been an arsehole. I've been stressed, and I've taken it out on you."

"I like it when you get moody, Detective Sergeant. It's sexy." Serge grinned.

"If it's any consolation, I didn't just take it out on you. I've spent most of the last two days shouting at officers so vastly senior to me, I probably need to get myself promoted before I get myself fired."

Serge's expression turned serious. "You're not joking, are you?"

Aaron closed his eyes and inhaled, considering the question. "No. I don't think I am. I think it's time."

CHAPTER EIGHTY-FIVE

SHE HADN'T EVEN READ the bloody message.

Nina banged the heel of her right hand onto her forehead in frustration. All that work crafting the perfect message for her mother yesterday, and she hadn't replied. Worse still, she hadn't even read it.

Tom had helped with the crafting, but the sentiments were all Nina's.

She slid the car into reverse and out of the narrow space she'd managed to squeeze into the night before. The car was low on power, but hopefully she'd be able to hook it up at the Hub. Working in a modern building with a modern car park was one big advantage when you had an electric car and no off-street parking.

There was a road closed in town, so she headed north through Bransty, early enough to avoid the primary school traffic, and out of town past Parton. She swung right, watching the rain beat down on the fields around Moresby Parks, and slowed as she reached the kids' play centre on her right. A man stood in the road, stopping the traffic as a truck reversed slowly into the car park next door.

Get a move on.

She wasn't sure why she was in such a hurry. If anything had happened overnight, she'd know about it by now.

She glanced right, into the car park. Two more trucks stood outside the warehouse, and three vans by the office next door. Men hurried through the rain, alone or in groups, carrying chairs, tables, filing cabinets.

Someone was on the move. They might have picked a better day for it.

The man in the road waved for her to go and stepped out of the way. Nina gave him a sympathetic smile as she passed. The rain was running off his hair into his face in rivers. *Poor bloke.* Beyond him, the others were still running and carrying, carrying and running. The sky was an unbroken grey in every direction; the weather wouldn't be shifting in their favour any time soon.

Nina turned her focus back to the road, her eyes sliding past the big sign with the company name on it. Half a mile down the road, wondering what was niggling at her, it clicked. She slammed on the brakes.

She waved an apology to the driver behind, who'd narrowly avoided driving his Audi straight into her back, and performed a hasty three-point turn.

Keep it calm. She had to keep it calm. Not just to avoid accidents. If she drove the way she wanted to drive, she wouldn't have enough juice to get to work.

She drove slowly back to where the man had blocked the road, humming *Suspicious Minds* to keep herself steady, and stopped, though there was no need to now. Within seconds, a man in a BMW was hooting at her.

CHAPTER EIGHTY-FIVE

Nina put on her hazards and flicked the wipers so she could see the words more clearly.

HARTLEY MORRISON, on the big board outside the warehouse.

FLOWERS & MILLER, on the smaller one beside the single-storey office block.

Ignoring the hooting, she did another three-point turn and drove, carefully and patiently, to the Hub, *Suspicious Minds* replaced with *Are You Lonesome Tonight?* and, when she'd been through that twice, *Love Me Tender*.

She'd driven past those buildings so many times. Seen those names, read them, forgotten them. They were just words. She hadn't known they were yet more front companies for Myron Carter's businesses.

She forced herself to keep calm as she hooked her car up to one of the spare chargers. When she was confident it was charging, she raced across the car park, up three flights of stairs and straight into DI Finch's office, where she stood, breathing hard, her back to the door, while the boss stared at her like she'd just fallen from the sky.

"Everything OK, Nina?" DI Finch asked after a minute.

Nina nodded and dropped into one of the chairs. "Sorry. Just give me a few seconds."

The boss continued to stare at her. "Well?" she said, after more than a few seconds had elapsed.

"These devices," Nina said. "Has Streeting told us where they are?"

"No." The boss shook her head. "He insists on being involved in their recovery. We suspect office locations, but we're not sure. Why?"

"Because I've just driven past a couple of Carter's front companies, and it looks like he's cleaning house."

"What do you mean?"

Nina outlined what she'd seen. "If it's this location—" She stopped as the boss shook her head.

"It doesn't matter if it's this location," DI Finch pointed out. "If Carter's clearing out one place, he's probably clearing out the rest."

"So if we're going to raid these places, we need to do it fast."

The boss nodded and picked up her phone. Nina stayed where she was. Even if she'd wanted to move, she didn't have the energy.

"Fiona," the boss said. "It's Zoe Finch. We have a situation."

CHAPTER EIGHTY-SIX

"Hiya," said the lawyer as they entered the room.

Tom paused. She was a short woman with a dark bob, young, probably not even out of her twenties, but with a professional, no-nonsense air. He was sure he'd seen her before, but couldn't place her name.

"Sue Sharples." She stood to shake his hand. "You're DC Willis, aren't you?"

Tom nodded. "And this is—"

"DS Keyes, right? I've read the files. And I've had a little chat with our friend here. He has some things to say. Don't you, Gustavo?"

Gustavo Arroyo nodded, staring gloomily at the floor.

The man looked awful. His skin had a grey tinge; his hair was a mess with clear signs its dark colour wasn't natural. His suit was creased where it shouldn't be.

A night in the cells hadn't suited Gustavo Arroyo at all.

"Everything OK, Mr Arroyo?" asked the sarge.

Arroyo looked at him miserably, dark patches under his eyes, mouth slightly open. He looked ready to cry. "Yes."

"Yes, what?" asked Tom.

"Yes. It was me. I took her."

"Hold that thought." DS Keyes held up a hand, started the recording, and ran through the formalities.

"You were saying?" he prompted.

"I didn't kidnap her," Arroyo said. "Not really. I just took the old dear to a hotel. She thought it was a treat. A nice little holiday. Ask her."

"And the damage to the house?"

Arroyo sighed and turned to his lawyer.

"It's like we discussed, Gustavo," she whispered, loud enough for Tom to hear. "They're going to find it all out, one way or another. Best for you if you just come clean."

"I'd better go back to the beginning, hadn't I?"

"I think that would be best," said Tom.

Arroyo looked up at him and blew out a long breath, as if readying himself for an ordeal. "You know Christian didn't really kill that man, don't you?"

Tom exchanged a look with the sarge, but neither spoke.

"This is why I'm doing this. Telling you. Otherwise, you're not getting a thing out of me."

"I'm sorry, Mr Arroyo," said Tom. "The Mulligan murder is no longer our investigation. It's being handled out of Durranhill. We can't promise you anything. But anything you say now, if it's relevant to Christian's case, it'll be put to the investigating team there. Is that good enough?"

Arroyo looked over at the lawyer, who nodded encouragingly.

"I suppose it'll have to do," he said. "OK, then. Christian was asked to do it, you know? Asked to confess to a crime he had nothing to do with."

CHAPTER EIGHTY-SIX

"Why?" asked Tom, but Arroyo held out a hand and Tom stopped.

Give them space. He'd learned that, on his interview course. Once they started talking, you had to give them the space to continue.

"He was asked to do it, and he said no, and that was fair enough. But when they came back and asked him a second time, they offered some money to sweeten the pill. A lot of money."

"A quarter of a million pounds?" suggested the sarge.

Arroyo nodded. "Christian said no again. I tried to talk him into it, but he insisted."

"Why did you try to talk him into it?" asked Tom.

Arroyo gave a short, bitter laugh. "You've met Christian?"

Tom nodded.

"He's absolutely lovely, Christian is. A gorgeous man, inside and out. But the thing about him is that he's ever so naïve."

"He had no idea how much you'd been spending, did he?" asked the sarge. "No idea how much debt you were in."

"Exactly," agreed Arroyo. "I needed that money. *We* needed it. Christian just didn't know it. So he had to be convinced."

Something occurred to Tom. "So you're saying he didn't commit the crime, right?" he said.

"Yes," replied Arroyo.

"And that's all very well," Tom continued. "But did the two of you know someone was going to be killed? Did you know what was involved? Because if you did..."

Arroyo looked horrified. "God, no. If we'd known that...

Well, we'd have told you. None of this would have happened."

"So what did happen, precisely?" asked the sarge.

"Christian was informed that there was going to be a crime, and that he had to be at a certain location at a certain time, where he'd be told what he'd supposedly done, and then he'd be given all the information he'd need to keep you busy for a while."

"He didn't know what this crime was?"

"No. We both assumed it would be something minor. We certainly didn't think anyone was going to die. And," he added, anticipating Tom's next question, "he was told there was no chance it would ever get as far as a trial. The idea was that he'd sow a little confusion and then go home. But he still said he wouldn't do it. Said no amount of money was worth getting involved with Myron Carter. He's always regretted selling him the business, and I've told him he wasn't to know what sort of man Carter was, back then, but he feels guilty, you know?"

Tom could see that. On the face of it, Carter was just a businessman. And Christian Ives had refused to do Carter's bidding, despite his husband's protestations. So what had changed?

Oh. Suddenly, it all fell into place.

"So you decided you needed another way to persuade him," Tom said.

A nod. "I got in touch with Carter myself. Told him I'd take care of it, gave him my bank account details, and then I nipped home while Christian was out and took the old woman out with me."

"And the house?"

"I had to make it look serious, and I had to remove the

CHAPTER EIGHTY-SIX

footage of me taking her. So yes, I came back and smashed up the security system. Left it like that for Christian to find, so he'd assume someone had genuinely kidnapped Matilda. It wouldn't take him long to realise it had to be Carter, finding another way to put the pressure on."

"Christ," said Tom under his breath.

The lawyer gave a sympathetic grimace. Arroyo could talk away his motives all day. He'd still kidnapped an old woman and tricked his husband into lying to the police. Abetted a murder.

Arroyo didn't react. "And the thing is, I just knew it would work. Once he saw his precious mother had been taken, Christian wouldn't have any choice. He'd *have* to turn up and do what they asked, and I'd get the money."

"And Mrs Ives? You weren't worried about how all this would affect her?" asked Tom.

Arroyo shrugged. "About time that bloody woman did something to earn her keep."

CHAPTER EIGHTY-SEVEN

"What's this situation of yours, then?" Fiona leaned back in her chair. "And sit down, for heaven's sake."

"We don't have time."

"You don't have time to sit down?"

Zoe frowned and took the seat across from Fiona. After a downpour, the sky was clearing, beams of light playing across the desk.

"Sorry. It looks like Carter's making his move. Preparing to disappear."

Fiona's brow creased. "We already knew that, didn't we? And last I heard, he was still in custody."

"We have new information. And yes, he's downstairs, but not for long. Unless we find those recordings, I don't see how we can get the evidence to keep him here. His lawyer's pushing for us to let him out now. And time's running out."

Fiona nodded and tapped on her phone screen. "I've already had a message from Becca Grey."

A voice Zoe hadn't heard before rang out. "Fiona? Becca here. Look, I've heard Myron's still with you there. It would save a lot of embarrassment later if you could just let him go, yes?"

The message ended. A breezy tone, like someone arranging to meet for coffee. Not like someone pressing for the release of a stone-cold killer.

"No help from the Chief?"

"Big Jo's still in the Bahamas, and even if she's checking her phone between cocktails on the beach, she's not going to respond to the likes of me." Fiona straightened in her chair. "Tell me why you think Carter's a flight risk."

Zoe related what Nina had told her.

"Fine. Let's do this." Fiona's voice was firm.

"You sure?"

"Isn't this what you want, Zoe?"

"Well, yes. But I thought…"

"You thought I'd push back. Be cautious." Fiona's eyes hardened. "I've been cautious before. Maybe too cautious. Maybe the IOPC are right about me. But not this time."

A knock on the door.

"Come in," Fiona called.

Morris Keane pushed it open.

"I had a feeling we'd need you for this, Morris." Fiona picked up her phone and dialled.

"Ops," said the voice on the other end.

"Superintendent Singer. I'm here with Zoe Finch and Morris Keane. The operation we discussed the other day. We need to bring it forward."

"To when?" he asked.

Fiona looked at Zoe.

"To now."

Morris sat beside her, his expression thoughtful. "I take it we've still got to drag Ralph Streeting along with us, Zoe. That right?"

She gave a rueful smile. "I'm afraid so."

"I can't tell you how much more complicated this makes things." Singer's irritation came through the speaker. "It's enough of a job recovering hidden assets whilst keeping our own team safe. Now we've got to keep that bastard safe too, and make sure he doesn't do a runner. Which means we'll need your people, Morris. Mix AFOs with unarmed officers. Which I *really* don't like."

"I'll ask for volunteers," Morris said. "I don't want to use a regular shift when it could be dangerous."

"Hello."

They turned to see a figure in the doorway. Tall and thin, wearing what Zoe thought was the same cardigan she'd seen him in months ago, in this same room.

"Oh. Sorry to interrupt. I just wanted to... It's OK. I'll come back later."

He turned to leave.

"Jeff? Hang on." Fiona gestured to the others. "This is Jeff. Resident IT whizz. He might know if these things are real."

"What things?" Singer asked through the phone.

"The bugs. Whatever they're called."

"Empress," Zoe said, the rest of the name lost in the flurry of facts crowding her mind.

Jeff nodded. "Empress SE400?"

"Yes."

"State-of-the-art stuff, that. Small, easy to hide, almost indetectable. Local storage."

"So they're real, then?" Fiona asked. "They do exist? Not just something from a Bond movie?"

CHAPTER EIGHTY-SEVEN

Jeff smiled. "They're real. Proper specialist stuff. You need me to look at something for you?"

"Not now. Thanks, Jeff."

He stood there for a moment, watching them, then turned and left the room.

"Right," Singer said. "Let's put this op together."

CHAPTER EIGHTY-EIGHT

"You going to call her?" Aaron looked between Nina and Tom. "Or do you want me to?"

Nina weighed up her options. After yesterday's bombardment, calling Kiki Carnegie wasn't exactly top of her list. But someone had to tell the woman what Arroyo had said.

And Nina Kapoor didn't back down from a fight.

She picked up her phone, found the number she'd called the previous day, and dialled.

"Carnegie," the DCI barked.

"This is DS Kapoor, from the—"

"I know who you are. What do you want now?"

No actual insults yet. Maybe the boss's comments had got through to her. Or maybe it was just too early.

"We've just been talking to Gustavo Arroyo."

"Talking to him? Coffee and cakes, is it?"

"We've been interviewing him." Nina bristled. Why was she on the defensive already? What was it about this woman?

"Good for you."

CHAPTER EIGHTY-EIGHT

"He's admitted taking Matilda Ives. Admitted he did it to put pressure on Christian to confess to the murder."

"Very public-spirited of him. Now we have both a murderer and a kidnapper in custody. I'm sure the Chief Constable'll be breaking out the champagne."

Nina paused, collecting herself.

"You still there, Kapoor?"

She took a breath. "Yes. Ives isn't a murderer, though. You know that. And now Gustavo Arroyo has confirmed it."

Kiki Carnegie's thunderous laugh boomed through the phone, making Nina jump.

"He's told you his husband didn't murder someone, and he's come up with some ridiculous story to explain it all away, and you think that's enough to justify releasing a man who's actually confessed to the murder?"

Nina blinked. The woman was wrong, she was sure of it. But when she put it like that, it was really quite convincing. Her phone beeped, and she checked the display.

Her mum was calling. She'd have to wait.

"His explanation isn't ridiculous," Nina said. "It's the most plausible interpretation of the facts."

"Arroyo says first Carter, and then he himself, applied pressure on Ives to confess, right?"

"Yes."

"How do you know the pressure wasn't to actually carry out the murder, rather than just confess to it?"

Nina opened her mouth to reply, but the DCI continued.

"Is Gustavo Arroyo the killer?"

"I don't think so."

"Has he told you who the killer is?"

"No, but—"

"So we have Ives, who's confessed to the crime, and we don't have anyone else. I'll tell you what, Kapoor."

"What?"

"You find me another killer, I'll let Ives go."

Nina stared at her phone. How could they find another killer if DCI Carnegie kept filling their screens with black crosses, refusing to let them even investigate?

The line went dead before she could ask.

She slumped back in her chair, trying to work out how the call had gone so wrong, then remembered her mum.

Maybe she would finally apologise. That would improve the day. She picked up her phone again.

Aaron tapped her shoulder.

"What?" she said.

"Briefing."

"Here?"

"Downstairs."

"What's going on?"

His eyes blazed with excitement as he held up his phone. "It's a strategy meeting to execute the warrant on Carter's premises," he said.

Her stomach clenched. "What?"

Tom swivelled her chair around to point at her screen, where the notice summoning them downstairs had just appeared.

"The raid," he said. "They're going in."

CHAPTER EIGHTY-NINE

"Bloody hell." Denise turned slowly to look around the room.

"Impressive, isn't it?" DI Finch said.

The basement briefing room was slick and gleaming with chrome and polish, twice the size of anything Carlisle had to offer. By the time Denise completed her three-sixty, she'd counted fifteen of Inspector Keane's Uniforms, a unit of six AFOs with their gear, plus DI Whaley, DI Finch, Detective Superintendent Kendrick, and another man with a bandaged hand who leaned against the wall, looking bored.

She turned to say something to DI Whaley but found him staring at the man with undisguised contempt. She turned back to DI Finch and nodded in the same direction. "David Randle?"

"One and the same."

"Not going to introduce him to everyone else?"

DI Finch looked astonished before realising Denise was joking. They weren't yet used to her sense of humour here. Given the tension she'd observed between the two DIs over

Randle, it probably wasn't the place for it. Before she could consider apologising, a burst of activity in the far corner distracted her – the AFOs checking equipment while the Uniforms looked on with ill-concealed envy.

Movement on her other side drew her attention. The team had arrived. Nina Kapoor. Tom Willis. Aaron Keyes.

Strange that she thought of them as the team. They weren't *her* team. They were targets, more than colleagues, potentially at least. Yet that was what they'd become over the months leading to the explosion, the days spent sparring with Nina, watching Aaron to see if he'd crack under his guilt, swapping surveillance shifts on Streeting with Tom.

Aaron walked straight up to her, arms out, then dropped them as he remembered where he was. "Good to see you. I didn't think you'd be involved in this."

"She's not *involved*," DI Whaley said. "She's observing."

Denise resisted an eye roll.

Nina gave her a friendly nod before heading to DI Finch, chattering about DCI Carnegie and someone called Gustavo.

None of it made sense to Denise, but it didn't have to. As DI Whaley had reminded her, she was merely observing. As was he. This wasn't really a PSD matter. There was only one reason PSD were there.

And here was that reason, being led into the briefing room by three custody officers from the sixth floor. Arms cuffed in front.

They weren't taking chances with Ralph Streeting.

The room fell silent as the procession advanced to the centre. There were people here who'd done dangerous things. People who'd shot people, who'd been shot, who'd

CHAPTER EIGHTY-NINE

seen friends die in front of them on duty. But no one present had ever seen anything like this.

Streeting made the same slow circle she had minutes earlier, eyes sweeping over Uniforms, DI Finch's team, AFOs.

His gaze stopped on her.

He stared. She stared back. His gaze moved up her face and down again, tracing her scars.

Scars that should have been his.

It had been Streeting's car that exploded. Streeting who'd been the target, not her. Yet here he stood in cuffs but intact, while she'd spent months in hospital learning to live again.

Their eyes met.

She wouldn't look away. It hurt seeing Streeting alive and well, seeing teams assembled to help him recover items he claimed existed, at his choice, on his timeline, when all this could have happened months ago.

She'd taken a full daily dose of painkillers before heading out – a reduction from recent days – but it still hurt. Even seeing him in cuffs did little to dull it.

Denise didn't think of herself as vindictive, but she wanted to see Ralph Streeting suffer.

He stared at her. She stared back.

Then he dropped his gaze. Slowly. Down her body to her feet. She was sure she could read something in the movement of his eyes. Not an apology. People like Ralph Streeting didn't do apologies.

But there was shame there. She was sure of it. And that made her feel just a tiny bit better.

CHAPTER NINETY

Singer was shorter than Zoe remembered, with shrewd green eyes and the same no-nonsense manner he'd displayed on the phone. He strode into the centre of the room with four others, surveying the assembled police officers with a critical eye.

The room fell silent.

"We understand there are three locations. Is that right?"

The question was addressed to Zoe. She glanced at Streeting, who nodded.

"Yes," she said.

Singer turned to Streeting. "You won't tell us where they are in advance, is that right?"

Streeting nodded.

"And you insist on accompanying the team, yes?"

Another nod. Singer turned slowly, taking in the room.

"We consider it likely that there will be armed resistance."

A heavy silence fell. If Streeting wasn't lying, if these

CHAPTER NINETY

devices existed, and if Carter got wind of it, he wouldn't go down without a fight.

"Yes," Zoe agreed, though it hadn't been a question.

"In that case, and without a sense of where we're heading to, I'm sorry, but I believe this is too dangerous."

Zoe stared at him. "You can't pull the op now. Not when we're so close."

"I'm sorry. But with this..." Singer pointed at Streeting, "impeding factor, and the urgency of the situation, which means we have only one team of AFOs instead of the three we hoped for, the raids can't be conducted simultaneously. They have to be consecutive, and we don't even have them all under observation. Unless we hit the jackpot first time out, they'll be ready for us. Mixing AFOs and unarmed officers is asking for trouble, even without this additional complication."

Zoe watched as Streeting's eyes locked onto Silver Command's. The silence grew, punctuated by fidgeting and anxious movements.

"Fine," Streeting said eventually. "I'll give you six addresses now. The three with the devices are among them."

"Why?" asked Zoe.

"I'm not going to be any more precise. The moment you turn up to one of Carter's places and know where you're heading, he'll realise I've been talking. I'll be exposed. My neck on the line."

It made sense – a horrible catch-22 of danger and distrust, but it made sense.

Streeting listed six locations. Some were familiar; others could have been anywhere.

"Where are these places?" Zoe asked.

"All close enough," Streeting replied, and silence fell again.

"Fine," came a voice from the side. "Can we stop pissing around and get moving?"

Zoe felt Carl tense beside her and reached out to put a hand on his arm. She turned to Randle, who'd spoken.

"This hasn't got anything to do with you, David," she said.

"Then why am I even here?" he asked.

"Bloody good question," Carl muttered.

Randle ignored him. "You can talk it over for the rest of the day and lose your chance, or you can strike while the iron's hot." He turned to Zoe. "Remember Bobby Silver?"

"What about her?"

"Remember what happened? You delayed. What did they say during the war? 'Loose lips sink ships.' Someone blabbed. She wound up dead. You were a few minutes too late, and those few minutes cost everything."

Streeting looked down at his feet.

Nina pushed herself away from the wall. "Hey, that's not—"

"And now you're doing these raids one at a time," Randle continued. "By the time you've messed up the first one, they'll have cleared out the rest."

"What can we do?" Zoe asked. "We don't have enough AFOs to go in simultaneously. Not unless we're willing to wait even longer. We've got to do this by the book."

Randle shook his head in what looked like disgust. He moved past her and towards the door.

"Where are you going?" she called after him.

He raised a hand in farewell without turning back.

CHAPTER NINETY

"No great loss," Carl muttered.
This time, Zoe thought he was probably right.

CHAPTER NINETY-ONE

Tom stood in the briefing room, memories of eight months ago flooding back. The last raid had left him hyperventilating, hands on knees, unable to go in. He'd been saved only by the fact they hadn't needed to enter after all.

The tactical gear felt strange, like playing dress-up. But this was real. He'd even bet Nina that someone's gun would be fired tonight.

And oddly, he felt at peace with that.

"You OK?" Sharon from Ops appeared beside him, dressed head to toe in black AFO gear that looked like something from a sci-fi film. She'd been there for the warehouse raid, too, though only in support. Now she was a full AFO.

"Yeah." His voice trembled slightly, but that was expected.

"You scared?"

"A little."

"Good. I'm scared. Everyone here's a little scared. Being scared is what keeps you alive. Only an idiot wouldn't be scared." She paused. "Oh, and Tom?"

CHAPTER NINETY-ONE

"Yeah?"

"Don't worry. We've got your back."

Tom grinned as she walked away. He surveyed the room. Silver Command was having a quiet word with the AFO team leader in the corner. Morris Keane briefed Martinez and the other volunteers. The DI and the sarge had been ordered to stay at the Hub by the super, to help run the op with Silver. They'd grumbled but accepted it, knowing she was right. DI Whaley and DS Gaskill had gone upstairs to monitor everything – which probably meant watching Ralph Streeting through everyone's bodycams.

Good people, both on the ground and back here. They wouldn't take unnecessary risks. And Sharon had his back.

Tom looked down at the floor, grounding himself.

This was happening.

"Ready?" Silver called out, looking directly at Tom.

Tom nodded.

"Good. We've just been given the first location by our friend here." The way Silver said 'friend' while pointing at Streeting suggested he wouldn't mind if the former DI caught a stray bullet.

Tom stepped forward with Nina beside him as the metal door rolled up.

Six vehicles waited. Everyone had their assigned places for the first op. Nina gave him a thumbs up after his weak smile.

Nina would be with Streeting, at least for the first raid. They'd have an AFO and two Uniforms, including Martinez, whose sole job was watching Streeting. Tom would ride with Sharon and two more Uniforms, with vehicles ahead and behind carrying additional AFOs and Uniforms.

The minibus-style vehicle had a long side door that could fit three people at once.

Tom took one final look back before climbing in.

CHAPTER NINETY-TWO

Jeff had worked fast, but the link to the screen in the team room wasn't live.

"This way." He led Zoe upstairs, past the super's office where the closed door muffled Fiona's voice, no doubt arguing with Becca Grey or another supposed ally.

Four doors down was a small office with one desk and chairs lined up facing a wall.

A screen divided into two displays, then subdivided further as they entered: four, then eight. Each feed had codenames rather than actual names in the bottom corner – standard procedure for AFOs.

"Welcome to the fourth floor AV Room." Jeff handed her a scrap of paper. "You should be able to see everything from here. Take my number. Any problems, give me a call."

Aaron and Denise sat while Carl paced. Jeff left, closing the door behind him. Zoe took a seat next to Aaron.

There was nothing for them to see or hear yet. Just engine sounds, quiet chatter, and dark tactical vehicle interiors.

Her phone buzzed twice, then kept buzzing. She pulled it out, shook her head, and returned it to her pocket. Ten seconds later, it started again.

She answered on speaker. "David, what is it?"

"I'm at the third site," he said.

"Hang up," Carl snapped. "We don't have time for this."

Zoe ignored him. "What site? What do you mean?"

"Streeting. He said Red Lonning. In his list of six. That has to be the site your DS saw this morning."

"What the hell are you doing there, David?"

"We can't risk them clearing these places out when they realise that we're moving."

Carl turned from the screens, face pale. "Bloody hell."

"Now, Carl," said Randle. "You need to calm down."

"No," Zoe said. "Carl's right. You have to get out. If they see you—"

"Oh, have some guts, Zoe!" Randle shouted. "Sometimes you have to make things happen. Like we made all this happen. I'm not stupid. I'll just sit quietly and watch. Make sure nothing happens."

"Listen to me, David. If you put this operation—"

"I'm sorry, but it's too late. And I owe you this."

Zoe scanned the room. Aaron looked confused, Denise's jaw was clenched, and Carl was oozing pure disgust.

"Zoe?" Randle's voice came through. "You still there?"

"We're here."

"Good. Look, I know you won't believe me, but what I told you the other day. It's true."

"We don't have time for this."

"We have all the time we need, Zoe. We're just spectators now. This is the perfect moment. I need to make it up to you all. I should never have..."

CHAPTER NINETY-TWO

His voice trailed off. She could still hear his breathing, and passing vehicles.

"David?"

"Hello," he muttered, as if to himself.

"David?"

"What's this?"

Then the line went dead.

"Shit." Zoe called back immediately. After eight rings, it went to voicemail. Her second attempt went straight to messages.

"Shit."

"He's blown it," Carl said.

Maybe he had. Maybe Carter's people had found him. Maybe he was already dead.

Or maybe it was nothing. Just one of Streeting's dummy locations.

But Randle had been right about something. They were just spectators now.

All she could do was hope.

CHAPTER NINETY-THREE

Nina hadn't noticed the convoy arrive. They'd glided in silently, their windows dark. Her attention had been focused inside.

Streeting clutched his left thumb so tight in his right hand that when he released it, the imprints of his fingers remained in the skin. He looked like someone having second thoughts about the whole affair, which brought a smile to her face.

Martinez and the other Uniform kept their focus on Streeting and their surroundings. Nina hadn't been keeping track of where they were, but at least these two were.

Mario had introduced himself with a grin. His bushy black moustache matched his famous namesake. He sat back in his seat, eyes half-closed, his body bouncing with the movement of the car. If it hadn't been for the big black gun at his side, he might have been anyone.

"You ready?" Mario asked.

Nina realised they'd stopped. Through the window, she

saw a car park beside several low buildings, some walls with big windows, others without.

Just another business estate on the outskirts of Workington.

The door slid open. Mario stepped out first, scanning in each direction. Nina followed him to the back of the vehicle and watched the others emerge – the unnamed Uniform, then Streeting, looking greener than before, and finally Martinez.

She spotted the other vehicles, the other AFOs, Tom.

Everyone maintained silence. Everyone was in position. Nina's phone vibrated in her pocket. She ignored it.

A woman they'd called 'Blue' in the briefing moved from her vehicle towards one of the buildings. Two more followed.

Then Nina.

She walked forward, one step at a time, glancing back to see Streeting following, Martinez behind him, and Mario bringing up the rear. He crouched, one eye to the sight, scanning their surroundings. He broke his concentration for a split second to wink at her before returning to his sweep.

At the glass-panelled entrance, the formation changed. Mario took point with another AFO. Nina looked back, her heart pounding. What looked like an army's advance guard surrounded the vehicles: AFOs, Uniforms, and more waiting in vehicles with faces in windows and gun barrels poking through doors.

If she was about to enter a potentially hostile building, this was exactly what she wanted backing her up. She'd bet Tom no guns would be fired today, but that was just to keep him calm. She didn't believe it herself.

She took a deep breath and turned back to the entrance.

Mario and his colleague had already gone inside. The door was closed.

She held her breath.

The door opened, revealing Mario's big, bushy moustache. "Clear!" he shouted.

Nina moved forward. Streeting fell in alongside her, then moved ahead with Martinez just behind him. They went through the door to find…

Nothing.

The Uniforms' lights in front and behind illuminated a vast, empty space. Scuff marks on the ground showed where furniture had been – desks and chairs, she guessed. Holes in the walls suggested partitions. Now there were only white walls, a white floor and a white ceiling with empty light fittings, darkness everywhere beyond their lights.

More people entered. More lights. Nina felt herself relax and realised she'd pulled out her phone.

Her mum had tried to call. Typical Mrs Kapoor, always ringing at the worst possible moment.

CHAPTER NINETY-FOUR

For a minute, Denise could only make out chaos on the screens. Silver's calm voice over the shared comm was the only reassurance that everything was under control.

"Clear," came another call.

Two screens went dark before showing brief flashes of light against walls. The remaining screens showed the outside world, until two more switched to interior views.

The lack of activity and the repeated calls of 'Clear' rather than 'Get on the ground' told Denise everything she needed to know.

Carter had known they were coming. He'd cleared out.

Floodlights from the cars illuminated the space now. The room was as big as an aircraft hangar, but completely empty.

Denise exchanged a grimace with Aaron. DI Whaley shook his head while DI Finch bit her lip, looking ready to tear someone apart.

Ralph Streeting appeared on multiple screens from different angles. Denise felt her own surge of anger watching him. She didn't want there to be a bomb, but if there was, at least Streeting would be there to face it.

He walked to the centre of the room and continued to the far wall. His hand traced up from the floor until he found something, then he turned to face one of the cameras.

"They knew we were coming."

"No kidding," Nina's voice came through the comm.

Streeting turned to them. "This was a working office last time I was here. They've taken everything. Even the walls."

"The device?" Silver asked over the comm.

Streeting looked around, confused, then remembered he couldn't see Silver. "No. There was a niche. A little gap I drilled into a stud wall. It was round here."

"It's gone, then?"

"The wall it was in has gone, so I'm guessing, yes."

"This must have been recent." Denise turned to Aaron, who tilted his phone towards her. He was already requesting CCTV footage of the area for the past forty-eight hours.

"Come on," Streeting said. "No time to waste. We'll go straight to the second location."

He walked out of shot, reappearing on the external camera feeds.

"Which is?" someone asked.

"Red Lonning," Streeting replied as he walked away.

Three frustrated sighs echoed through the room.

"Shit," Denise muttered.

"Hello," DI Finch called out. "Can you hear me?"

Multiple voices responded, "Yes."

"You may have a problem at Red Lonning. David Randle's gone there."

There was a moment of stunned silence.

"He's done what?" Silver asked.

"He called. A few minutes ago. Said he was there."
"Well? What's he seen?"
"We don't know. We lost contact."
"Bloody hell," someone muttered.

Streeting reappeared on the screen. "You let him do it." He stormed up to one of the camera operators, jabbing his finger. "Why? He'll have screwed the whole—"

"Shut up," Silver commanded, and Streeting fell silent. "We'll just have to see. Come on. Let's move out."

CHAPTER NINETY-FIVE

"Was he like this earlier?" Tom pointed at Streeting.

Martinez shook her head. "No."

Tom didn't bother whispering. It wasn't like he had to pretend to like the man.

He'd switched with Nina, so she was with Sharon and the team, while he rode with Streeting, Martinez, and the AFO with the big moustache who called himself Mario. Tom wondered what had come first, the codename or the moustache.

Streeting was shaking, muttering to himself, cursing under his breath like someone with a compulsion. Tom hadn't wanted to ride with Streeting, but he had to prove something to himself: that he wasn't afraid of Ralph Streeting.

And that meant sitting two seats across from a man who wouldn't stop mouthing obscenities.

"What's that?" The other Uniform pointed out the window.

Tom couldn't see what had caught his attention. They'd

CHAPTER NINETY-FIVE

made their way south, now slowing as they reached Whitehaven's outskirts. Suddenly there were sirens.

"We're supposed to be going in silent, aren't we?" Tom asked.

"That's not us," Mario said.

"Fire engines," Martinez said.

The car turned and slowed. Tom saw it.

Smoke.

The door slid open, and the full scene hit him.

Everything was ablaze.

He'd driven past this place countless times. Nina had driven past it just that morning. A big board stood outside the warehouse – Tom could make out three letters, SON, at the end of one line. The rest had already gone, the warehouse burning steadily nearby.

Tom followed Martinez out of the car. Streeting's cursing had grown louder, and Tom felt tempted to join in.

There might have been a board outside the office block, too, but it was gone now. The office block itself was just a blackened inferno.

"We need—"

Something slammed into Tom's stomach, pushing him back against the car as an explosion thundered in his head. His eyes filled, and everything went silent except for a high-pitched ringing.

Where was he? Where was everyone else?

What the bloody hell had happened?

Stay calm.

Tom's eyes cleared momentarily. He opened them to a wave of black smoke.

He shut them, then blinked and tried again, managing a few seconds before they were forced closed.

An explosion. There had been an explosion.

A voice sounded in his ear.

"Get back in the car."

He turned and felt his way back, heard movement, and found a seat to slump into.

"Is everyone—?" he said.

"All units, welfare check." Silver's voice came over the comm.

They went through the roll call, name by name. Tom waited his turn.

"DC Willis, clear," he said.

A minute passed.

"Roger," Silver said. "No injuries. Update, please."

"Major explosion. We don't know what—"

"Gas," Streeting cut in. "Jenson & Marley stored their gas supply here. Carter must have triggered it. Bloody Randle."

"This place was being emptied this morning," Nina said over the comm.

"There probably wasn't anything there anyway."

"Any sign of David Randle?" Silver asked.

Four voices responded: "No."

"Car," another voice said. "Grey Astra."

"That's his," DI Whaley said.

"Site three, please," Silver said. "Location?"

"Shouldn't we wait for the fire crews?" Nina asked.

"No. Location, please."

Streeting gave the address, and the car started moving. The door slid open, and Nina jumped in.

"What?" Tom asked.

"Out you go. You've had your fun. My turn now."

"Fun?"

"Out."

CHAPTER NINETY-FIVE

He nodded and slipped from the car, straight into the open door of the vehicle beside them. Sharon smiled at him, and he found himself smiling back.

Mario was fine. Mario would have looked after him if needed.

But Sharon had his back. She'd said so.

He was better off with Sharon.

CHAPTER NINETY-SIX

"Where... What?" Zoe scanned the faces in the room, searching for answers.

Carl knew the unspoken question before she'd even formed the words. "I don't know. We don't know. Maybe he's fine."

Hopefully not, he thought. David Randle ranked low on his list of concerns right now. He turned back to the live feed, showing the interior of various vehicles, catching occasional glimpses of faces.

At least no one was injured.

He glanced at Denise. She'd winced when it happened, taking a step back and drawing long, measured breaths. She leaned against the wall now, as if it was the only thing keeping her upright.

"You OK?" he asked for the second time in two minutes.

"Fine. Let's just—"

The door banged open as Detective Superintendent Kendrick strode in.

CHAPTER NINETY-SIX

"Don't stand," she said, not noticing they were already on their feet. Her eyes went to the screen. "Anything?"

"Nothing good," Zoe replied.

Carl felt conflicted. Part of him wanted to comfort her, while another part wanted to shake some sense into her.

"Well, sorry to add to the shit pile, but Carter and his lawyer have pulled some strings. I've just had the ACC's office on the phone again."

Zoe's sigh seemed to drain all the energy from her body. "They want us to let him out, right?"

"They're demanding immediate release," the super confirmed.

"They can't do that," Zoe pointed out.

"Technically, no. In practice, well, it's the ACC, Zoe. They can do what they bloody want. Unless something new's come in, Carter's about to walk. And there's nothing new, right?"

She turned to the screen, showing only empty vehicles.

"Come on, then," Zoe said, heading for the door behind the super.

Aaron Keyes stood staring after her, shaking his head.

Carl felt a tug on his arm and turned to find Denise's face inches from his.

"We're still looking into them, right?" Her voice was barely audible.

"Who?"

"Us. PSD. Looking into them. Those people."

He nodded, noticing Aaron frowning at them.

Not his business. And that was probably best for Aaron Keyes. What he didn't know wouldn't hurt him.

"We'll talk about that another time," Carl whispered.

Denise nodded in response.

CHAPTER NINETY-SEVEN

Zoe knocked and entered Interview Room Four. Myron Carter leaned back in his chair, a smile curling his mouth.

Clarissa Bexley sat beside him, her gaze fixed straight ahead with her usual severe, disapproving expression.

"Has someone got themselves into trouble?" Carter's eyes glinted.

"What?"

"You look flustered. Upset. Is someone making you do something you don't want to?"

Zoe forced a smile and studied the man before her. He wore a different suit today. Navy pinstripe with precise lines, paired with a crisp white shirt.

She noted his freshly shaved face before turning to Bexley.

"Fine. You probably knew it before I did, but we'll be commencing the process of your client's release shortly."

Bexley leaned forward, elbows on the table. "Shortly?"

"Releasing Myron Carter back onto the streets isn't the

only thing I have to do right now." Zoe smiled. "I'll leave you to... to get on with things."

She hadn't approached the table or taken a seat. All that remained was to turn and walk out.

"This isn't over," she said, striding from the room. At the custody desk, she instructed Clive Moor to begin the release process.

"No big rush, though."

Clive nodded.

She sprinted up three flights of stairs to the AV Room.

"Are they there yet?" She burst through the door.

Four heads swivelled towards her.

"No," Carl said. "Nearly."

Zoe looked at the super. "You're sticking around?"

Fiona nodded. "Last throw of the dice, Zoe. You never know. We might actually get that double six. And if we do, I wouldn't want to miss it."

Zoe glanced at the bank of screens showing alternating patterns of darkness and light as cars sped through the late morning sunshine, then back at Fiona's face. The super looked as nervous as the rest of them. Tense, excited, just the right side of terrified.

But she still seemed to think they might get that double six.

At least someone was feeling optimistic.

CHAPTER NINETY-EIGHT

Nina wanted to kick herself.

She wished she could rewind time by ten minutes, just long enough to stop herself from saying "Shouldn't we wait for the fire crews?" in front of everyone on the op. But since she couldn't, self-reproach would have to do.

When no one was looking, of course.

She glanced around the car. Streeting was muttering curses about David Randle, hoping he'd gone up in flames. He probably had.

No great loss, she thought, remembering DI Whaley's words as Randle had stormed out of the briefing.

Martinez and the other officer maintained their focus, as they should. Mario frowned at her.

"You OK?"

She nodded. He wouldn't remember her stupid comment, and if he did, he'd dismiss it as meaningless. He wouldn't know *why* she'd said it.

Tom might figure it out though. She'd need to watch for that.

CHAPTER NINETY-EIGHT

Mario's concerned gaze prevented her from properly berating herself. She settled for mentally calling herself an idiot.

What had she been thinking?

The car slowed, turned, accelerated again. She barely registered their location.

But she knew exactly what had been going through her mind.

I look pretty cool in all this ops gear. I look pretty damn sexy in black. Wouldn't be such a bad thing if Skip from the fire crew turned up and saw me like this.

At least she hadn't said that part out loud. "Shouldn't we wait for the fire crews?" had been bad enough.

"You sure you're OK?" Mario asked, still frowning.

She nodded again.

"Look lively, then." He gestured towards the door.

It was open. They'd stopped. Mario dropped out onto the ground. Nina scanned the car once more before following, glancing back as the others emerged. First the unnamed Uniform, then Streeting, then Martinez.

No dramatic burning building this time. Just a car park, mostly full of ordinary vehicles, with a few people walking towards the office building Streeting indicated.

"It's in there," he said.

"Where?" Nina asked.

"I'll show you. I—"

A scream cut through the air. Nina ducked and spun around to see a woman by a neon pink Ford Fiesta staring at Mario and his gun.

More shouts erupted as others spotted the armed officers. The woman screamed again as she noticed two more AFOs.

Someone needed to take control. The situation was

spiralling. Her head throbbed – probably from the Red Lonning explosion, though that hideous Fiesta wasn't helping.

Her phone buzzed. Silver's voice came through her earpiece.

"Move out," he ordered.

Blue led the advance toward the building. Civilians backed away as they registered not just the three officers in front, but Nina, Streeting, Martinez, the other officer, Mario, and the AFOs.

Nina maintained her pace and kept quiet.

Another scream pierced the air, not quite human this time.

Someone else would handle it. She focused on their target: a glass door with a trembling security guard inside, his walkie-talkie in one hand, the other raised half-heartedly to stop them.

The inhuman scream grew closer. Irritated, Nina turned to see a black vehicle bearing down on her.

She froze.

Absurdly, she found herself staring at the approaching Mercedes badge, thinking black was a much better choice than neon pink.

The car swerved left and stopped.

Through the open window, something dark shifted in the shadows.

Nina heard shouts from Blue's team behind her. Ahead stood Streeting, Martinez, and the other officer.

The shouting ceased. In the sudden silence, the shadow moved, light glinting off a gun barrel.

Nina's body moved before her mind caught up. No one had pushed her – her instincts had taken over.

CHAPTER NINETY-EIGHT

She slammed into Streeting, throwing him down and covering him with her body as gunfire shattered the silence.

CHAPTER NINETY-NINE

Jesus Christ.

Aaron looked from feed to feed, struggling to make sense of the chaos unfolding before him. The audio channels erupted with overlapping shouts.

Denise Gaskill's voice cut through from within the room. "That wasn't..."

"Gunfire," Detective Superintendent Kendrick interjected.

Silver's usually steady voice cracked with urgency. "Update from scene, please!"

"Don't move!" came another voice.

"Suspect down!"

"What about Nina?" Aaron heard himself shout, his own voice surprising him. *What about Nina?*

"I'm good," Nina's voice came through the comm.

"Urgent update from scene!" Silver commanded, initiating the roll call.

Aaron's tension eased at Nina's words. *I'm good.* He waited through the roll call, each name confirming everyone was safe.

Streeting's voice came through the comm. "Bit bruised. Someone could do with losing a bit of weight."

"Sod off," Nina retorted.

The situation became clearer as Silver continued to give instructions, pulling back unarmed officers until they were confident everything was safe. One of the AFOs had spotted and neutralised the shooter before they could fire. Aaron recognised Sharon's voice downplaying the praise from her colleagues. She'd be drinking free for weeks after this.

"Suspect?" Silver asked.

"I've got her," Blue responded.

DI Finch pointed to a screen showing a black car. A woman with dyed red hair slumped in the seat, her hands visible and empty.

"Medical on its way," someone reported.

"How bad?"

"She'll live."

DI Finch leaned forward. "I know her."

"Get me a bloody doctor," the woman demanded.

"Well, well," DI Finch said. "She can speak English after all."

The room fell silent as DI Finch explained. "She's called Kaciaryna. That's what she claims. We picked her up last year. Warehouse raid, trafficked women. She posed as one of the victims and escaped. Pretended she couldn't understand English."

"Can someone get me a doctor?" Kaciaryna repeated, but Blue had already moved away.

"We're going in," Blue announced.

Aaron watched through the feeds as the team entered past a cowering security guard and terrified office workers.

Streeting led the way with Nina close behind him, refusing to let anyone between her and Streeting. After Carter's attempt on his life, her protectiveness made sense.

They moved through an open-plan office where workers lay face-down, hands over their heads. The team continued into a corridor and small room, where Streeting approached a conference table.

"Give me a hand," Streeting said. The other uniformed officer stepped forward, and together they pulled the table apart.

Streeting reached into the gap between the halves. The tension in the room was palpable.

His hand emerged holding a small black box, a smile spreading across his face. Aaron grabbed his phone.

"Clive?"

"Alright, Aaron?" Clive Moor, the custody sergeant, replied. "What can I do for you?"

"Has Carter left yet?"

"Nope. Still being processed."

"Good. Do me a favour, will you? Make it slow."

"Something happened?"

"I'll find out shortly. But we might just have rolled a double six."

CHAPTER ONE HUNDRED

"She'll be OK," Martinez said. "Needs blood, but no major organs hit, by the look of it. Paramedics are on their way."

Tom stood at the open car door, surveying the scene outside. "It's not her I'm worried about. I've never shot anyone myself, but I don't think I'd feel like this afterwards."

Ten feet away, Sharon the AFO sat back against one of the vehicles, her head down as she was violently sick on the ground. Those of her colleagues who weren't tending to the woman she'd shot stood around her, offering sympathetic arms on shoulders and smiles when she looked up. They grimaced at each other when she looked away.

Silver had confirmed the op was over. Tom felt relief wash over him, but there was a tiny bit of disappointment, too. He'd won the bet. There had been gunfire. But no one had shot at him.

He shook his head. If he was upset that no one had shot at him, it was probably a good thing the op was over.

Mario slipped in beside Tom and slid the door shut. "Oh,

she'll definitely be OK. It's the adrenaline. Bloody good shot, too. She saved your bacon, that's for sure."

Tom turned to see Nina nodding in agreement.

Behind her, Streeting shrugged.

Bastard wouldn't know gratitude if it hit him in the face.

Tom's phone buzzed in his pocket. He pulled it out and answered on the speakers. "Boss."

"Is Nina OK?" DI Finch asked.

Nina leaned forward from the row behind. The arranged order of things, who was supposed to be in what car, it was all shot now. *Like that woman*, Tom thought, and giggled.

Maybe Sharon wasn't the only one suffering the effects of too much adrenaline.

"I'm fine," Nina said. "We've got the device."

"Play it," said the boss as the car started up and they began to make their way back towards the Hub. There was an urgency in her voice that dried up the laughter in Tom's throat.

"What's it worth?" Streeting said. He was still holding the thing.

Tom turned around, reached back, and pulled it out of the former DI's hands before he knew what was happening.

It was tiny. So small he could close his palm around it and barely feel it. It was matt black, broadly cuboid, and heavier than it looked. Apart from four tiny black buttons, each raised no more than a millimetre above the thing, its surface was unbroken.

"Come on," urged the DI's voice.

Tom looked meaningfully at Streeting. "Well?"

Streeting smiled back at him. "I guess I've got a little more leverage than—"

Tom turned away and leaned forward to talk to the

CHAPTER ONE HUNDRED

driver. "You can stop here. One of our passengers will be making his own way back."

"You can't do that," Streeting pointed out.

"True," Tom admitted. "But we don't have to put you back where we got you from."

"What do you mean?"

"There are plenty of places we can put a suspect on remand. Some of them are less secure than others."

The colour drained from Streeting's face.

"OK," Streeting said. "Point taken. Here. That one to play." He indicated the third of the four buttons. "The one at the end to stop. And the other two just rewind and go forward. Recording is automated."

"There you are," Tom said. "That wasn't so difficult, was it?"

CHAPTER ONE HUNDRED ONE

Standing in the AV room, a few doors from her office, Fiona Kendrick heard her heart pounding.

She glanced at the wall to her left. Her desk was through there, buried under papers, data reports, budget analyses and the bloody IOPC. All politics and bureaucracy.

But in here, none of that mattered. In here, it was pure policing. She'd forgotten how good that felt. When things fell into place, when the first dice landed six up and you waited for the second one to stop rolling.

A buzzing noise filled the room.

"What's that?" Zoe Finch asked.

"Static," Tom Willis said through the comm.

"Take it forward," Ralph Streeting instructed.

Fiona watched the feed intently. Someone's fingers tapped on the device.

Tom's fingers. He'd stepped up lately. Nina Kapoor, too. They'd all risen to the challenge.

Tom tapped again. The static persisted, with something else underneath – a clicking noise, quiet, fast, irregular.

CHAPTER ONE HUNDRED ONE

"That's a keyboard," Fiona said.

"Carter's typing," Streeting confirmed.

A liquid sound filtered through.

"Coffee." Streeting's voice was matter-of-fact. "He gets through about six cups every morning."

"Not a complete monster, then," Zoe said.

Fiona smiled. She was enjoying this, but they still had nothing usable. And Carter would be leaving any minute.

"This is no good," Nina Kapoor said over the comm.

"It'll be there," Streeting replied. "Just be patient. Take it forward again."

Tom repeated the sequence. This time, a voice emerged.

"Leave it with me," Streeting's voice came through the recording.

"That you?" Tom asked.

"Yes. You went too far forward. Go back."

Tom adjusted and hit play again. After a moment's silence, another voice spoke.

"That's the man." Carter's voice, clear as day.

"You're sure?" Streeting asked on the recording.

"Yes. The one I pointed out to you last night. Parlick."

"And you definitely want to do this?"

"Yes." Carter's impatience was evident. "Do it. Use his boat or something. I want to send a message."

"A message?"

"Yeah. If you work for me, you don't talk to the cops. No exceptions."

Fiona turned to Zoe, finding the DI's eyes already on her.

"Well?" Zoe asked.

Fiona smiled. "I don't care what Joseph Carghillie and his people think. Get downstairs. Get that bastard back here."

CHAPTER ONE HUNDRED TWO

Zoe found herself in the custody suite, standing by the desk without remembering how she'd got there. She scanned the area. No Carter. No Bexley. The only person in sight was the PC she'd seen earlier – Parton, she thought, not Stones – walking towards her with a grin.

"Can I help you, DI Finch?"

"Carter. Where is he?"

His face creased into a frown. "We were told to process his release. Is there a problem?"

Zoe forced a smile. "No problem. Just need to know where he is."

Parton shrugged and pointed towards the main entrance. "Only left a couple of minutes ago. Might still be around."

Zoe turned and ran down the corridor. Footsteps kept pace beside her. She slowed for the door, pushed it open and glanced left.

Denise wore an expression of sheer determination as she moved. She caught Zoe's glance and grinned. "Come on."

The entrance area held fifteen or twenty people, but

CHAPTER ONE HUNDRED TWO

none were Myron Carter. Zoe scanned the room methodically, left to right and back again.

"Come on," Denise said again, moving towards the main doors.

They stepped out together into the cold air. The wind hit them, along with sporadic, heavy drops of rain.

"There," said Denise. A hundred yards away, two figures standing by a large grey car.

Zoe ran.

The figures became clearer – the shorter one talking, the taller one nodding with a bored expression, hand reaching for the driver's door.

"Myron Carter," she shouted from twenty yards away.

They turned. Clarissa Bexley's frown was visible even from this distance. The lawyer had been here before, in this very spot, watching her client get re-arrested after walking free. That was over two years ago. Zoe wondered if Bexley remembered.

She slowed to catch her breath. Denise stopped beside her, breathing hard.

"Myron Carter," said Denise, then turned to Zoe.

This was Zoe's investigation. Zoe's arrest.

"You're under arrest," Zoe said.

"Not this again." Bexley stepped forward as Carter backed away, his eyes darting between Zoe and Denise.

"You're under arrest," Zoe repeated.

Bexley walked right up to her. "You played a good game, DI Finch. But you lost. You've been instructed to release my client. This is nonsense. You have no new evidence. No grounds for this. Please stop harassing my client."

She stepped back with a confident nod.

"You're under arrest for conspiracy to murder Victor Parlick."

Carter's face fell. Bexley jerked as if slapped. Zoe savoured the moment as Denise began the formal caution.

She turned to look back at the building, her gaze drawn to a particular window on the fourth floor. Even through the dirty glass and Cumbrian rain, she could see Fiona Kendrick was smiling.

CHAPTER ONE HUNDRED THREE

NINA WASN'T sure why she'd been chosen to make the call, but she didn't mind.

"Who's that?" she asked.

"This is Skip. I'm responsible for the—"

Her heart missed a beat. "Oh, I know who you are." She looked around the team room at the sea of confused faces. "Fire chief," she mouthed.

"Who's that?"

"Cumbria Police. Nina Kapoor. DC. I mean DS."

"I remember you," said Skip. "Didn't we—"

"Can you tell me about the fire?" No need for everyone to know about his attending the fire at her place. Or what state her bedroom had been in.

He outlined the basics. The fire at Red Lonning – Site Two, they were calling it – was under control but not yet out.

"As it happens, I was just about to report this. We've found what we think are human remains."

The whispering around her in the team room stopped.

The boss stepped back, bumping against the spare desk. Nina watched her eyes meet DI Whaley's, something complicated passing between them.

She wouldn't get involved in that. If David Randle was dead, as people kept saying, it was no great loss.

She thanked Skip and took down his direct line while everyone else's attention turned to the recording they'd managed to copy before entering it into evidence. She joined the others at Tom's computer, straining to hear the words that would surely spell the end for Myron Carter.

"Nine hundred Euros sounds steep," said Dean Somerville's voice.

"You won't get girls like this cheaper anywhere else," replied Carter.

Nina's stomach churned even as triumph surged through her. Carter couldn't wriggle out of this.

Tom tapped his screen and skipped to another section.

"When can you have her delivered?" Mick Halfpenny's voice made Nina freeze.

Mick Halfpenny. The man who'd captured her, tied her up, put her in a bag. The man who would have killed her if he'd had the chance.

The man who had killed Daria Petrescu.

"She'll be there, don't you worry," said Carter. "Give me a day and I'll have the details. And don't forget, it's important to me that this works out for our mutual friend."

Tom glanced past the antimacassar on Nina's chair to meet her eyes, then tapped his screen again. That was enough Mick Halfpenny.

Over the next ten minutes, they heard Carter discussing arms dealing with Lucas Wright, the man they'd arrested for Noah Cane's murder. They heard Carter and Streeting

CHAPTER ONE HUNDRED THREE

discussing keeping Dean Somerville quiet after his arrest, and trying to work out who from within Carter's organisation was betraying him.

"I don't want to hear a name," Carter said, "unless you can follow it with the words 'is dead'."

Tom hit pause.

"Was that what I think it was?" asked Denise Gaskill.

"Yes," replied Aaron. "That was the order to kill Bobby."

Nina saw the same mix of emotions in his face. A victory, but hard to hear.

Aaron and Bobby Silver had been friends, after all.

Tom hit play again. They waded through static and irrelevance before another voice blared out.

"What is his name?" A female voice, heavily accented.

"Morrigan," replied Carter. "No, that's not it. I don't know. He's Ralph's number two."

"*Was* Ralph's number two," the woman corrected. Nina had heard that voice recently.

Carter laughed. "Anyway, I don't want old Ralph getting too comfortable."

"What do you mean? He is in prison. In some cell in some horrible place. It will not be comfortable."

"I mean that I don't want him forgetting that I can get to him whenever I want. Or if not him, people close to him. Get rid of Morrigan. That should send the right message."

Tom stopped the recording and turned to look at Nina. She could see in his face that he'd realised the same thing she had. There were things they could do now, downstairs or here in the team room. Questioning Carter, liaising with Stella's team, talking to the CPS, figuring out what to do about Ralph Streeting. Important work right here at the Hub.

But there were other important things that couldn't be forgotten in all the excitement.

Nina walked to the door, Tom a step behind her.

"Sorry, boss," she said. "Tom and I need to sort something out."

CHAPTER ONE HUNDRED FOUR

The woman in the hospital bed frowned as Tom and Nina approached. She lifted an arm, pointing in their direction.

"You," she said. "I have met you before."

A man stood in the room with her. Tom couldn't see a weapon, but he had little doubt one was concealed somewhere.

Nina turned to the man. "Can you give us some privacy?"

The man nodded and stepped out. They weren't in danger from Kaciaryna. She had half a dozen tubes snaking around her body and wouldn't last ten minutes without whatever was being pumped in and out of them.

"Yes," Kaciaryna said. "You were at the warehouse, both of you." She fixed her gaze on Tom. Despite the tubes, armed guards outside, and her current helpless state, those cold blue eyes made him shrink back. "You were sick, weren't you?"

"No," Tom said. It was true – he hadn't been sick during the warehouse raid months ago when they'd found the trafficked women and Kaciaryna hiding among them. He'd had a panic attack, but there was no need to mention that. "You're being interviewed under caution. Do you want a lawyer?"

"What is the point?" Kaciaryna asked.

"What's your name?" Nina said.

"You can call me Kat. All my friends do."

Nina tapped into the team inbox. "Please listen to this."

The recording played: "He is in prison. In some cell in some horrible place. It will not be comfortable."

"Is that you?" Nina asked.

"It is me," Kat confirmed.

Nina played the rest of the conversation.

"The other person in the recording," Nina said. "Who's that?"

"It's Myron Carter."

"And the topic of the conversation?"

"Myron Carter is instructing me to kill Detective Sergeant Kieran Mulligan. Myron has trouble with names, sometimes."

"And did you?" Tom asked.

Those cold blue eyes turned back to him. "Did I what?"

"Did you kill Kieran Mulligan?"

"Oh, yes. I'm afraid I did. I have seen you before that, you know."

"You have?"

"You would not have seen me. You were in the car behind. I was in the car with Ralph. I saw you in the mirror."

"After..." Tom said.

"After Ralph had shot Bobby Silver, yes. That woman and her damned parrot."

Tom pushed away a smile. She was right about the parrot. He glanced at Nina to find her watching him.

"Would you like to do the honours, DC Willis?" she said.

"Certainly, DS Kapoor." He turned back to the bed. "Kat... Er, what's your full name?"

"Kaciaryna Ilinich."

He nodded. "Kaciaryna Ilinich—"

"Oh, bloody hell," Nina interrupted, staring at her phone with wide eyes.

"What is it?" Tom asked.

"Look." She passed him the phone.

It was a text from Nina's mother: *Nina Kapoor, for an experienced detective sergeant you really are a bloody idiot. I wasn't trying to set you up with him. I was just trying to tell you, as delicately as I could, that I have been dating him myself.*

"That's the first time she's shown any interest in a man since Dad died," Nina said. "Ten years."

"About bloody time," Tom replied.

"About bloody time," Nina agreed.

"Hello?" Kaciaryna called. "I am still here."

"Sorry," Tom said, turning back to her. "Kaciaryna Ilinich, I am arresting you in connection with the murder of Kieran Mulligan."

CHAPTER ONE HUNDRED FIVE

"Look," Carl said. "I don't want to argue with you. I just want to understand."

They were in Zoe's office. Zoe sat behind the desk, Carl opposite her. Like normal people having a normal workplace discussion. But Carl knew there was nothing normal about this.

She wouldn't meet his eye.

"Understand what?" she said.

"Zoe, please. Just look at me."

She looked up, her eyes wet.

"I know this is about David Randle," he said.

She shrugged.

He wanted to shake her. "Please help me to understand why this man's death seems to mean more to you than the deaths of all the decent, innocent people you've investigated over the years."

She gazed out at the rain-soaked fells, where the setting sun picked out lines and shadows with its dying rays. Then she looked back.

"I know," she said. "It's ridiculous, isn't it?"

Carl felt something melt inside him.

"I know it doesn't make sense, Carl. I know we're not going to agree on what he was like at the end, on whether he meant what he said about regretting it all, and even then, I know he wasn't a good man. And even if he had been, he wasn't someone I ever actually liked."

Carl felt a smile edge onto his lips. Zoe gave a weak laugh.

"He was a real arsehole, wasn't he?" she said.

"A real arsehole."

"He was patronising."

He raised an eyebrow. "Corrupt."

"Devious."

"Greedy."

She frowned. "A bad, bad boss."

"A selfish, calculating, sneaky bastard."

"And," she concluded, "he was the sort of misogynist who hides in plain sight, pretending not to be. But he was still someone I worked with. Someone who helped, in the end."

They could argue about that until the end of time, Carl thought. No point starting now. Not when they were finally eye-to-eye on everything else. He waited.

"And there's something else," she said.

"What?"

"Now he's gone, how the hell are we going to find Olivia Bagsby?"

He frowned. Olivia would help the case, certainly. But now they had these recordings, her evidence wouldn't be the crucial plank it had once seemed. Just the last nail in Carter's coffin.

"I don't—"

"It's not the case, Carl. It's her. She needs to know what's happened. And she needs to know Carter's in custody. She's safe now."

"Is she?"

Zoe smiled and shrugged again.

"OK, maybe not. But she's closer than she's been for years. And now David's gone, I don't see how I can find her."

"Ah," said Carl.

A short silence fell.

Zoe turned away from the window, back to face him, frowning. "Ah?"

"Yes," he said.

"Yes, what?"

"Olivia Bagsby. Finding her. I might just be able to help with that."

CHAPTER ONE HUNDRED SIX

"I can't just click my fingers and make him appear, DS Keyes." DCI Carnegie folded her arms across her chest.

Aaron stood in the reception area at Durranhill, knowing full well that in this place, Kiki Carnegie was as close to God as they had. "But he's coming, yes?"

"Yes."

"You've processed the release?"

She sighed. "Bloody hell. Yes. We've processed the release. Christian Ives will be a free man within the next twenty minutes."

Aaron thanked her and sat down as she walked away. Twenty minutes. He looked at his watch.

Twenty minutes was fine.

You find me another killer, she'd told Nina, *I'll let Ives go*.

They'd found that other killer. They had the woman under armed guard at the West Cumberland Hospital and on tape from her hospital bed, confessing to the murder, far more convincingly than Ives had. In all the chaos and excitement, Ives might have been forgotten, but Nina and Tom had realised what the voice on Streeting's device meant. Realised it proved what they'd believed all along.

Christian Ives was an innocent man.

Innocent or not, Christian Ives kept Aaron waiting twice as long as Kiki Carnegie's twenty minutes. Just enough time for Sammy Knight to walk past, spot Aaron, do a double take, and carry on walking as if nothing had happened. In the past, Aaron might have assumed it was racism or homophobia, and it was always possible it was.

But some people were just arseholes, and Sammy Knight was one of them.

When Ives finally emerged, he shuffled alone into the entrance hall with fresh bruises, peering around as if expecting another beating. Aaron stood and approached him, palms out, and saw the man visibly relax.

"Come on, Christian. Let's get you home."

Ives nodded but didn't speak. Aaron stepped towards the door, realising after a few steps that Ives wasn't with him.

He hadn't stopped. He just couldn't keep up.

It was impossible to know what they'd done to him – no doubt there were plenty of undetectable injuries underneath the visible ones. But he was exhausted, worn out by the questions and the beatings and the knowledge that in just a few days, his life had fallen apart.

Aaron waited, then took the man's arm. Together, they approached the door. The sensors weren't working, so the heavy glass panel had to be pulled open. Aaron let go of Ives to manage the door, uncertain if the man could stay upright without help.

A diminutive figure stepped smartly past them and pulled the door open, then waited. As Aaron stepped through, he turned and recognised the woman.

CHAPTER ONE HUNDRED SIX

"Song?"

"That's DI Hae-Won, Aaron." She smiled. "Haven't seen you in an age."

"I've been busy." Aaron's eyes darted to Ives.

DI Song Hae-Won nodded. "We must do this again some time." She stepped back inside and let the door fall shut.

It took five minutes to cross the short distance to Aaron's car, anxiety building over the final yards. Twenty minutes might have been fine, but forty-five minutes was a long time to leave someone sitting in a car.

Not that she was a dog. He'd left the window open. She had water and an egg sandwich. He'd have to get rid of the smell.

"Mother?" Christian Ives' face contorted into something that was close to a smile.

Matilda Ives patted the seat beside her.

"They let you go?" he said. "It's really you?"

"It's me. Come on, Christian. This nice man just made me a lovely egg sandwich. I'm sure he can find something for you."

Aaron slipped into the driver's seat and glanced in his mirror to see the smile breaking out on Ives' face.

Good. Let the man relax. Let him have something good in his life. Aaron would have to tell him about Gustavo before they got where they were heading. Half an hour's joy was the least he deserved.

CHAPTER ONE HUNDRED SEVEN

It couldn't have gone better, but now Denise was home, the pain had returned with a vengeance.

Excitement and painkillers had kept it at bay during Myron Carter's arrest – the second one, the one that counted. That had made everything worthwhile.

Her whole body ached. She'd taken four pills and more than a splash of whisky, yet the pain persisted.

Building up a tolerance wouldn't be ideal. Not when she was ready to get back to work.

She settled in front of the TV and selected a historical drama with beautiful costumes. Simple enough to follow, she thought, but within five minutes she'd lost track of the characters and plot.

Work consumed her thoughts. Not just today's success, but the work still to come.

The projects. The people she needed to investigate. The lies and corruption she had to expose. She'd spent months confined to bed rest and sitting around. Time to get moving.

She paced through the house – living room to kitchen, up

the stairs, into each room, and back down. Three circuits. She sat down but found herself up again within minutes.

The doorbell rang. She checked the camera app on her phone and her breath caught.

Bloody hell.

She stared at the woman's face in partial silhouette against the garage opposite, debating whether to answer or retreat upstairs and pretend she wasn't home.

But Denise couldn't avoid her forever. She walked to the door, removed the chain, and pulled it open.

The woman strode past her into the hallway, turning to meet Denise's gaze.

"You're looking well. Better than I expected, anyway."

Denise remained silent.

The woman's eyes scanned the room until they found their target. Her smile widened as she turned back to Denise.

"I see you got my flowers. I thought maybe you'd call."

"Why should I call?"

"Come on, Denise." The woman tilted her head in that once-endearing way, her lustrous waves of hair falling to one side.

How long had it been?

"What do you mean, 'come on'?"

"Can't we at least be friends?"

Denise let out a harsh laugh. "I don't think so. I think it's a bit late for that, Sinead."

CHAPTER ONE HUNDRED EIGHT

Darkness had fallen over the hills, and the moon hid behind clouds which spat occasional bursts of cold rain.

Zoe had been watching the house for twenty minutes. A faint light glowed in a window at the far end of the building, but nothing suggested movement.

Carl might be wrong. Randle could have realised he was being followed, led Carl into the middle of nowhere, then doubled back. Or Olivia might have fled already. Anyone could be in that house. Or no one.

But Zoe could feel it. Someone was there.

She took a breath and had just slid her car into gear when her phone rang.

Ignore it.

The display showed *Nicholas*. She glanced back at the house. If Olivia was there, she wouldn't leave on foot. And the only road out was the one Zoe was on.

She tapped to answer, feeling the warmth of her son's voice fill the car.

"What's up? Big stake-out?"

CHAPTER ONE HUNDRED EIGHT

"How did you know?"

"Very funny. You're sat in your office staring at half a dozen piles of papers, aren't you?"

Zoe closed her eyes and smiled. "Something like that. How are you?"

"Good. Great, actually. Listen, Mum, I've got news."

"Go on."

"I'm moving back to England."

Her heart leapt. "What? When? Where?"

He laughed. "One thing at a time, Mum. You know it's not been the same here since Mo moved away. And you know I mentioned postgrad? I was looking to go somewhere else for that anyway. An opportunity came up, and I applied. Didn't actually think I'd get it."

"You need to have more faith in yourself."

"Well, maybe. Because I got it. The actual course doesn't start for nearly a year, but I can head down there any time from January and start research."

"Where?"

"That's the thing, Mum. It's not really any closer to you than bloody Stirling is. It's in Exeter."

She smiled. From what she knew, the South West was the sort of area Nicholas would love. Warmer than Scotland. Warmer than Cumbria. And she could visit Lesley when she was down there.

They chatted for another fifteen minutes until she glanced up and saw the light was out.

"Shit."

"What?"

"One of those piles of paper needs urgent attention. Can we talk tomorrow?"

"You bet."

She could still hear his voice echoing in the car as she slid into gear and crunched up towards the house.

Still no light.

She stopped on the road. No one would get past, but it wasn't exactly busy here. She pulled the handbrake – the slopes here were unforgiving if you forgot – and stepped out.

The rain had stopped. No birdsong, no cars. Wind rushed through distant trees, and the clouds parted, allowing weak moonlight to fall onto the house.

It was bleak. Old stone, weathered and replaced over generations. People had lived lives out here, hard lives. Short ones, probably.

She stepped up to the ancient wooden door, tapped, and took a step back.

Nothing happened. She tried again, louder.

Still nothing. After a minute, she bent down, put her mouth to the wood, and shouted. "Olivia, it's me!"

The wind picked up, whistling past, sending scree tumbling down the road behind her.

"Olivia! It's Zoe Finch! You need to open the door!"

She put her ear to the door and listened. There – footsteps from inside.

"Olivia!"

As the clouds parted and moonlight picked out the building's shape, a voice came from inside. "Who is it?"

"It's Zoe Finch."

"I don't believe you. How do I know you're not lying? How do I know it's not someone pretending to be Zoe Finch?"

Zoe took out her phone, found the torch, shone it onto her face. "Look out of the window!" She moved along to stand outside where she'd seen the light earlier. Movement came from within as Olivia went from door to window.

"We've arrested Carter. We've charged him with murder. He can't get you now, Olivia."

"Where's David?" Olivia's voice came through the window.

How could she answer that from the wrong side of the glass?

Zoe shook her head.

There was movement before the door opened. Olivia Bagsby stepped outside.

"Seriously?"

Zoe nodded.

She stepped towards Olivia Bagsby – the woman she'd been trying to find for two long years. In the moonlight, she could see the shock on the other woman's face.

"No," Olivia whispered.

It was a quiet protest, more doubt than defiance, but Zoe felt it just the same. She took another step, and Olivia moved towards her. Then another step, then a third, and they were together. Tears fell from Olivia's eyes.

Zoe opened her arms and held the other woman as she wept.

I hope you have enjoyed reading *The Port*. The story continues in *The Marsh*. You can also read about Zoe's move north to Cumbria in the novella *The Castle*, which is free as ebook or audio to members of my book club at rachelmclean.com/the-castle-book or you can buy the paperback from book retailers.

Happy Reading!
Rachel

THE CASTLE, A PREQUEL NOVELLA

DI Zoe Finch has a big decision to make

Will she stay in Birmingham, clinging to the wreckage of her beloved team as it breaks up and leaves her behind? Or will she follow her partner Carl to Cumbria, a new job and a new life?

Carl's already decided. He's heading up north, revelling in the lakes and fells and excited about his new job chasing down dodgy coppers.

And Zoe's future colleague DS Aaron Keyes is perplexed. A man has been found dead at Egremont Castle – a man who left a voicemail for him just before he died.

Can Aaron track down the killer? Will Carl be able to work out exactly why members of Cumbria police are acting strangely? And will Zoe decide to make the move up north?

Find out by reading *The Castle* for FREE in ebook or listening for free in audio at rachelmclean.com/the-castle-book or buy the paperback from book retailers.

READ THE CUMBRIA CRIME SERIES

The Harbour

The Mine

The Cairn

The Barn

The Lake

The Wood

The Port

The Marsh

Buy from book retailers.

ALSO BY RACHEL MCLEAN

The DI Zoe Finch Series – buy from book retailers.

Deadly Wishes

Deadly Choices

Deadly Desires

Deadly Terror

Deadly Reprisal

Deadly Fallout

Deadly Christmas

Deadly Origins, the FREE Zoe Finch prequel

The Dorset Crime Series – buy from book retailers.

The Corfe Castle Murders

The Clifftop Murders

The Island Murders

The Monument Murders

The Millionaire Murders

The Fossil Beach Murders

The Blue Pool Murders

The Lighthouse Murders

The Ghost Village Murders

The Poole Harbour Murders

The Chesil Beach Murders

The Beach Hut Murders

...and more to come

The McBride & Tanner Series – buy from book retailers.

Blood and Money

Death and Poetry

Power and Treachery

Secrets and History

The London Cosy Mystery Series by Rachel McLean and Millie Ravensworth – buy from book retailers.

Death at Westminster

Death in the West End

Death at Tower Bridge

Death on the Thames

Death at St Paul's Cathedral

Death at Abbey Road

The Jurassic Coast Mystery Series by Rachel McLean and Millie Ravensworth – buy from book retailers.

The Swimming Club

The Empty Easel

The Shattered Bauble

ALSO BY JOEL HAMES

The Sam Williams Series – buy now in ebook, paperback and audiobook.

Dead North

No One Will Hear

The Cold Years

The Art of Staying Dead

Victims, a Sam Williams novella

Caged, a Sam Williams short